FACE

FACE

by Tim Lebbon

Night Shade Books | San Francisco

First Edition

ISBN
1-892389-19-3 (Trade)
1-892389-20-7 (Limited)

Night Shade Books
348 Pierce Street
San Francisco, CA 94117
books@nightshadebooks.com

Please visit us on the web at
http://www.nightshadebooks.com

For Nan and Granddad, wherever you are.
You did a good lot.

CHAPTER ONE

Later, they would all wonder how they had not guessed the truth. He was waiting in the snow, but after climbing into the car he did not seem cold, his breath did not condense, he appeared calm and composed. He did not act like a man that needed help.

As they first approached him he looked like a tree, struck by lightning decades ago and rotted down to a six-foot stump, standing proud of the snowbanks as if still striving for the sun. And then he turned his head and his shadow followed; maybe a split second later, maybe not. It was still snowing heavily, and the wind sent sheets of snowflakes waving across the road and into the darkness beyond. Perhaps this explained why the headlights had not picked him out very clearly at first away. For an instant the space he occupied in the world was a black hole, swallowing light and logic, disbelief and doubt.

Minutes later they knew him as a human being and for a while they ignored the fleeting doubts, fears and concerns they had felt in those first few moments. They would return later, these fears, and the family — Dan and Megan and Nikki — would try to sort truth from lies. And they would come to know that hate misleads, fear distorts and love blinds.

To begin with, they thought that they were safe.

Some days all Nikki wanted was to be a little girl again. They'd been driving for four hours on what was normally a two hour journey. She had begun to feel sick, she wanted to ask if they were nearly there yet, and she needed the toilet… but she knew her parents were in no mood for any of this. She was a teenager with a level of behaviour to adhere to, after all. So she simply sat back and shut up, bit her tongue, wondered why she was feeling like this more and more. She thought that all the anger and angst were supposed to be left behind with puberty.

Snow threw strange shadows across the window beside her, like shaky footage of nebulous creatures of the deep. Everything today was white. The radio had called it a whiteout, an expression she'd heard before on television, and only then from America or Switzerland or the Antarctic. Never had a whiteout in Britain, she was sure. And certainly not here in Monmouthshire, of that she was positive. No, that would be just too exciting.

She caught sight of something she recognised — a small gatehouse discernible only by shape, because the blizzard ate size and colour — and she knew that they were only a few miles from home.

Her dad was driving, a dark hunched shape dressed against the cold so that he looked like a chrysalis sitting in the driver's seat. Nikki wondered what he would turn into, and she spent a few idle minutes speculating to divert her mind from her uncomfortably swollen bladder. Most of her ideas were bad. Dad would not be a butterfly, he would be a moth. Her mum said he had lost sight of his youth — the childlike wonder, the freshness, the miracles — many years ago. He collected those old books, but his interest in them was like a photograph of himself as a child; nostalgic rather than fresh. Often she thought of asking exactly when he had grown old, but she was too afraid to know. She was terrified it had happened the moment she was born.

A forest emerged by the roadside. Beyond it their house and one other lay surrounded by woodland and mock-wild meadow. Boughs were loaded and ready to break. Nikki imagined different shapes dodging the headlights, silhouettes between the trees, fleeting glimpses of things never known. But there was only the snow. Silent and insistent, it buried the world she knew beneath its misleading shroud…

Her mother sighed and her father shifted grumpily. This was no time or place for imagination to be let loose; it would be thwarted by the emotionally staid, sterile atmosphere. So instead Nikki thought about *The Rabids*, wondered when they would secure their first gig, where it would be, and which record company spotters would be there to see them play.

"Poor sod," her father said.

"It's a tree," her mum muttered.

Nikki leaned between the front seats and tried to squint through the misted windscreen. A shadow appeared out of the snow next to the road, a daring shape standing upright against the worst storm nature could muster, turning and staring at the car as it closed in. And in the early dusky twilight brought on by the blizzard, its eyes caught the headlights and fired them back.

How romantic, Nikki thought, a stranger in the snow! Imagine him sitting in the car next to me, dripping and shivering but trying to sound polite and grateful for the lift. He'd be no more than a few inches away, his cold flesh tingling as blood circulation recovered, and if I shifted over just a little he'd feel my heat —

— so how do I know it's a he?

"You just *have* to pick him up," Nikki said.

"He's a hitchhiker," her dad said.

"For Christ's sake, Dad — "

"Nikki!"

She tutted. "Sorry, Mum." And thought, well, for *fuck's* sake then.

The Land Rover Freelander slowed as it approached the figure, her dad obviously keen for a glimpse of who would — or could — be out in this horrendous storm. The shape seemed to grow faster than perspective allowed, until by the time the vehicle came to a halt it was standing right there in front of them, bare hands seeking the warmth of the bonnet, head thrown back and mouth open to catch snowflakes on a dry grey tongue.

It *was* a him.

His hair was long and black, shining like oil-slicked leather in the poor light. His cheekbones were so high and pronounced that they caught a few flakes and held them there, frozen. His eyelids were shut and snow gathered there too, rough white pennies on the eyes of a cadaver.

Holy shit, Nikki thought. He's a fucking god!

Then he opened his eyes and looked straight through the windscreen. Nikki heard her mother mutter something beneath her breath, and her dad gasped. Nikki could only nod to herself. A god.

"Around here!" Her father waved to the man, motioning him to the passenger side of the Freelander. He turned in his seat and smiled quickly at Nikki. "Honey, open the door and let him in. Poor sod must be half frozen."

The shadow moved out of the headlights and passed Nikki's mum's window, walking slowly, dragging along the side of the car and snapping ice crystals from the paint work.

"He should be dead," her mum said.

Nikki strained against her seatbelt and flipped open the door, letting in a waft of snow and startlingly cold air. She sat back and huddled into her corner, all fanciful notions of sharing warmth vanishing as the solid shape filled the doorway.

"Help me, I need guidance," a voice whispered, and for a horrible moment Nikki thought it was her mother. Her mum was staring straight ahead, not turned around in her seat to watch the stranger climb into the car. Her lips did not move but the voice came again.

"Help me."

"Nikki, give him a hand in."

Nikki's dad nudged her shoulder. She glanced quickly at him, and then her mother turned around to see what was taking so long. She looked bored and tired, not frightened as Nikki had imagined. Of course the voice was not hers. How could it have been?

This time she unclicked her seatbelt and shimmied across the seat. The man was trying to climb in but he appeared too weak to help himself. His right hand lay on the leather like a landed fish, twitching its life away. Nikki grabbed it and started to pull. It was warm, not cold as she had been expecting. And as soon as she curled her fingers around his she felt strength, not weakness.

The man looked up and smiled in gratitude. His eyes shone. His skin was as white as candle wax but for the red flushed cheeks. Nikki remembered the scene in *Ben Hur* when Charlton Heston gave a cup of water to Christ, and Christ looked up at him. You never saw his face, you had to guess at his expression, the mystery made it all the more enigmatic... but now she would never need guess again.

The man started climbing into the car and Nikki had to brace her feet on the floor. She was sliding along the seat. He was big, heavy, and his weight was pulling her out. She was about to shout — the panic was rising, a cold fear congealed from thoughts of abductions and rapes and all the things she read about in the papers every day — when the man sat in the seat, sighed, heaved the door shut behind him and rested his head back against the headrest.

Trying to pull me out, she thought. Out into the snow.

"It's so cold tonight," he gasped. "Thank you." He was still holding onto Nikki's hand.

She loosened her grip and he let go a split second later. Her hand felt cold without his there to keep it warm.

"What were you doing out there?" Her dad had turned fully and was flipping the top from his hip flask.

"Waiting for a lift."

"Someone stood you up?"

The man shook his head, leaving wet marks on the headrest where the snow in his hair was finally melting. "No, not yet."

"Hitchhiking in this weather?" He offered the stranger his flask.

The man smiled and nodded, taking a long swig, closing his eyes and swallowing noisily. "Hmm... Jameson's." There was an uncomfortable silence as they waited for him to answer the question. He took one more sip from the flask and handed it back to Nikki's dad. "Most grateful." Then he turned and stared from his window.

"How long have you been out there?" Nikki asked. She was still pressed against the door, trying to shy away from this stranger who seemed to take up so much of the back seat.

The Freelander was a big vehicle, but she could have easily reached out and touched his face from where she sat. Not that she wanted to. Not really.

The man turned to look at her. The corner of his mouth furthest from her parents hitched into a wry smile. She saw the scar there, a thin white ridge running from his right cheek down to his chin. Dashing, like a duelling scar. Cool.

"Long time," he said. "Seems like forever."

"You don't look so cold. You look... comfortable."

Nikki's mum glanced around at this, looking at the man to see what her daughter was talking about. Nikki saw her eyes widen slightly, her nostrils flare, her posture change from tired to alert.

The stranger shrugged. "I'm dressed for the weather. Where are we going?"

"Home," Nikki said.

"Sounds like a good place to be."

Her dad turned back to the windscreen and the Freelander began creeping forward once more. "Where's home for you?" he asked.

"Nowhere and everywhere."

"Right. So, you want me to drop you where?"

"Where." The man had rested his head back and closed his eyes, but Nikki could see crow's feet deepening and his scar flexing as he smiled to himself. In profile he looked very strong.

Again, a loaded silence. Outside sounds were muted by the snow. Even the Freelander's engine seemed quieter than usual. Inside, the atmosphere had turned strange. Any conversation not following normal conventions can leave an odd feeling in the air, a sense of anticipation, an idea that someone will say something soon to tie up all the oddities being uttered. Loose ends, Nikki thought. None of us like loose ends. Already this stranger had created several, and they flailed at the heated air like snakes — maybe deadly snakes — just waiting for her or her parents to grab hold.

"What do you want?" she asked, because she was sure he wanted something. A lift maybe, but something else too. It was obvious from the way he sat. He was just thinking of how to say it.

The man glanced at her and smiled again, the twitch at the corner of his mouth which her father would never see in the rearview mirror, not unless he was really looking for it. And Nikki hoped his concentration was on the road.

"Why thank you," the man said.

"What?" Nikki's dad said.

"What I want is, a moment of your time." He seemed very pleased with himself. This time after speaking he did not close his eyes, but sat there watching the family, his gaze moving from mother to father to Nikki, then back to his window as if seeking an answer from out there as well.

I'll bet he'd like *The Rabids*, Nikki thought.

"Well, we're not going anywhere." It was the first time her mother had spoken. It did not sound very friendly, and neither was its meaning clear.

"A moment of your time... " the man said.

"What's your name?" Nikki asked, suddenly uncomfortable sitting next to someone who could have been anyone.

"Brand," the man said. "As in burn, mark, seal, scar of ownership. I have a brand, its meaning is one and all. Would you like to see?" He raised an eyebrow and moved his hand towards the front of his coat.

"No thanks," Nikki said. She wondered what he meant. A scar? A tattoo? And where was it, this brand, this seal on the pasty skin of the stranger who only wanted a moment of their time?

"I think you should tell me where you want to go," Nikki's dad said, slowing the car even though there appeared to be no obstruction in the road ahead. "Really, we're only a few miles from home, we've been travelling for hours, I don't have time to divert that far... tell us where you want to go and I'll see how near we can get."

"I want to go up your daughter."

"What!" Nikki pushed herself back against the door, certain she had heard him right. Doubt crept in straight away, however, because her parents did not react. He said it, she thought. He did! "What do you mean?"

"I mean we don't have time to go anywhere else," her dad said impatiently. "So if Mr Brand will tell us where he wants to go, we'll see what we can do."

"Anywhere will be fine," Brand said. He did not look at Nikki. She was sure he'd said it, she'd heard it so clearly... and she had felt a twinge as he spoke, as if the words themselves could caress where they hinted at.

"Look — " her dad began again.

Her mother spun around in her seat. "Just get out of our car."

"I only want a moment of your time." Again, Brand glanced outside at the driving snow. Nikki could see his face reflected in the window. The scar looked very fresh and red. He was smiling.

"You've had a moment and now you're starting to... annoy me. Please, leave the car." She turned to Dan. "Stop, Mr Brand's getting out."

"Mum... " Nikki began, but her mother's glare silenced her instantly. Let me handle this, it said. I know what's best for all of us. It was something her mother told her so often that she no longer needed to speak for Nikki to know what she was thinking.

Brand shook his head as the car slowed, glanced across at Nikki, then stared at her dad in the rearview mirror as if he'd had a sudden thought. "It's very cold out there," he said. "I might freeze."

The Freelander coasted to a halt just before their turning into the woods. A mile away lay their house. Two spare bed-rooms, the heating programmed to come on four hours ago, a full fridge, hot food within the hour. We could help him, Nikki thought. I think he needs help.

"You're dressed for it. You said so yourself." Her mother was turned around in her seat now, unwilling to present her back to this man. She pressed herself against the dashboard, as far away from Brand as possible. Nikki still sat against her door. Brand took up most of the space inside the vehicle.

He looked imploringly at her dad. "A moment of your time? Are you sure you can't spare me just a moment of this mad, merry-go-round existence of yours? Attention spans are so much shorter nowadays, you know. Blame it on television or computers if you want. Me... I blame it on God."

"What do you mean?" Nikki's mum asked.

"Well," Brand said, "if he wasn't such a useless fuck he'd have sorted us out centuries ago."

Nikki closed her eyes.

"Get out!" her mother screamed. "Get out of this car now! Leave us!"

Nikki kept her eyes shut. She heard the door click open, the sound of movement as Brand slid from the seat, the hard crunch of wet snow as he landed in the fresh fall. A gust of cold air touched the moisture around her eyes and across her top lip... she hadn't realised she'd been sweating... and then the door slammed shut.

"Where is he?" her father said.

Nikki opened her eyes. Brand had gone.

Her parents both looked around for several seconds. "Into the trees," her mother said. Not because she knew for sure, but because it was the only place the tall man could have disappeared to so quickly.

Into the trees.

"I want to go home," Nikki said. "I feel sick. I need the loo. I want to go home."

He was left to unload the car. Screw equality and 'Noughties Man, when it was cold and snowing outside, when the bags were heavy, it was down to him. Normally Dan would not mind. But tonight felt far from normal. This evening, everything was as strange as hell.

There was the blizzard, never letting up, throwing down layer upon layer of snow in an apparent attempt to erase the landscape from existence, and then memory. There was the oddball stranger they'd picked up, the weirdo who'd said his name was Brand, probably still wandering around out there even now. Dead by morning, Dan thought. Just like that guy in that famous photo from the American mid-West, he'd be tangled on barbed wire until the thaws came and the cold let up, allowing the rot to begin. And finally there was the fact that Megan, his wife of eighteen years, had told him today that she wanted to move back to the city. Back to the place where the bad stuff six years ago had effectively forced their new life out here; a life he was immensely happy with, and which he had believed Megan was happy with as well.

No, nothing was normal about today.

Dan struggled between the Freelander and the house five time, amazed at how they always seemed to bring more junk home from a holiday than they ever took with them in the first place. They'd only been away for three days, spending the time at a year-round guest-house in Cornwall, but their bags seemed to have multiplied in that short time and become heavier. Or maybe the snow was wearing him out. It had been a long drive, after all, and he wanted nothing more now than to slouch down in front of the fire with a good book and a beer.

He hoped Megan was sorting out something warm to eat while he unloaded. Nikki was upstairs already, no doubt, preening herself in her full-length mirror and twitching to get on the 'phone to Jeremy, her dopey boyfriend. The first thing the kid had said upon meeting Dan was, 'Hey, Mr Powell, call me Jazz', since when Dan had called him Jeremy as much as possible, purely out of principle. He was a nice enough kid, relatively concerned about his future, conscious of his appearance, quite bright… but he was also going out with Dan's one and only daughter. He persuaded himself that it was a father's right to be sarcastic and worried, because he remembered himself at that age. A walking gland.

Shit, Nikki was seventeen. She was a pretty girl. Dan knew that he to face up to these things.

On his final trip out to the car he saw something moving in the woods. Surely he can't have made it here yet? Dan thought, and by allowing his subconscious fears to the fore he realised just how much Brand had shaken him. The guy was not only weird, he was spooky, and the way he'd been glancing at Nikki… Dan had seen him in the mirror, a little sideways look every few seconds. He was sure his daughter hadn't known she was being sized up, surely not, surely she'd have said or done something? Of course she hadn't known… she was only seventeen. And then all that odd talk, asking for a moment of their time when they'd already stopped to offer the idiot refuge from the blizzard. Home sounds good, the guy had said. And then he claimed he had no home. And then the God stuff, really the last thing to say in front of Megan, guaranteed to drive her into a righteous frenzy. And indeed it had. Almost as if Brand had known his words would antagonise Megan, draw her out of the silent shell she'd been in for virtually the whole trip.

Maybe that's what had annoyed Dan most of all. He hated the idea, but he also hated the fact that it was Megan who had driven the fruitcake from the car in the end, not him. His job was protector... he'd failed once before, true, but he never would again... and still, tonight, his wife had been the decisive one. She had acted while Dan had prevaricated.

Well, he'd been ready to pull over and drag the guy from the back seat if he had to.

Another movement deep within the trees. Perhaps it was snow dropping down through the canopy, laden branches snapping them off at the trunk. Following an abnormal storm like this, Dan knew, there would be many more trees than usual damaged by the weight of snow. He paused, trying to see beneath the tree canopy, the heavy bags in each hand making his shoulders begin to burn.

A face. Dan saw a face between tree trunks, too large and out of perspective, surely, but it was there, and it was smiling. A curtain of snow blew across the driveway, shoved by a sudden gust of wind, completely obscuring his view of the trees for several seconds. He squinted and hunched his shoulders, bending his knees so that he could rest the bags on the snow, tucking his face into the neck of his jacket to protect it from the cold surge of air. It passed as suddenly as it had arrived and he looked up again. The face had gone. In its place was a branch, snapped from one of the trees at the edge of the wood and now standing upright in a three-foot-high snowdrift. The fleshy yellow wound where it had broken from the trunk was clearly visible. Nothing else. No Brand, no stranger, no leering idiot watching the house from the dark.

Dan turned and walked inside, nudging the door shut with his heel. He dropped the bags onto the kitchen floor, turned and shot the bolts at the head and foot of the door. Better safe —

"Locking up already?"

"Jesus!" Dan jumped.

"Dan… " Megan gasped, surprised.

"Sorry, love, you scared me. Yes, thought I'd lock up now. Why? You thinking of going for a walk?"

She smiled and shook her head. "The furthest I'll be walking this evening is to bed. But first… " She indicated the microwave with a flourish, whipped a tea-towel over her arm like a hoy polloi waiter and opened the door. "Chicken tikka massala, a can of Caffreys, and your armchair awaits, good Sir."

"What about 'Noughties Man?" Dan asked, breathing in the spicy aroma.

"Forget that. You unload car, strong man. I cook tea!"

Dan hugged Megan to him and buried his face in her hair. It still sparkled with drops of cool water, all that remained of the snow she'd caught on the way in. "And then I'll take what's rightly mine, woman!" He grabbed her bum and growled.

"Oh, that is just so disgusting," Nikki said from the doorway.

Dan and Megan giggled, a defence, neither of them eager to admit that they were embarrassed in front of their daughter.

"Thought you'd be calling Jeremy," Dan said, enjoying the brief look of annoyance on his daughter's face.

"Jazz is out."

"In this?" Megan asked, surprised.

"Walked to Jesse's. What's for dinner, Mum?"

"A freezer full of ready meals and a microwave."

Nikki tutted, then darted to the microwave to snatch Dan's meal.

"No way, you!" He beat her to it. "Bread and water for you, if you like. And tomorrow, if you're a very good girl and you wear your gloves and scarf, I'll take you out to build a snowman."

Nikki rolled her eyes at the ceiling and wandered out towards the sitting room. Megan smiled at him and said she was going to the loo. Dan was left alone in the kitchen with his curry, his Caffreys and the dreadful sense that all this was coming to an end.

I want to move back to the city, Megan had said. *I need more friends. And really, it's no more scary than this place, is it? Late at night, anyone could come out of those woods and break in…*

The attack had happened in the city. Six years ago, short years in both of their memories. She must *really* hate it here.

Dan looked around the kitchen at the flagstone floor, the Rayburn hot and heavy in the corner, the antique Welsh dresser scarred by time and generations of kids and cooking. And he knew how serious Megan was, because she had said it only once. To labour the point would be to dilute her determination. She must have been thinking about it for a long time. And the worst of it was, he had not even had an inkling. He loved his wife, he cherished her, he looked forward to growing old with her... but sometimes he did not know her at all.

Outside in the snow, something cried out.

Megan felt the need to pray.

In the Freelander something had *made* her turn, not only in the seat, but in her mind. Something had nudged her passive sense of boredom aside and made her spin around and snap at the man, be rude to him, be afraid of him, make him go, *need* him to go, demand that he leave them alone. All this and he had barely done anything wrong.

She used the toilet and then went to their bedroom, sat on the bed and picked up her Bible from the beside table. She hugged it to her chest and closed her eyes.

I was a stranger, and ye took me in.

They had taken Brand in, but only for a few minutes. Only until something had changed in the car. She could not tell exactly what had altered, nor when, but it had bitten at her furiously, sunk its teeth into the situation and urged action.

For a second, as she had started into Brand's eyes — shouting at him to leave them alone, get out of the car, *leave them alone* — she had known that they would see him again. This did not scare so much as worry her, because a man like that might want revenge, a man like that —

Like what? A man like what? A cold traveller (although he had looked quite warm when she turned to face him, pale but warm); a weary walker struggling through the blizzard (but he'd been standing still by the roadside, waiting for a lift he'd said, waiting...)

Megan muttered the Lord's prayer under her breath because it took her closer to Him, brought Him closer to her. And when she opened her eyes she realised at last why Brand had terrified her so much.

She had seen eyes like his before.

The eyes of the man who had attacked her.

She opened the Bible and flicked through the pages, her breath stuttering in her throat, heart fluttering. Good God, she remembered those eyes, she had never forgotten how they had stared down at her, heartless and remorseless and laughing as their owner pummelled and hit. And she had hoped and prayed that she would never see their like again.

It had been dark in the car. She'd been tired. The man... Brand... had said some strange things. Of course she didn't know what she had seen exactly, and sitting there for the whole journey thinking about a return to the city could not have helped. She had been musing upon it for months. That morning in bed it had just come out. Not a great way to finish their short break, she knew, because Dan loved this place. Perhaps her heart did tell her to leave, but did it also tell her to break her husband's heart in doing so? And could she really vilify a man because of the look in his eyes?

She didn't know. She was confused. It looked like night outside even though it was barely seven o'clock, there was a blizzard in April, maybe her husband hated her today, just a little. And Brand's eyes...

She was tired. A long journey, concern over what she had told Dan, the stranger in the car... Nikki growing up, so quickly! So, so tired.

She put the Bible down, curled under the duvet and closed her eyes.

The next thing she knew it was morning, and her world would never be the same again.

Later, with her mum and dad in bed, Nikki sat at her bedroom window and looked out across the fantastic landscape. It had stopped snowing an hour before and the clouds had parted and cleared, lighting up the snowfield with moon- and star-light. She was tired and it inspired a dreamy feel, as if she was just coming down from smoking a joint or had been drinking heavily the night before. She was trying to think of a song. *The Rabids* did lots of covers, but she was sure the only way to get anywhere was by writing their own material. Jesse and Mandy agreed. Jazz thought it was dull.

Nikki simply wanted to write poetry. If they could put it to music, all well and good. But her mind was a blank.

The scenery was beautiful. A million specks of starlight hung in the woods, every snowflake reflecting its own signature, each icicle an exclamation mark in the night. There were vague tracks in the driveway from where they had driven in hours before, but they had mostly been filled in by fresh drifting snow. And it was silent, so silent. Normally there were sounds in the night, but tonight the snow dampened everything. If there were cars passing on the main road a mile away, she could not hear them. If any creatures were abroad in such terrible weather they were moving quietly, their hunt for food or shelter silenced by the snow which may yet kill them.

And still, no words came. She sighed, closed her eyes, saw Brand.

Her eyes snapped open and she searched the edge of the woods. Where would he be sleeping tonight? What warmth would he find out there?

"Warmth in my bed," she whispered, afraid to speak too loud in case it carried across the snow and found him. She was merely trying the words for size, after all. Weighing them up. Seeing what they felt like in her mouth.

There was no movement beneath the trees, but that did not mean that Brand was not there.

Nikki moved to her dressing table and brushed her hair, staring in the mirror with the window just over her shoulder, a white square shining in the night. She teased the knots from her long auburn hair, brushed and brushed until it was straight, rubbed some cream into the wind-burned skin of her cheeks and chin, removed her eyeliner as best she could. And all the while, her gaze kept flickering to the window reflected in her mirror, the snowfields beyond, the virgin falls waiting to be branded with footprints.

She turned on the bedside lamp and undressed for bed with her curtains half-open.

THE BOOK OF LIES

Love is a warm brain, not a leaping heart. Scientists say they have proven this, as they have also shown that association with a place will not necessarily endear a person or a thing to that locale. Place is important, of course, but love is more so. What is a place without a love to be there? An empty venue, a stage without surprise, a concert hall with no acoustics to transfer the thoughts and emotions of a composer left desperately wanting.

So listen to this, let me tell you the truth… it's who you're with, not where you are.

A place can be anywhere at any time. Take where you are at this moment. Ten million years ago perhaps it was a swamp, trees thrusting from the murky waters, vines winding their way up to the sunlight, fat leaves giving life to the trees and shelter to the hundreds of small creatures living beneath them. Lizards, scorpions, insects and birds of all varieties, nesting in the branches, eating leaves, burrowing into moist, living bark, roosting for one night and then no more. And the waters, the swamp, rancid with the dead yet giving life, lizards living and dying in its embrace. Sometimes, a splash as something bigger comes through — a bear or a wolf, perhaps — but most of the time the only disturbances are water snakes venturing to the surface to breathe, or dead things falling from the trees and adding themselves to the fertile swamp bed. The air smells of rot and blossom, the rains taste fresh and pure.

Five million years later. A desert, perhaps, swept free of flora by centuries of drought or an unforgiving decade of rain that rotted the plants, driving them down into the ground and giving the sand the chance it needed to blow in and take over. There are a few animals, but none of them reflect those which had lived here before, none echo or impersonate the bones beneath them. The smells are hot and dusty, the air tastes of nothing but heat, no hint of moisture there at all.

And now, where you sit, where you read… do you call it civilised? Do you glance around without a second thought to the swamps and the deserts lying below, and far behind you in time? Of course you do, because change is the way of things.

A place can die and be born again as something totally different, many times. A place is not eternal, because evolution does not allow that. Nature moves on. Without advancing, changing, it will grow stagnant.

Love, however, is immortal. And eternal.

If place comes before professed love, then it is a love that never was.

CHAPTER TWO

From the moment she woke, Megan felt unsettled and agitated. She reacted like this whenever she dreamed of the attack. Time had made those dreams few and far between, and when they did come they were nowhere near as bad as they once were, suggestions rather than graphic replays of the terrible nightmare she had survived. But she had not dreamed of the attack last night. She was certain of that. Her face did not ache from the bastard's fists.

Her dreams last night had been of dark places splashed with isolated patches of light, and pounding from light to dark and back again had been something invisible, something running and crunching ice underfoot, cracking it and sending shards into the air to glisten or melt away. And sometimes the footsteps sounded dark, although dark only had a sound inside dreams. Less often it sounded light, it smelled good, it tasted as if it belonged... but even these positive elements were a deceit. She knew that, even as she remembered those spidery feelings of unease. The thing in her dream had been cunning and clever. A pretender.

She lay in bed for a few minutes, staring at the ceiling and the peculiarly even light reflected there from the snow outside. Birds twittered in the trees around the house and further away in the woods, perhaps in awe of this new landscape, the total whiteout that awaited them this morning. Or maybe they were already mourning their own demise. There would be little food for them today.

Megan would feed them. The family had been away for three days, the bird feeders must surely be empty by now. Dreams forgotten for a moment — shoved to one side, at least — Megan stood, slipped on her dressing gown and wandered downstairs. Dan was already awake and she could hear him in the kitchen, the smell of bagels and bacon and strong coffee luring her down. The flagstone floor was cold and she went on tiptoe. She didn't mind; it made it easier to kiss him good morning.

"Sleep well?" he asked.

"Hmmm." She still felt distracted and upset. If she could recall her dream fully maybe she could dispel the mood, but it only existed in flashes, strange, elusive ones at that.

"Is that a good 'Hmmm', or a bad one?"

She kissed Dan again and sat down at the breakfast bar. "Sorry. Weird dreams."

Dan did not turn around but she saw his shoulders tense, his turning of the frying bacon slow down.

"Not that," she said. "Don't know what, exactly, but not that dream. It's just left me feeling… weird."

"Bacon bagel coming right up, ready to scare away all nasty dream thingies!" Dan took a bagel from the oven and threw in two rashers of bacon, a fried egg and a thick slice of cheese.

"That," said Megan, "is about as unhealthy as you can get."

"Strong creamy sweetened caffinated coffee?"

"Of course."

He poured, she bit into the bagel.

"It's lovely outside this morning. I think we should take a walk. Wake Nikki and see if she'll come along, too."

Megan shook her head and tried to mutter something, chewing into the hot mouthful before she could speak. "Nope. I'm feeding the birds, then I've got to sort out the stuff we brought back. Do some washing. Back to work tomorrow."

Dan came over and kissed the top of her head, kneading her shoulders. "Yes, but last day of the holiday today!" His hands moved down over her breasts and he squeezed lightly.

Megan closed her eyes and the pounding of heavy footsteps cracking through a frozen crust of snow came back to her, along with the uneasy sense of the footsteps sounding dark. She shrugged his hands away and finished her bagel.

Nikki surprised them both by rising before ten o'clock. As she zombied into the kitchen Megan went outside to fill the bird feeders.

Stepping into the garden was like slipping through to a slightly altered reality. The sounds were different, for a start. It was as if the snow had cleaned the air; the chirping of birds and the drip of water from gutters was as crisp and clear as the snow itself. As Megan walked across the frozen garden her footsteps sounded incredibly loud, like shed leaves being crunched and rustled right beside her ears. The sensation was incredible: her foot pressed down, passed through the first skein of resistance, sank lower, met more resistance, lower still. Each step consisted of a dozen movements. It took her a long time to reach the dead apple tree.

Dan had wanted to cut the tree down as soon as they moved in, but Megan had fought to keep it. She loved dead trees. She liked living ones more because they were God's work, and there was nothing more glorious than that, but dead trees looked… timeless. And besides, it was out at the edge of their garden. Hardly in the way at all.

There were eight feeders hanging around the tree in various states of disrepair; the squirrels had a lot of answer for. Megan began filling them from the bag of seed she'd brought, conscious of the excited twitter of birds sitting along the fence. Some of the braver ones hung around the upper branches, ready to hop down to one feeder the moment she moved onto the next. She looked up. Blue tits, siskins, marsh tits… she'd even seen a woodpecker in the garden once or twice, and she hoped it would come across from the woods today for some food.

She moved around the tree, and it was only when she reached the branches furthest from the house that she saw the marks in the snow. She stopped. They could have been anything: holes where birds had dived in; prints she'd left herself just now; a curious melting effect. But the ice crust on the snow's surface was too thick for small birds to penetrate, she had not started this far around, and icicles hung from the apple tree's branches, solid, not dripping. There was no thaw and nothing to cause these holes, nothing at all… .

And then she saw that they led away left and right, staggered like footprints but too widely spaced to be her own. Whatever had made these had been running, loping across the virgin surface. The holes were the wrong shape for human feet. Instead of long and thin they were round, as if whatever made them had been walking on fisted hands. They reached the fence and continued on the other side, heading across the meadow toward the trees. Snow was still mounded on the fence panels, undisturbed; whatever made the prints had hurdled the four-foot fence.

Must have been a deer, Megan thought. They wandered down from the wooded hillsides sometimes, and once or twice she and Dan had found evidence that they'd vaulted the fence in the night and wandered around the garden. Now, in this awful weather, perhaps they were becoming more daring or desperate. She decided to follow the trail to see what damage had been done to their plants. Dan was the real gardener, he put in all the hours digging and tending and nurturing, but she appreciated its beauty as much as he. She'd hate to see all his hard work trampled or eaten.

Megan followed the prints away from the fence, walking alongside so that they remained undisturbed. Why she wanted to preserve them she did not know. For Dan? Perhaps. But she knew it would feel wrong to follow in these footsteps. And not only wrong… unsafe, as well. As if whatever had made them was still here, possessing the space above them, and to step into that space would be to know what had been there before.

Pounding, crunching, running footsteps, all tasting wrong…

The trail curved across the lawn towards the house, and as Megan struggled through the foot-deep snow alongside, the sounds and sights and smells changed around her. She glance up quickly, thinking for a moment that it was a literal change, but then she realised what was different. She no longer felt alone out here. She was walking almost in the footsteps of something; perhaps these were her dreams senses she was still using. She felt as though she was being watched.

Megan looked back over her shoulder at the woods, and

just as she did so a tree shed its frozen weight. It hit the ground and snow puffed into the air, drifting back into the trees and out of sight. It was still dark in there. Light out here now that the sun was up, but the woods were darker than ever, the canopy thickened by snow clinging to bare branches, blocking out the sun.

Megan hated dark places, had done ever since she was a little girl. Her mother had been unreasonably afraid of the cellar in their house, and that fear had translated to Megan as an undefined horror of the dark. Until she became an adult. Now she knew exactly what scared her: the Devil could be in there, watching and waiting, ready to tempt her God-fearing soul into depraved acts —

She shook her head and turned around, and Dan was right behind her.

"Jesus!" she screamed. Her cry shocked Dan — his eyes widened and his jaw actually dropped, she'd never seen that happen before — and he almost fell backwards into the snow. She laughed, shocked into a giggling fit.

"Megan, what the bloody hell!"

He'd almost shouted. That proved that she'd really startled him. She tried not to laugh again but failed miserably. What had she heard? People laugh when they're scared? And he'd scared the hell out of her, as well. With these prints, strange and regular and apparently with purpose, and that darkness huddled beneath the trees… she realised she was spooked and the thought upset her. Spooked in her own garden by nothing worth being afraid of, and finally by her own husband. She offered up a little prayer to God and felt slightly better. *There is nothing covered, that shall not be revealed, and hid, that shall not be known.*

"I thought you were filling the feeders," Dan said. "Then I saw you from the kitchen window following something in the snow — "

"These," she said, pointing down between them.

He looked and glanced back up. "Footprints."

"Well, yes. But what made them? That's all I was wondering."

The back door opened and Nikki peered out, biting a thick

slice of toast. "What's wrong?" she called, crumbing the snow before her.

"Nothing, honey," Dan shouted back. "Just scaring your mum."

"He is!" Megan called.

Nikki rolled her eyes and closed the door. Megan and Dan smiled, both knowing what their daughter was probably thinking: *Parents!*

There was a commotion in the dead apple tree, birds fighting over the fresh food Megan had just put out for them. So much like us humans, she thought, fighting amongst themselves when sharing would work just as well. Really, we're not as bad as all that.

Dan knelt in the snow and put his hand into one of the holes. He leaned to one side so that he could see how far down it went. "It's deep," he muttered. "I can see grass down there. Went all the way through the snow. Strange."

"Why strange?" Megan said. "A deer has long legs, if it was running it could have sunk straight down. It was still pretty powdery in the night, it probably froze early this morning."

"Hmm." Dan pushed his hand in deeper, up to his elbow. "Yes, but you'd expect some snow to be compacted at the bottom of the hole." He shook his head. "Definitely grass... "

"Oh, so you're Dan Walking Tall now, are you? Great Mohawk tracker?"

Her husband smiled and stood up, flicking snow at her. "You going to finish those feeders or stand around gassing?"

Megan grinned, glanced over his shoulder and stopped smiling. She moved to one side to see better, though she thought even then that maybe she did not want to. Not at all. Some things, frightening or important, are best left unseen. Best left covered, she thought.

... A moment of your time...

The words came unbidden but remained there, like a hated song repeating itself again and again in her mind.

"Dan, the prints stop at the house." She looked up. What was she thinking? No, stupid, impossible... but there they were again, depressions in the snow on the roof, the slates visible in places where whatever had made the prints — *what-*

ever had run across their garden and over their house — had displaced it. "Dan… "

As he turned around the back door opened again. "Mum! Dad! You've got to hear this! They said on the radio the Devil was running around in the snow last night. And they've even found a load of footprints!"

Something grabbed Megan inside, an ice-cold stone in her chest, and it felt for all the world like a fist closing around her heart, squeezing until the blood ran cold, froze, broke down. She closed her eyes and a disgusting stench made her retch, but when she snapped them open the smell had gone. Like her dream, it smelled all wrong.

"Dear God," she began. But she had no idea what else to say.

Just stupid, obviously. Dan quite liked silly news stories like this — in his book collection there were a dozen volumes dedicated to just this sort of hoax, from Charles Fort to Arthur C Clarke — even though he knew that they were make-up covering all the terrible things going on in the world. He wondered how many murders, car crashes, drunken fights or abductions there had been in the country last night, and which the news this morning chose to gloss over with a fanciful story of devilish footprints.

It had always been this way. Whenever it snowed, humanity seemed to rediscover its childish sense of wonder. It never lasted for long.

Nikki was unfazed by the news item, munching steadily through a second bowl of cereal without once glancing up. And Megan… Dan knew how she would react, and he hated it.

His wife stared wide-eyed at the radio, sitting up straighter whenever news updates came along, holding her breath when the local radio station newscaster told of the trail of prints found across the countryside that morning. The reason the subject was considered so newsworthy was twofold. Firstly, many of the prints had been found in odd places: stamped into windswept snow stuck to the sides of barns; scurrying back and forth across the thin ice of a barely-frozen pond; passing easily beneath low hedges and bushes; halting at the edge of a doctor's surgery and commencing again on the other side. And yes, across the roof as well.

The second reason was that it had all happened before. February 9th, eighteen fifty-five, so they said. Devilsh hoof-prints trailed along the south coast of Devon. The newscaster had an amused lilt to her voice whenever she moved onto this story from something more serious.

"More tea?" Dan asked. Nikki shook her head without looking up from her depleted bowl. Megan did not respond.

Damn it, he hated it when she was like this. Religion was supposed to be a balm, a healer, surely? But since they'd moved out to the country, it was the one thing still able to drive an invisible, yet hefty barrier between them. Sometimes he could not talk to her at all.

"Megan? Tea?" He spoke louder than he should have, he supposed, but he wanted to stir her from this reverie. If he turned the radio off she'd only switch it on again, but at least he could try to distract her from whatever spiralling course her thoughts were taking.

Her eyes were wide and moist, he could see that now as she looked straight at him. She was truly terrified. He felt ashamed for thinking so badly of her, and angry that she could think herself into such a state. "Right across our roof," she said. "He walked... he walked right across our roof!"

"Huh?" Nikki looked up, interested in something at last.

Dan shook his head. "Megan, honey, it was a bird or something, you know — " "Those prints were not made by a bird! They were... they were huge. And unnatural."

"A fox — "

"Over that distance?"

"How do *you* know how far a fox travels at night?" His voice was harsher than he'd intended. He turned away and closed his eyes briefly, desperately seeking something to grab onto, something to steer Megan away from this. The last bloody day of our holiday, he thought, and something like this has to happen. She'd obsess upon this for days. He knew that already, but it did not stop him from trying.

"Footprints!" he said suddenly, remembering something he'd once read in The Unexplained magazine. "Small prints in the snow can melt out into larger shapes as it thaws. The prints distort, too... "

Megan looked away from him, dismissing him completely.

"Right across the house?" Nikki asked.

Dan shook his head at her, sending her a warning glare, but she was caught. She scraped her chair back and hurried to the door. "It went right across our house, huh?"

Megan watched her leave. For a moment Dan thought she was going to call their daughter back, tell her to beware, tell her that Satan was out there and that he'd scoop her up with a ton of snow and melt them both together into a gruesome pink mess. But she let Nikki go.

The back door closed.

"Megan," he said.

She was tapping her fingers on the table, beating a tuneless tattoo with bitten fingernails. Her nails were always bitten. And she drank too much sometimes, and her occasional cigarettes were becoming more than occasional. He would ask her what was wrong, but she never gave him a straight answer. Was it the attack? So long ago now, but still there, still echoing in her mind and dreams. Was it this place they had moved to, its sedate pace driving her to distraction?

Was it him?

"Megan, it's just a piece of rubbish — "

"Right across our roof, Dan."

" — designed as a bit of sensationalism because the local radio channel needs some publicity."

"You're saying some disc jockey worried about his job planted the footprints?" she said in a monotone.

Dan shook his head. "No, they didn't *do* it, it's just something they can manipulate, latch onto. You know as well as I do we only hear the news they think we need to hear." Another news update rattled its way through the jingle on the radio. That was one of Dan's pet hates: the fact that radio producers believed listeners needed background music to keep them interested in news.

The item this time was slightly longer, and it contained details of where the trail of prints started and ended. It also stated that they were cloven prints, and that in places there were drag marks in the snow between them, as if made by a long tail.

"My God, they finish just at the end of our road!" Megan muttered.

For a moment Dan could not breathe — perhaps subconsciously awaiting more news to follow after the end jingle — and then he sighed deeply and quietly. Megan hadn't caught on, he was sure. And if she saw his surprise at where the prints were purported to commence and finish, it would be something more to worry about. Somehow his poker face held.

"A mile away, through the woods," he said. "There, I told you it was a deer." But for the first time, Dan actually wondered whether something or someone else had left that trail through the night.

It started five miles away, took a huge circuitous route across the countryside, and ended on the other side of the woods, right next to the main road.

The exact locations where they had picked up and dropped off Brand.

Nikki walked around to the side of the house — across her dad's favourite flower bed, but it was under a foot of snow and she'd feign ignorance if there was any damage once the thaw came — and looked up at the roof. At first she could see nothing marring the white slope, but the more she backed away, the clearer the prints became where something had, apparently, moved up the incline to the ridge. And as her parents had said, the trail began directly above where the prints on the ground ended.

"Woah," she murmured. "Can't be real." She glanced around at the silent landscape — the dead apple tree brought to fluttering life by the birds; the garden fence half-buried in places by drifted snow; the evergreens standing moodily at the edge of the woods — and then retraced her steps closer to the house. Where the mysterious prints ended there were two wider holes next to each other, as if whatever it was had run this far and then squatted to jump. She glanced up at the stone wall but there were no marks or scratches, no scrapes in the snow clinging here and there. Whatever had leaped onto the roof had made it in one go.

Springheeled Jack come do your thing,
Your every thought just makes me sing.

Nikki felt embarrassed muttering the lyrics aloud. They were from a song that Mandy and Jesse had written for *The Rabids*, a weak tune called 'Springheeled Jack Come Back'. They said it was based on a legend about some guy who'd been able to jump over houses. Nikki had a vague memory of it — probably something her dad had wittered on about once, a tale from one of his old books — but it was an odd subject for a rock song, and for once she and Jazz had agreed on something to do with the band. Musical differences, she thought. Now there was a good title.

A moment of your time. That's all Brand had wanted. The memory of his voice made her colder and brought up goosebumps. More words echoed at her, something she was not even sure he'd said: *I want to go up your daughter.* And then she wondered why she was suddenly remembering the tall stranger at all. Perhaps because she liked to imagine him having a moment of her time, and doing what she thought he'd said? Those dark eyes, long hair, the charisma that Jazz tried but failed to exude, but which came naturally from Brand. Oh yes, she could imagine it. She had not seen beneath his coat — he'd almost shown her, he'd teased her — but she could picture it, she could see them together in the snow, not noticing the cold because they were making each other so hot —

Jazz was still a boy. He was her age, but when it came to sex she felt superior, in control. Her own experience hardly made her and expert — a sticky, fumbled few times with her previous boyfriend — but with Jazz she felt so much *older.* He was a little baby with a new toy, while she only ever wanted to be grown up. But thinking of Brand made her feel like a little girl again. Her experience would be nothing to his. She would be putty in his hands, a jumble of disparate words which he would make into poetry.

She wondered where and what his brand was, and what would have happened if he'd actually shown her. She also wondered who had branded him.

Nikki turned around and scanned the treeline, knowing he would be there. He was. He hid behind a trunk, but she knew he wanted to be seen. He may have been a part of the tree itself but for his long hair snapping at the breeze, and his coat billowing open to reveal something dark underneath. He did not move. He did not indicate that he had seen her, or that she had noticed him.

She raised her hand to wave but thought better of it, brushing it through her long hair instead. Weird. He was just standing there as if he'd been there forever, watching and waiting, a natural part of the forest and all its secrets. She walked sideways across the snow-covered lawn to try to get a better view. He seemed to become more camouflaged moment by moment, and by the time she reached the house she doubted that he'd ever been there at all. Maybe all she had seen had been part of a tree. Twigs twitching with the weight of snow. Shadows dancing as the sun shone down through the laden branches.

The back door opened behind her and she let out a little squeal of surprise.

"Boo!" her dad said.

"Dad!" She sighed, wiped at her forehead and noticed she'd been sweating.

"Jazz on the phone. Said he can't live if living is without you."

Nikki stamped her boots in the porch and cringed as her dad ruffled her hair. Sometimes he still thought she was seven, not seventeen.

"Mum still listening to the news?"

Her dad snorted behind her, and mumbled: "What do you think?"

"Don't worry Dad, she'll forget about it all by this evening." She opened the kitchen door and went in without waiting for a reply. Her mum was sitting as she'd left her, hunched at the table, eyes wide as the radio threatened more news updates at eleven o'clock.

"Okay Mum?"

No answer. Nikki left the room quickly, not wishing to get caught up in Mum-and-Dad stuff. She hated when they rowed. Hated it even more when they just ignored each other. So she ran upstairs, grabbed the cordless phone from its wall mount on the landing and went to her bedroom.

"Hi," she gasped into the mouthpiece, breathless from pounding up the stairs.

"Wow, what have you been doing? Thinking of me?"

"Just ran upstairs. Out of breath."

A moment of your time, she thought, the memory again unbidden. It made her deliciously uneasy.

"Sounds sexy," he said.

She adjusted her breathing to mimic the cliched heavy breather.

"Not sexy anymore. Forced. I like you natural."

"That's not what you said when I wore the leopard-skin bra."

"Well... that's natural, isn't it? A leopard? Grrr!"

There was a pause for a moment as they both giggled. Nikki looked out at the icicles hanging from the guttering above the window.

"You have a good time?" Jazz asked.

She rolled her eyes as if he could see her. "Mum and Dad bickered, pretended they were enjoying it, made me go for a stupid walk along the cliffs. Three bloody hours! Then on the last day the snow started, and the journey home was... interesting."

"I'll bet. I thought you might get snowed in somewhere, or something." There was a lilt in his voice that gave her a thrill, a sense of power.

"Would you have cared?" she asked, knowing the answer but wanting to hear it.

"'Course I would. I missed you."

"Missed you too," Nikki said. She wondered how true that was, thought of Jazz with his long blond hair, his still-spotty face, his belief that he could play his guitar like Clapton, not clapped-out, his love of strong cider and weak cigarettes, the way his eyes widened with a childlike glee on those few occasions they'd tried sex... and how that sex had been uninspiring.

And she tried to convince herself that she really had missed him.

"So what was interesting?"

"Dad picked up a hitchhiker."

"Your old man? A hitchhiker? Get away. That's too... interesting."

"Well, he did. Odd guy... just standing out in the snow. Brand."

"Huh?"

"Brand, that was his name."

"Sounds American. Weird. Where'd you take him?"

"Nowhere." *Nowhere and everywhere*, he'd said.

"Don't geddit."

"Dad kicked him out. Well, Mum did really, after he started slagging off God."

"Your Mum? Kicked a guy out of the Freelander? That I wish I'd seen." Even the static behind Jazz's voice sounded amazed. "Although thinking about it, if he did dis God I can almost believe that... "

"Not physically. She... you know, told him to leave."

Jazz fell silent, and for a moment Nikki thought the line had been cut. Then he shouted down the phone and made her jump. "Hey, you see the news? About the Devil?"

"There are footprints in our garden."

"You're kidding!"

"Really. Up on our roof as well. Reminds me of 'Springheeled Jack Come Back'."

Jazz grunted. "Trash."

"We can write good stuff, you know."

"Can we? Who's 'we'?"

"Well... I write lyrics." Nikki thought of the poetry book in her bedroom drawer and squeezed the phone. The thought of someone seeing, reading, *singing* her words sent acid shivers through her.

"Yeah, but you never show us any!" Jazz's voice whined like a kid asking for more sweets.

"That's because none of you appreciate them."

"It was only once, Nikki."

"You took the piss." She lay back on her bed and stared at

the sloping ceiling, imagining the footprints — *hoofprints?* — only feet from her nose.

What had passed above her as she slept?

"Well, I'm sorry. I've already told you that."

Perhaps it had paused on the roof, looked down at the fresh snow between its feet, sensing her heat, hearing her light breathing… smelling her, tasting the subtle tang of sweat on her skin.

She shivered and dropped the phone. It clattered to the floor as she stood on the bed, ran her fingers across the ridged Artex ceiling as if an impossible truth lay ingrained there.

The phone crackled as Jazz shouted at her. Nikki ignored it. She leapt lightly from the bed, landed on her toes, walked to the window. Water had begun dripping from the icicles, landing on her window sill and holing the snow piled there. The dead apple tree had shed most of its snow, though whether that was more down to the feeding frenzy of birds rather than a thaw, Nikki was not sure.

Further away, beyond the garden, along the edge of the woods, movement caught her eye as snow began losing its frozen hold on the trees and finally hit the ground.

The phone still buzzed. She sighed, picked it up and listened.

"Nikki? Fucking hell, Nikki, don't get so pissed about that just because — "

"I'm not, Jazz. I was looking out the window, that's all. The woods look so nice from here."

"Oh. Well. Do you want to come over?"

"Maybe tomorrow. The snow's still pretty deep, and I'm tired from the trip yesterday." And maybe, she thought, Brand is still around somewhere, waiting to tease me again from within a tree's shadow.

"Okay. Tomorrow, then. Missed you."

"You too." She blew him a kiss and turned off the phone.

For the next hour she sat on in window seat and watched those strange footprints melt away into memory.

THE BOOK OF LIES

Associations are often made too easily. Here and there, this and that, why and wherefore, they slip together without question, without the observer trying to realise what is going on. It's far too easy to accept what the brain is telling you without attempting to discover why.

You believe your own thoughts far too often. Form an opinion and that's it, that's all there is, there's no other way or meaning or route by which this opinion can be changed. Variety is good, lies are good, experimentation... experimentation in anything is good. I was once a Mormon, but circumstance made me question my beliefs. Hell, I got bored. I dabbled in Buddhism for a time, then Catholicism grasped me and barely let me go. I don't want forgiving. Paganism and Wicca followed — fun, but without the challenges — and then I dipped my toe into the darker beliefs, eventually shunning everything in favour of a comfortable atheism. That way I offend everyone. All of theses were contrived periods in my life, brave yet pitiful attempts to fit in, to be a part of something that needed me far more than I needed it. It took me a long time to see the lies behind these beliefs... and ever since then, it's been harder to find truths.

Now, I believe in whatever I need to in order to get by.

I'm not saying I'm better. I can see through lies easier than most, and lie to them myself, and that's why I'm writing all this down. Trying to help rather than hinder. Impart what I know because I think it's worth knowing. Although when you eventually read this, you may not want to know he truth.

I've lived by questioning everything I see or sense. Just because food tastes rank, that does not mean it's bad for you. Simply because something looks unpleasant does not mean to say you cannot grow to like it, use it, love it, given time.

Take a footprint. Hide its source. Give it a cloven hoof. To any fervent Christian, the Devil has come to town.

Honest.

CHAPTER THREE

Dan always hated the slow transformation from snow to slush. It was a leftover from his childhood, when a snow-covered landscape was a place of joy and fun and adventure. The slushy remains of the thaw meant a resumption of normality, a return to a school previously closed down by iced-up pipes.

Nowadays, in his darker moments, he could not help but compare it to how his life had turned out. Vivid and clear and full of potential, transmuting as time passed by to stained and grey, slowly fading away to nothing. He felt bad thinking these things, and he knew that reality was never as perfect as a child's imagination led it to believe. But sometimes when honesty cut in he would stare at a wall, listen to slow, deep music and mourn something forever unattainable. It wasn't that he did not like his life. It was just that sometimes, life no longer liked him.

He sloshed through the melting snow to the Freelander, pockets full of loose change, fleece zipped up under his chin. Megan would normally drive him to the pub for pool night so that he could have a drink, but this evening she was unsure, still nervous of skidding on black ice even though Dan assured her it was all but gone. And perhaps, he thought, she was concerned that on the way home, she may run into whatever had made the prints in the snow.

So tonight he was sober. Pity. He played his best pool after a few drinks.

The Freelander started first time. Dan drove along the driveway, edging out onto the shared lane that snaked between the trees and out to the main road. The thaw seemed to be speeding up now, even though evening was rapidly leeching light from the sky. There was movement all around as he drove between the trees, melting snow hitting the forest floor. The headlights danced along the treeline, picking out fallen and falling branches along with the pale scars they had left on the trunks.

Dan turned on the stereo for company. He grabbed a tape blindly from the rack and pushed it home, and his spirits lifted instantly when Thin Lizzy crashed from the speakers. The sound of Lynott professing to still being in love eased away tensions Dan did not even realise he had. His shoulders felt lighter and aches gave way to a dull, fuzzy warmth in the muscles around his neck and arms. He'd driven a long way yesterday through horrendous weather, but now he was heading out for an evening of relaxation, chat and pool with his mates. And if he had to stay sober… well, he'd have the pleasure of watching them drink themselves into the foolishness he usually acted out as well. Megan had once called them a bunch of sad old men trying to relive an even sadder wasted youth. It gave Dan great pleasure to agree.

He glanced in the rear-view mirror and a shadow sat up in the back seat. He jumped, gasped, sighed with relief when the light shifted again, passing hard-edged shadows across the upholstery where the main road lamps shone through iced-up windows.

Lizzy rocked, Dan bopped and sang along, the Freelander purred its way through the melting snow. In twenty minutes he would be at Bar None. It was a strange name for a pub, but on his first visit several years ago he had instantly fallen in love with the place. On the outside it gave the impression of being a quaint old British country pub, but upon entering that illusion was shattered… and its shards were broken down even more as one passed through the lounge and into the bar.

The landlord and his wife were obsessed with dead people.

The lounge walls were lined with bizarre portraits of 'late' famous people. Jimi Hendrix riffed the customers through the hallway and into the lounge proper, and Janis Joplin, Bill

Hicks, Laurence Olivier, Graham Greene and Steve McQueen glared down at patrons as they ordered their first drink. Each portrait had some unusual aspect to it... Greene was naked, McQueen had piercing red eyes, Hicks' likeness was created wholly in cigarette ash and filters. Above the fireplace hung a huge, portrait-sized mirror, bearing subtle irregularities in its surface. Pretty strange, many casual visitors would comment, odd but interesting.

Upon passing through the frosted glass door from the lounge into the bar, any previous perceptions of strangeness demanded serious and instant re-evaluation.

Dotted around the bar were several skeletons, all bearing some strange and disturbing mutation, giving hints of the flesh and bone monstrosities they had been: one skull had three eyes sockets; another skeleton had only four ribs; yet another displayed bulbous evidence of grotesque malformation, nodules and humps and whorls of bone decorating its surfaces, a plastic Elephant Man. Norris the landlord always claimed that every skeleton was genuine, purchased at great expense from dubious contacts he maintained in South America. Dan knew as well as anyone that they were in fact cast for him in Cardiff, created by a young student doctor with a knowledge of, and a penchant for deformity.

Still, it made for an entertaining locale in which to play pool. Norris called it his pub at the end of the world. Naturally, some folks in the village took exception.

The pool table was the only standard item of furniture in the room, surrounded as it was by false cadavers, bone-tables and amputated-limb chairs. At the cueing — off end a heap of congealed plastic on the floor allegedly marked the spot where a witch was once burned at the stake. However much construction work went on above this point, Norris said, however many times the flooring was renewed, her cooked guts always found their way back above ground. It was a disgusting, repulsive idea, but it was also a foot rest. Dan was tall enough, but his friend Justin was a little over five-two — wide as well as tall — and he found it useful.

He was also very loud.

"Oh, Danny boy, Danny boy — " Justin shrieked as Dan

arrived.

"Fuck off, fatty."

The two exchanged more unpleasantries until Brady emerged from the Gents'.

"Hi Brady," Dan said.

"Hello Dan." Brady — real name John Williams — was one of the quietest, humblest, most pleasant people Dan had ever had the pleasure of knowing. He wouldn't simply lean over backwards to help a friend in need, he'd put himself in need *for* them. If ever there was someone who'd take the rap, the blame or a bullet for his friends, it was Brady. Unfortunate, then, that he bore an uncanny resemblance to the notorious Moors Murderer as he had appeared in the mug-shots of the time. John Williams's gaze was doleful instead of evil, his thick hair unmanagable instead of unkempt, but ever since he had hit sixteen Williams had been Brady. When he tried to change his appearance to lessen the likeness, he simply looked like Brady trying not to look like himself. It was a nasty nickname, unfeeling and cruel, but it had stuck so hard that even his elderly parents now used it on occasion. People no longer considered its origins. Not even Brady.

"No Ahmed?" Dan asked. Ahmed Din Mohammed was usually the fourth member of their pool team, a tall, dryly witty man with a particular love of old science fiction books and terrible B-movies. He would provide the witty counterpoint to Justin's outright crudeness, just as Dan was lively and talkative next to Brady's thoughtful silence.

"He couldn't get his car out of the drive," Brady said. "Gave me a ring this afternoon. Totally snowed in, and even if he could get out his wife didn't want to drive so he'd be sober all night."

"Him and me both," Dan sighed.

"Never mind." Brady took a long, luxurious swig of his Guinness and smacked his lips. He lived five minutes from Bar None.

"Bastard," Dan muttered under his breath, but loud enough for Brady to hear.

Brady smiled sweetly, tipped his glass again and emptied it. "Get you a Coke?"

Dan slapped Justin around the back of the head as he bent down to line up a shot. "Alright fatty?"

"No probs."

"How did you get here?"

"Walked."

"You? Walking? You never even walk when it's a pleasant seventy in the shade, the sun is setting and cars have been banned from all major and minor public roads."

"Well, you know... it's snowing."

"You big kid!" Dan gasped. He shouted across to the bar. "Hey Brady, fatty here wanted to play in the snow!"

Brady looked back, his face giving nothing away. "Freak."

The three men spent a few minutes chatting, gossiping, swearing and cursing, taking the affectionate piss out of each other as was their wont. Ahmed would have made the group complete, but they made do with what they had and reserved especially harsh judgement for their absent friend. There were only a few other people in the bar, most of whom Dan knew to nod a polite hello to — a local farmer, a young couple who lived in a converted barn just down the road from Bar None, an old widow who still inhabited a virtual shack at the edge of the village. Rumour had it she was paying to have a gas line installed as an eightieth birthday present to herself. She had two walking sticks with her tonight instead of the usual one, and she wore so many layers of clothing that she looked like a jumble sale drinking a double malt.

Dan began to relax. The stresses and strains of the past few days — and holidays with his family always contained hidden pressures amongst the enjoyment — melted away like snowflakes on skin. Nikki's teenaged mood-swings, Megan's surprise revelation that she wanted to move back to the city, that weirdo yesterday afternoon, Megan's panic this morning over the supposed Satanic hoofprints in the snow... all in all, it had been a rough three days.

The longer he stayed, the more tempted Dan became to have a few drinks and walk home. But it was several miles, and he knew that he could freeze. He was above all else a sensible family man... so he stuck to the fizzy drinks, burped and watched his friends getting drunk.

"Good holiday?" Justin asked.

Dan shrugged. "Apart from the freak blizzard turning the easy journey home into Damnation Alley, yes, not bad. Oh, and Megan told me she wanted to move back to the city."

"You're moving?" Brady said, looking up from the table.

"No, I just said Megan wants to move back."

"Shit…" Justin trailed off. "What a bastard." He drained his beer, frowned and went to buy another round.

"So," Brady said, leaning against the wall next to Dan. "You're moving."

Dan laughed and shook his head, but inside a bitterness was welling up. Yes, Brady was right, they were moving. Megan had stated her intent and that was it, she was as serious a hell… and wouldn't she love *that* comparison… and so, eventually, they would be going back to the city. Once Megan said something like that it was only a matter of time before she had her way. Sometimes it took months. Dan resented her because he knew his capitulation was a form of sympathy. But he hated himself more for giving it.

He wouldn't be surprised if she'd already made an appointment to have their house valued.

"I dunno Brady," Dan said quietly. "I thought she loved it here. Thought she was happy. Away from the dangerous city, away from where she was attacked…"

"Maybe she's got over it and wants to go back to her friends."

"She has friends here!" But Dan could not convince even himself of that, let alone anyone else. Megan was slow to get to know people at the best of times, and out here in the country the chances had seemed less frequent. Although, Dan thought, she rarely tried to make her own opportunities.

Justin returned with the drinks and he and Dan began a frame. The harsh clacking of the pool balls calmed Dan and drew him away from family problems for a while. He forgot the melting snow, the beautiful, moody woman his little girl was becoming, the strange man who had slipped in and out of their car and left the memory of himself behind like a bad smell, and he thought about placing his stripes over the top pockets, planting doubles and leaving the cue ball on the cushion. Considering he was sober he played quite well, but Justin won the game so Dan let Brady to the table.

Dan strolled to the bar. "Hey, Norris, two more beers for the gruesome twosome over there." As the publican pulled the pints Dan glanced around. "Any new stiff additions?"

"They're cadavers, Dan, as well you know." Norris's eyes twinkled as he spoke. He talked about the false skeletons as if they were his own kids.

"Well if one of your patrons decides to walk home in this, you'll have another one to add to the collection. I'd like to hang above the bar, I think."

"You driving tonight?"

"Yep. Megan didn't want to drive me up here in this, which is fair enough."

"Dangerous out there." Norris moved off to pour another whiskey for the wrapped-up old lady.

Dan chose some music from the jukebox — an old wall-hung unit whose playlist had not been updated for about five years — took the drinks to his friends and started a frame with Brady.

The Cure agonised from the speakers. Brady planted a ball into a side pocket. Norris coughed behind the bar, a true hawking that sounded like a tin of dog meat being emptied. Dan thought about the book fair he was going to next weekend, wondering what treasures he may uncover in dusty corners. He hadn't looked at his books since they'd been back. He would tonight. A glass of wine when he got home, and maybe a browse at the illustrated Dante's Inferno he's pickled up two weeks ago. Some gorgeous etchings in there. He closed his eyes, sighed.

The bar door rattled in its frame.

"I bet Nikki's pussy tastes fine."

Dan opened his eyes. Justin and Brady were leaning against the pool table, chatting.

"What the fuck did you say?"

"Huh?" Justin asked. Brady looked as tired and bemused as ever.

"Just then. In my ear. You whispered something about Nikki."

"Something about Nikki," Justin repeated, bemused. Dan

could see that it was no joke.

He looked around, wondering who else could have said it but knowing there was no one. Norris was changing an optic bottle, The Cure obsessed about love lost in a forest, the young couple were putting on their coats, the old widow still sat in her corner, her whiskey glass doing its best to drink in the single wall-light above her. No one close enough… and no one likely to say what Dan had heard.

Tinnitus, he decided. Blocked ears. Ran in his family. And maybe family problems didn't flee when he was here with his friends, maybe they just went under cover until he was looking the other way.

He bent over to line up a shot. Looked across the pool table at the woman in the corner. Saw that she had taken off some layers of clothing and her headscarf, so that her long black hair, which previously had been grey, flowed down over her shoulders like a slick, and her whiskey glass travelled to her lips to be emptied in one gulp, the hand holding it large and strong and long-fingered.

"You," Dan said, not knowing whether to be angry or scared.

Brand stood from his seat and approached the bar, never once glancing at Dan. He walked stooped like an old man, and he was not as tall as Dan had at first thought. Five-ten, maybe. Certainly no giant.

"What did you say?" Dan said, loud enough for everyone in the bar to hear him above the music. As if on cue the song ended, a loaded silence replacing it.

The young couple looked at him, the old farmer in the corner aimed a rheumy glance his way, Norris looked up from counting change at the bar, but Brand simply stared down into his glass, waiting for it to be filled.

"You," Dan said. "Oddball. What did you just say to me?" He realised how thuggish that sounded, the cliched *You looking at me?* which he'd heard many times in pubs in the city but never out here. It wasn't Dan, that type of behaviour. He was as much a hooligan as Megan was a rock star. But this guy had offended his family, insulted his daughter… and frightened him, truth be known. He had frightened him badly.

Just how the hell did he whisper into my ear from all the way over there?

Norris poured. Brand drank and smacked his lips, settling the glass back on the bar with a reverence usually reserved for churches. Dan noticed the scarring around his left eye; raised, rough skin, his eyelid twisted, as if someone had attacked him with a cheese grater. He was surprised he hadn't seen it in the car.

Then Brand glanced at him, almost dismissive, a casual look with hooded eyes. "I didn't say anything," he said. "I'm here for a drink. It's cold out there, you should know that. And the last thing I want to do… " He indicated his glass to Norris, who dutifully refilled it from a bottle of Glenlivet. "… the very last thing, is to talk to you, Dan."

"How do you know my name?"

Brand paused with the glass halfway to his lips, frowned, looked up at the ceiling and closed his eyes.

Got him, Dan thought. He can't answer that one. But his triumph vanished when he mentally asked the question once more: How *does* he know my name?

"Let's see," Brand said, and now Dan was aware that the rest of the pub were watching. Norris had even turned the jukebox down, so that Paul Weller sounded so far down in the tube station that he could hardly be heard. "You picked me up in the blizzard, took me a mile or two, ejected me from your car into the worst snowstorm this county has known in living memory, left me for dead… and you're worried that I know your name."

"I'm worried about what the fuck you're doing following me! And if you mention my daughter one more time — "

"Dan," Brady said, touching his shoulder.

Dan shrugged him off. "No, Brady," he said, without taking his eyes off the tall, dark-haired whiskey drinker. "This guy's up to something. Just look at him — "

"Dan" Norris said from behind the bar, "you really should calm it a little. I may have a pub full of cadavers, but I'll not have any trouble in here, especially from one of my regulars."

"Norris!" Dan said, disbelief hitching his voice. He heard the door open and looked just in time to see the young couple quietly slip out. Fleeing a forest fire, Dan thought. Leaving the party early.

"The man's just having a drink. He's been waiting for a lift, he says, and he's keeping himself warm. And he has taste. Glenlivet."

Dan glared at Brand for a few seconds, the taller man returning his gaze with an expression so devoid of emotion that Dan had a brief, crazy idea that Norris had hired him as just another corpse.

"You stop talking about me and my family," Dan said. "Then we have no problem."

"Okay. Whatever." Brand nodded, eyebrows slightly raised in innocent surprise.

"And you don't talk to me. Say anything like that again — "

"I didn't — "

"Anything!" Dan shouted. "Anything like that and I'll make you regret it!"

"Jesus Christ, Dan," Justin said from the pool table. Dan could hear the shock in his voice, the surprise that his mate was acting the thug.

Dan turned his back on Brand and looked across to his two friends. The atmosphere was hazed from Justin's cigarettes, thickened in a very different way from how alcohol usually narrowed the room for him. This was not tunnel vision, it was a blurring of sight, something that made everything more confusing instead of targeting his concentration at one specific point. Brady and Justin stared back at him, the latter openly aghast.

He turned back to Brand. "And let's leave it at that," he said.

Brand nodded. "Of course." He lifted the glass to his lips.

Dan walked back to the pool table, feeling small and foolish even though he'd just scored an important victory, for himself as well as his family. He was certain of that. A victory.

"Still," a voice said, "I'll bet her tight little cunt tastes of honey."

Dan spun around, and his turning body — his anger, his frustration, his hidden weaknesses that even he was sometimes unsure of — added momentum to the swinging pool cue in his hands.

It would not happen, he knew. He could never win now because he never had before, never did, never would. Brand would duck and wrestle the cue from him —

— it was the thick end, the grip end sweeping through the air, heavy enough to do some real damage —

— and turn it around, handing out the beating Dan intended for him, giving it back. Because Dan never won. He never *succeeded*. He had not been there for Megan as she suffered, and he was rarely ever there for himself. There was an angry person here, true, someone trying to defend his family's honour, but it was Dan, and he could not walk away having triumphed. By trying to help he would only hurt himself some more. That was simply how his life ran.

He had not been there for Megan, not when she needed him most. He had dabbed her blood and bathed her cuts and bruises, but when the bastard was actually hurting her, beating her —

The thud as the pool cue connected with Brand's head shocked Dan back to reality.

Did it!

The impact juddered the cue in his grip, but he managed to keep hold as it glanced from Brand's skull, hit the ceiling and dropped back down. Dan went limp for a moment, the cue resting on the floor, but then he lifted it again and brought it up in a short arc into Brand's back. He held it tighter this time and felt the meaty hardness of the man's shoulders beneath the wood.

He remembered the sight of Megan's wide, white eyes glaring from a mask of her own blood. The way she had stared at him, no emotion there other than fear, not feeling safe even when he hugged her and whispered that everything was alright, she was safe, there was only the two of them in the house now…

Brand slumped to his knees and rested with his forehead against the front of the bar. He had a bald patch on top of his head. Nobody's perfect, Dan thought, and he hit him again, a short sharp smack to the back of the head that split the cue. He could not see Brand's face — his long hair swung forward and concealed his expression from view — but his groans told the whole truth. Brand was only half conscious. His left foot twitched and thumped a brief, loud tattoo on the bar floor.

Loud, because all else was silent. Dan was trapped with his own breathing and pounding heartbeat. The others in the bar — Norris, Brady, Justin — all stared at him with vacant disbelief.

Their wide eyes reminded him of Megan.

He had not been there for her. She may have forgiven him, but he had never forgiven himself.

"Bastard!" Dan hissed. He dropped the cue, stepped in and kicked the kneeling man in the back, hard, aiming for his kidneys and hoping that tomorrow he'd piss blood. Each time his foot connected — lower back, shoulders, head as Brand slipped to the floor at last — he felt sicker, but prouder. With the last kick he slipped in Brand's spilled drink and sprawled on his back, grunting as the air whooshed from his lungs. He heard a giggle from the man on the floor. Hands closed around his upper arms. Brady and Justin hauled him upright and, winded, he could not resist.

"Dan, for Christ's sake!" Brady pleaded. "Dan!"

"Did you hear what he said?" Dan asked, and verbalising the question made it sound so stupid.

"No," Justin said. "Didn't hear anything. Poor fuck just came in here for a drink. What the hell's wrong with you?"

Dan did not struggle but Brady kept hold of him, fingers digging into his bicep. He stared down at Brand. The man squirmed on the floor, and Dan smiled as he reached around to the back of his head and his hands came away bloody.

I did that, he thought. Made him bleed. Made him bleed for Nikki.

"I'm calling the police," Norris said.

"No," a voice whispered, and for a moment it was right beside Dan's ear again, so close that he turned to see whether Justin was whispering something to him. But then the voice came again, and he realised that it was Brand.

"No… don't worry." Slowly he stood, head down, hair still obscuring his face. A couple of droplets of blood fell and bloomed into rosettes on the floor.

More dead stuff for Norris, Dan thought.

Brand looked up and his face was a mask of blood.

"Jesus," Justin said. "You might need stitches."

Dan felt shock closing in. He began to shake and a sense of unreality widened the space around him, pushed him deeper down into himself. His brief game of pool minutes ago seemed days in the past, as did his family's recent holiday, but his battering of Brand was still there in the here and now. His hand throbbed where it had been bruised by the cue, as if the impact was still occurring. His heart thumped. He was sweating.

"That's just not you, Dan," Brand said quietly, so quietly that Dan was sure only he heard the words.

"You leave my family alone!" he warned, more scared than he could understand, more disturbed by Brand's words than he could explain.

"Dan, for fuck's sake, he's not doing anything to your family," Brady said, digging his fingers cruelly into his friend's arm before letting go at last.

Norris still had the telephone receiver in his hand, and an impersonal voice was telling the room to *Please hang up and try again later*. "I'd like you to leave, Dan," he said.

He looked at Norris and nodded. What else could he expect?

Brady and Justin frowned and said goodbye. They watched him leave the bar without moving to see him out. Whatever brief madness had overcome him, they obviously thought it had now passed. Either that or they were afraid it was catching.

Brand had stood up and now leaned on the bar. His hair covered the new whiskey glass he held cupped in his palms. He did not look up, did not even register the sound of the door opening and closing as Dan left. The back of his head glistened blackly in the hazy atmosphere. The blood on the floor had smeared and already looked dry.

"See you around!" a voice whispered, promised, as Dan left the building.

The cold clapped around his ears and sucked breath from him, but he still found the energy to run to the Freelander. His footprints punched into the melting snow, waiting for morning and the sun to remove them from this place forever.

CHAPTER FOUR

Nikki could hear her dad bustling in the kitchen. Her bedroom curtains were open. Sunlight flooded in. Reality was fluid, and it was a few seconds (who am I, why are the curtains open, why's Dad up so early, where's Brand, what time is it, what *day*, what *year*) before she sat up, rubbed her eyes and remembered everything.

The snow had mostly gone. She'd never seen such a sudden thaw. Birds flurried past the window, larking around now that the ground and trees were partially exposed and they could eat again. There was no one watching the house from the treeline, although perhaps there had been last night, staring as she undressed in front of the lit window and offered her young secrets for view. She felt weird thinking that. Last night it had seemed sexy, delicious, ghost-tongues of cool air teasing her nipples without touching. This morning it felt all wrong.

Two days left of the Easter holiday. Her dad was back in work today; that was why he was up, that was why he was making such a noise downstairs. Nikki always held the belief that he hated going to work when she had no school and could lie in. True, she should be revising. A-levels weren't that far away, and then perhaps university, and then… what? What followed the life she knew? A life she had no inkling of, that's all she could bank on. In the past few years she had dreamed of becoming: a vet; a nurse; an architect; a musician; a music shop owner; a traveller (during one of her darker moments, when responsibility seemed too smothering and the romanticised freedom of the road lured her); a checkout girl (similar feelings, but less rebellious); and a solicitor. At present, her heart and dreams lay in *The Rabids*. Her mum and dad knew and honoured this, although she could see the desperation in their eyes whenever the subject came up. They often tried to talk to her about realistic chances, luck, talent, drugs and money. They'd both lived their lives working at normal, mundane jobs. Neither of them had ever seen the band play.

It would be unfair not to humour her dreams, and they knew it, and she knew they knew. Her dad, after all, often expressed a desire to make a living from his antiquarian book dealings. Musty old things smelling out the dining room and the study, that's all Nikki thought of them, but he seemed to love their feel and texture and stench. Occasionally he'd buy something and sell it on for a good profit, but the money usually went to pay for a new freezer, or a holiday, or to negate the upward-spiralling balance on a credit card. He had as much chance of succeeding there as she had of becoming the next Tori Amos. But of course, she'd never say that to her dad. She wouldn't be that unfair. That was her mum's job.

She'd see Jazz today, talk about *The Rabids*, give him a kiss, hand him his present and see his face drop when he realised it wasn't a bottle of scrumpy. She liked a drink, but Jazz often went one further until drink liked him. Sometimes that was just a bit too much. He thought it was cool, but it made her cold.

Nikki pulled on some jeans and a shirt and padded downstairs barefoot. She heard her mum humming in the shower as she passed the bathroom and realised with a brief pang of excitement that she would be alone in the house today. Maybe she'd tell Jazz, maybe she wouldn't. Perhaps — even better — she'd tell him, but not invite him over. She thought about last night again, the dark reaching in through the window to goosebump her skin, the coolness between her legs where the brisk air touched... dark thoughts all, alien and daring, exciting and frightening.

"Hi Dad."

He spun around, dropping a slice of toast. It landed buttered side down. He stared at her for a few seconds, mouth wide, eyes as well.

"Dad?"

"Hi hon," he said, expression hardly changing. "Sorry. Startled me."

"You okay, Dad? Look like you've seen a ghost."

"I'm, well, I suppose — "

"HAA!" Nikki star-jumped, shouting as loud as she could, choking on a laugh even before her feet met the kitchen floor again. Her dad dropped the butter knife — it skittered greasily across the tiles — and stepped back two paces, bumping against the sink. His eyes went even wider. His hands jerked up into a warding-off gesture.

Oh Jesus, Nikki thought, he's having a heart attack.

One of his hands looked black.

"Dad!"

"Nikki, don't bloody do that first thing in the morning." He shook his head and bent down to pick up the knife and toast, hiding his startled expression.

"Sorry Dad," she said quietly.

"In fact, don't do it ever."

"Sorry." Quieter. She felt like a little girl, being told off like this and simply accepting it. But her Dad's face had really scared her then. Sometimes, she thought about losing him.

He looked up at her again and tried a smile through the icy glare. It looked like a face trapped under ice. "You'll give your old man a coronary."

"Don't say that!" she scolded. "And what's that on your hand?"

He cringed. His hand looked like a dead spider, fingers clawed, palm black and swollen. "Accident with the pool cue last night."

"The pool cue and somebody's head, more likely!" she said, giggling even as her dad turned around to the worktop to make fresh toast.

"Went to swing it around my head when I beat Brady. Caught the end on the table and it jarred my hand. That's all."

"Silly sod," Nikki said.

"Watch it you!"

"Two slices of toast please Jeeves, and make it snappy."

Nikki sat on a barstool at the breakfast bar, sighed, ran her hands through her hair, trying to pull out the knots but succeeding only in tangling it more. She looked through the pile of papers and magazines and found the local free rag, four pages of news and twenty of adverts for tree-surgeons, honey sellers and garden shed manufacturers. It was usually full of junk and her dad used it to light the Rayburn, but this week's front page caught her attention.

"When did this come?" she asked.

Her dad placed a plate in front of her with two thick, black slices of toasted brown bread. Her favourite. "It was through the door when I got up. Some poor kid must have been delivering them at six this morning."

"It's got those footprints on the front." Nikki buttered her toast and scanned the story. There were various claims as to what could have caused the prints: a deer; a badger; a wounded buzzard unable to fly. Most column space was taken up by the Devil.

"Oh shit," she said. "Better bin this. Mum won't be too happy with it."

"Don't swear. Happy with what?"

And of course, her mum was standing behind her. Nikki crouched low over the paper, pursed her lips, wished that sometimes she could think before speaking. "Morning Mum."

"Hi honey. All ready for your long hard day of doing nothing while your father and I slave for the good of society to earn a crust to keep you in hairspray and nail polish and all manner of leather clothing?"

"You're my parents. It's your job." Nikki smiled and took a bite of toast.

"And what wouldn't I like?" Her mum leaned over and pulled the paper from under Nikki's arms.

Now she'd be pissed, Nikki knew, as much at me for saying that as at the article itself. She glanced at her Dad but he had already given up, turned to the sink, run the water and waited for the explosion. It always went like this. Good banter, a bit of fun, a bit of piss-taking — she was old enough now, her mum treated her as an adult even if her dad did still sometimes ruffle her hair and object to her short skirts — and then religion interrupted and wham, bam, fireworks.

Religion. And she'd always thought it was sex that was supposed to come between a mother and her daughter.

"Deer... badger... and the Devil." Her mother read the options out quietly. She put the paper down. "Well, the foot-prints have gone now. Let's just pretend they were never there."

And incredibly, amazingly, that was it.

Nikki's parents left at around eight thirty, offering her a lift to Jazz's, but she said he wouldn't even be up yet, and that he'd probably come around to pick her up on his motorbike. Wear your helmet, her dad advised, frowning slightly. Be careful, her mum said, covering all manner of possibilities in one phrase. She smiled at them both and waved them away. Then she smiled for herself because she loved them. All the way down the drive her parents faced forward, and if they were talking to each other they did so without turning their heads.

Nikki spent an hour wandering from room to room, brows-ing books — new ones, not her dad's smelly old things — listening to some Rob Zombie at earthquake-inducing volume. Then she showered, dressed and had a cup of coffee. And all the while she was looking from the windows at the surround-ing landscape — trees on two sides, the Wilkinson's house on a third, the lane to the main road on the fourth. Watching for someone.

No, not someone, Brand. Watching for Brand. Because she was certain that he was still out there.

She had heard his voice in her dreams.

Sweet, he had purred as she hovered on the edges of sleep. *Fine.*

Honey...

Jazz's arrival just after eleven o'clock was announced by the whooping rattle of his old motorbike. It was a 50cc machine, an asthmatic mongrel Nikki's dad usually commented, but for Jazz it was a sleek mean road hugger. And although he looked vaguely ridiculous pulling wheelies or burning down skid-marks on such a small bike, he seemed so proud that Nikki could never find it in her heart to take the piss.

Today, as she watched him perform a clumsy half-moon stop on the wet driveway, she felt a surprising tug at her heart. She was actually pleased to see him. He pulled off his helmet and leaned over to kiss her without dismounting. She kissed him back, closed her eyes, losing herself for a moment and enjoying every second of it. She held his head and wrapped her fingers in his long hair. For a few brief moments she was kissing someone else.

"Missed you," he said.

"Me too." She hugged him and pressed her chin into his shoulder, looking past him at the woods. The constant shadows sat there, watching. She wondered what moved within them and she suddenly felt very sexy. For a few seconds she considered inviting Jazz inside, taking him upstairs... but she knew that she'd close her eyes as he kissed and caressed her, be with someone else. And in a strange way, after the last two nights, it would feel as if she was *betraying* someone else. The shadows beneath the trees would dislike her betrayal. She did not know what they could do about it, and she did not want to find out. The snow had melted away, there was no way of telling what had been wandering their garden late last night, but she could smell something strange. Unknown perfumes in the still air.

"We meeting up with the gang today?"

Jazz nodded. He looked to the house and back. Nikki knew what he was thinking, he had that frantic sparkle in his eyes. "Yeah, in a couple of hours, old man Warrington's said we can use The Hall again. Jesse and Mandy have written a new song." He shrugged. "It's alright, I suppose."

"What's it about?"

"Don't know." He was still sitting astride his bike, legs wider than necessary as if it was a Harley rather than a hardly. "They called it *The Origin of Storms*, but it's all hot air to me." He grinned.

"Ha ha, Sid Little."

"Invite me in, I'll show you I'm not little." That look again, a sort of temporary madness, eyes so wide open that Nikki was amazed he wasn't drooling from the corner of his mouth as well. She glanced down at his combat trousers. He already had a hard-on, probably had one all morning thinking about seeing her again. But right now she wanted to get away, leave the house and the woods, go into the village.

She glanced over at the trees, suddenly certain that she was being watched. Surely he can't still be here, she thought. He isn't really watching me undress at night, is he? He can't honestly have hung around so long without someone else seeing him?

"Let's just go and see the guys," she said, climbing on behind Jazz and wrapping her arms around his waist. She nuzzled his ear but kept her hands high. "Maybe later," she whispered.

He handed her the spare helmet and revved up, spitting a skid of gravel behind them as he pulled off along the driveway. With two on board it was not even worth pretending that the bike was fast, so he settled for a safe ride through the woods and out to the main road, turning right and heading toward the village of Tall Stennington.

An occasional smudge of snow still lay like roadkill on the verge, grubby and sad now that the rest had vanished. It was cold, the sky was clear, there was no breeze, Nikki felt her cheeks freezing and her eyes watering, and she loved every minute of it. Leaving the house and the woods behind, seeing the first buildings ahead — Bar None and the village garage — gave her a thrilling sense of freedom, as if she was leaving responsibility behind as well.

Jazz tried to squeeze some more power from the bike. They screamed over a little stone bridge and into the village square, past the few shops and fewer shoppers, past the monument to the town's war dead, the old church and the youth centre. Then they exited the village only a minute after entering it. Fields opened up on either side, heavy hedgerows flashing by. Nikki glanced back over her shoulder. She wanted to stay there. She wanted to sit in Magenta's, the village café, drink coffee for a couple of hours, smoke some cigarettes and chat to Jazz about the painful few days they'd had away. Maybe she'd even tell him some more about Brand, her idea that the big man had been trying to pull her from the car, hug her out into the snow with him, instead of climb into warmth and safety.

"There they are!" Jazz shouted. Nikki turned forward again

and they bashed helmets. The bike swerve and wobbled, Jazz revved down and braked, and for a terrible few seconds Nikki knew that they were going to crash. But somehow Jazz pulled them around into a skid instead, locking the front wheel and turning them a full one-eighty, spraying Jesse and Mandy with grit from the side of the road.

"Fuck," he whispered.

"Sorry," Nikki said.

"Hey, cool spin!" Jesse ran to the bike and clapped Jazz on the shoulder.

"Looked more like an almost fatal accident to me," Mandy said. She was leaning picturesquely against The Hall.

"Yeah, well, I wouldn't dream of giving you the satisfaction." Jazz kicked down the stand and he and Nikki dismounted.

Nikki was shaking slightly, from the cold and the fear and the pleasant thrill she felt at having her friends around her once more. She was more keen than ever to pick up her bass and start strumming. It would end in shouting and arguments — every jamming session did — but that was just the way things went. Besides, as Jazz always told them, any good band worth their salt fell out all the time. Just look at Oasis.

"Hi Mandy, Jesse."

"Nikki. You look scared shitless." Mandy was puffing casually and in a precisely choreographed manner on her menthol cigarette. Everything Mandy did was intentional, each expression and comment analysed and probably rehearsed in front of a mirror. The same age as Nikki, she was more aware of herself as others saw her than anyone Nikki had ever met.

"Just glad I get to climb off Jazz's big chopper for a while."

Jesse sniggered, too loud and for too long. The other three all privately agreed that he was still a virgin, though he professed to having 'done' Emily Walker at her brother's wedding party the previous summer.

"Have a good holiday?" Jesse asked. He scratched his face as he spoke, picking at a fresh slew of whiteheads.

"Shit, thanks. I'd tell you all about it but I wouldn't want to bore you into a coma." Jesse nodded, still stared at her, still picked his spots. Nikki wondered whether Jazz ever noticed the looks Jesse sometimes gave her. She hoped not. They didn't need another wrench in the band's cogs.

"Hey," she said, "I hear you guys have written a new song!"

"It's great!" Mandy produced a folded sheet of paper from her pocket, waving it open and handing it to Nikki with a flourish.

"You do the lyrics again, Jesse?"

He nodded shyly.

"What's it about?"

"Read it and see," he mumbled.

Nikki glanced at the paper. Mandy's scrawled notes and attempts at musical arrangement promised hours of arguing and snapping back and forth this morning, but Jesse had printed his lyrics clearly enough. She scanned them, then read them through a second time, feeling a flush of jealousy. Jesse could write. Angry, scared, silent, shy, introverted… maybe it was a good thing he had never been laid.

Perversely, Nikki was pleased for Jesse that his talent made her jealous. "This is fucking great," she said. She smiled at him.

"It's pretentious crap," Jazz said.

Mandy lit another cigarette. "I like it."

"'Course you do, you bloody wrote — "

"I did the lyrics," Jesse said.

Mandy held Nikki's shoulder. "Your Jazz thinks we should do a cover of *Creeping Death* instead of the new song."

Your Jazz. Nikki hated that. And she hated those voices, being raised even before they'd strummed their first note of the day.

She closed her eyes and waited until the argument had reached a crescendo before shouting: "Shut the fuck up!"

They all looked at her, a different form of hurt on each face.

She nodded at The Hall, saw that Mandy had borrowed her dad's car to bring their kit, suddenly wanting nothing more than to get inside and start playing. Drown out all the strangeness of the last couple of days.

Sweet… fine… honey…

"Let's do both songs," she said. Ever the diplomat.

The Hall should really have been named The Shed.

The band went through the main door, past the toilets and into the hall — there really was little else to the building. A rear room had once been used as a bar, but it was now boarded closed and accessed only from outside, home to a dinosaur lawnmower that Warrington used two of three times each summer to tidy up the roads leading into and out of the village. The local council carried out the bulk of the work, but never to Warrington's satisfaction. His own gouging attempts made matters worse, but the villagers turned a blind eye.

"What did he charge this time?" Nikki asked.

Mandy grunted. "Bottle of Scotch."

"Hope you bought him the cheap stuff."

"Took one from my dad's stock," Jesse said. "He'll never miss it."

Nikki smiled. Warrington was probably holed up somewhere even now, pissed to high Heaven and cursing the very youth he profited from. There was probably a lesson to be learned from that, but she wasn't sure what.

They set up their equipment, each of them performing familiar tasks and entering their own private world for a few minutes. Jesse unpacked his meagre drum kit, Mandy set up her microphone and the two small speakers she jokingly referred to as her PA, Jazz removed his guitar from its wooden case, polished it with his sleeve, almost cooing over its shine as he wired up for sound. Nikki looked around as she plugged in her bass guitar and monitor. She knew them all well — they were, she supposed, her best friends — but even if they'd been strangers she could have summed up their personalities from the way they touched their gear, how they moved as they clicked sockets and trailed leads along the front of the old box-staging units.

Jesse's slow, ponderous movements and the gentleness with which he fixed each drum — quietly, so as not to attract too much attention — testified to his shyness. Nikki had always felt herself drawn to him, but more as a sibling than anything else. If she'd had a brother, she liked to think he would have turned out like Jesse. His coyness was s symptom of his inherent selflessness. Or perhaps a cause.

Then there was Mandy, singing louder than was necessary to set the microphone volume. The opposite of Jesse, she demanded attention, and if she did not receive it naturally she forced it upon herself. I've fucked a sheep, she sang, I've fucked a goat... Then she did doh-ray-me, slipping on the final high note and bending over into a forced cough to provide an excuse, then continuing with that when she realised it was something else which would turn heads, then pouting and strutting when it did not work... And yet, Nikki really liked Mandy. They had been friends for a long time, and as they grew into their teens together Nikki began to see the taller, prettier girl for what she was: a loser wearing a winner's medal. Mandy was quite intelligent and came from a wealthy background, but despite all her show and tell she was destined for a life of mediocrity. There was nothing really to her. Nikki knew that friendship based on pity was wrong, but then she'd remind herself that not many people understood Mandy. Maybe not even Mandy herself.

And then Jazz. Pompous, funny, arrogant, romantic at times. He wore his guitar slung low over his shoulder, smiled at Nikki when he played, pursed his lips as he launched into a solo, then exaggerated the pose when he saw others watching him, smiling at their smiles. Knowing, behind all the bravado, that they were actually laughing at him... and not really caring. Some people thought Jazz was thick as shit — her dad included — but Nikki knew the truth: his confidence was so sincere that he was simply happy to laugh at himself.

"Let's hit it," she said. As usual she took on the role of band leader without anyone complaining. Even Mandy would shut up and let Nikki run things for a while, just until the arguments kicked off. But hopefully they had a while to go now before that happened. Nikki had a few days of shit to play away.

"Fuck it," she said, "let's do *Creeping Death* to clear the cobwebs."

Mandy hated the song, she made no secret of that, but she loved *The Rabids*. They all did.

They played badly, but sounding like they meant it.

The Rabids went through *Creeping Death* three times, and each time Mandy sounded more and more pissed off. That was good. It suited the song. But after the last chord of the last run-through she stormed to the toilets, slammed the door and stayed there.

"We ever have a gig it'll be the shortest in history," Jesse said.

"We'd better do the new song, I suppose." Jazz was sweating, his long hair dark and knotted where he'd been swinging it around his shoulders. Nikki was constantly amazed at how it avoided his guitar strings, but she had to admit it looked pretty cool. Jazz, however, now looked freaked and dizzy. That's why he wanted to do *The Origin of Storms*. Nothing to do with Mandy. He was tired.

Jesse went to fetch their moody singer and, pleased at the attention, she deigned to come out and perform the new song. They played it five times before it even started to come together, then they took a break for a beer and a smoke. As usual, Jazz had brought some pot. As usual, Mandy snorted her derision.

"Weed!" she hissed.

"Resin," Jazz said.

"Not *it*. *You*."

Nikki sat back and listened, leaning into Jazz's embrace as he made a great show of smoking. The tangy cloud built around them and she tried to pick out tempestuous shapes where it floated around the smoke alarm on the ceiling. If that went off they'd have to get a broom to smash it in. Not as if anyone would hear it from where they were now; The Hall was half a mile from anywhere. And anyway, likely as not its battery was dead.

Brand would be tall enough to reach it. He could stand there in The Hall on tiptoes, stretch up until his fingertips just brushed the base of the dusty alarm, nudge up an extra half-inch to crack the casing. Even though the ceiling was almost twelve feet high she imagined him doing it, filling The Hall with his presence and his build, casting out the tainted air because he did not want it, did not need it, to breathe and be and belong.

He was the first thing she had thought about that morning, the last thing she would think about tonight. Jazz felt suddenly cold next to her, a distant heap of flesh she had nothing in common with. Another puff of smoke billowed into her vision she felt him slumping down some more.

"You smoke any more and you won't be able to play," she said.

"'Course I will! I'll be a speed demon, baby."

"We're not playing thrash now, you know. Jesse's and Mandy's new song doesn't need some doped out psycho... "

He sat up and she felt the hurt as he stared at her, glassy-eyed and white-faced. He never liked to admit that the cannabis made him feel ill, sick, cold and sweaty. He thought it was too cool for that.

"Nice to see you back from holiday, too," he muttered. Then he stood and picked up his guitar, scratching out a few angry chords, distorting them as his own senses were distorted.

"Fuck!" Jazz shouted. He threw the remains of his spliff at a dusty window. It hit the glass and spewed sparks in death.

"Sorry, Jazz," Nikki said, but he spun around and shook his head.

"No, there was someone out there watching us," he said. "Scary bastard. Big."

Brand...

"Great, now you're hallucinating," Mandy said through a nasty smile. "Was he dressed as a Mars Bar, this big scary bastard?"

Jazz shook his head, exasperated. "Really. There's someone watching. Just startled me a bit, that's all." He took a step towards the window to try to regain some sense of cool, but only one step. Whatever he'd seen really had shocked him.

"Let's go see," Mandy said.

Brand, Nikki thought. I imagined him and now he's here, watching me through a window like he has been since we picked him up. A shiver crawled down her front and into her groin as she thought of undressing before her lit window, wondered what he'd been doing as he was watching...

Mandy strode across the dusty floor, giving her behind a little twitch for Jesse's and Jazz's sake, and pushed her face up against the glass. Nikki could see her breath condensing on the panes. It was still cold, and although the Hall had an old gas heater, none of them felt brave enough to light it. They all shared a fear of seeing The Rabids become famous in flaming, gas-fuelled death.

"Nothing out there," Mandy said.

Jazz had barely moved. "You sure? I saw this face looking in, can't you see in the dust on the window? Where he was pressing his face — "

"Oh my God!" Mandy screamed, staggering back, one foot kicking at the heel of the other and dropping her heavily onto her rump, coughing up a cloud of dust from the floor. Air whooshed from her chest as she hit the boards, and her hands slapped down with a painful smack.

"What?" Nikki shouted. *What, a tall man all in black...?*

"Arsing us about," Jesse said.

"What's out there?" Jazz shouted, almost screamed. His guitar still hung comically from around his neck but both hands had gone up to his mouth in an unconscious gesture of shock and burgeoning panic. A dropped façade, once again.

"Arsing us about," Jesse muttered again. The sound of a snare drum being tickled added a bizarre background theme to the proceedings.

Mandy's shoulders began to shake with laughter as Nikki stepped forward.

"Bitch!" Jazz hissed.

"Told you she was arsing us about."

"What was the fucking point in that? I did see someone, you know... "

"Mandy, for someone so stunningly beautiful you're such a childish little girl," Nikki said, and Mandy's shaking stopped, shoulders still high, tense. Nikki could almost see the muscles knotting in the other girl's arms and neck. "Oh shit, Mand," she muttered, wanting to tell her sorry, forget it, but those words would just not come. Hardly ever for anyone, and especially not for Mandy. Stuck up bitch.

"Well I'm going outside for a look," Jazz said. If he expected a reaction he was disappointed. Nikki glanced at him and raised her eyebrows, as if to say why bother, but he'd said it now. Blustered up by Mandy's mockery, he could not back out. He unslung his guitar, laid it gently in its box, lit a cigarette — just plain tobacco this time, Nikki noticed — and went slowly for the doors.

"I'll come," Jesse said.

"Cheers, mate."

"Me too," Nikki said. She tried to convince herself it was for Jazz, to show solidarity with him in front of Mandy. But it was more for Brand, who may be out there even now watching through another window, imagining her undressing at night, perhaps wishing he'd tugged that little bit harder when he'd tried to haul her from the car...

So what if he was a stranger, tall and scary and antagonistic, warm when it was cold? So what if he wanted a moment of their time? As far as Nikki was concerned he'd already had that from her. And besides, she could handle herself.

The three of them left The Hall and stood outside on the gravel, kicking at weeds, avoiding dog shit, looking around and wondering who would be the first to venture around the corner of the building.

The Hall backed onto a field, and in between stood an explosion of a hedge, a great overgrown mass that hadn't seen the business end of a saw or pair of shears for decades. Brambles mixed with hawthorn; nettles nudged their way past dock leaves; an old rambling rose grew thick and gnarled, rejoicing in its wildness; dead trees rotted down while others struggling heroically to push their way up to the light. Even as a kid Nikki had played in there on occasion — hide and seek, or just plain hide — but now it held no nostalgia. Only a strange sense of foreboding, a fear that if she went back in — the place where she'd been a child before growing up, before discovering herself as a woman and not just a little girl — she would see or feel things she did not like.

"I'll go this way," she said, heading for the corner of The Hall nearest the road. Safe that way. Besides, that was the side Jazz reckoned he'd seen the face, so in a way she was the brave one.

"I'll take a look round back," Jesse said.

Jazz shuffled from foot to foot, puffing at his cigarette, kicking an empty snail shell on the ground and crushing it slowly beneath his boot. "I'll just wait here," he said.

"Mind Mandy doesn't jump out on you," Jesse muttered. Nikki giggled to herself as she reached the corner. He'd mixed sarcasm and innocence just right so that Jazz could not quite be sure of what he meant. Yes, she liked Jesse. He was a good guy.

She rounded the corner and walked alongside The Hall. There was only a narrow grass verge between the building and the roadside, and she kept her eyes down, looking for signs of their mysterious watcher. She recalled the strange prints in the snow a couple of days ago, though now they had gone and there was no chance that any new ones could distort, mutating from normal to something abnormal. *The Devil*, her mum had whispered. Funny. Annoying. Depressing. Sometimes she wished her mum would just calm down and enjoy life instead of worrying about what happened when it ended.

There was no traffic on the road. There were a few birds singing around her, and the distant purr of an unknown engine, but other than that her footsteps were the only sound. She could not even hear Jesse pushing his way between the shrubs and the corrugated wall of The Hall on the other side.

She passed the window where Jazz had said he'd seen a face — looked down, checked the ground, saw no footprints in the mud — and rounded the second corner.

Brand stood fifteen paces from her. He was at the far edge of The Hall, back pressed into the hedge where it bulged out, apparently trying to extend its domain and creep along the end of the building in a vain attempt to reach the road. He was staring at her, smiling, his long hair tied back in a ponytail. He had two dark bruises on his face — one on his cheek, the other at the side of his mouth — and a cut across the bridge of his nose.

Some bastard's been picking on him, Nikki thought, but instantly realised what nonsense that was. No one could pick on Brand, he was just not that kind of man, he was strong and capable, and anyway, she guessed that the other person was probably looking a lot worse —

"You're a very sexy girl, Nikki," he said, though his mouth did not move.

"What?" She'd imagined it, she must have, although it *had*

been his voice.

Then he did speak. "You're a very sexy girl, Nikki. And you play bass well."

She smiled, but it didn't feel right. She shrugged. She was useless, hopeless, not knowing what to do or say.

He turned and walked behind The Hall.

"Wait!" she shouted, running to where he had been, slipping in a mud-puddle and banging her shoulder and head on the wall as she went down, feeling the cold mud suck at her leg and hip, seep into her shoe. "Wait!" She scrabbled in the puddle, trying to stand. Pain flared in her head and she was sure she'd cut herself. She paused, listening for Brand pushing his way through the undergrowth, but there was nothing. He was waiting there for her. Standing just around the corner, listening to her shouting and cursing, probably giggling behind his hand, maybe even smelling her blood…

Nikki stood and walked the last few paces, swinging herself around the corner and wincing as errant twigs plucked at her cheek and neck.

There was no one there. The bushes and trees pushed up against The Hall, branches and creepers actually appearing to penetrate the outer shell and disappear inside, though she had never seen any sign of them within.

Brand was not there.

She'd been here as a little girl, hiding under this very tree as her mum and dad looked for her, called, cried and called again, and she had only come out when it had started to rain. The memory came back hard and fresh and sad. It was the first and last time she had run away from her parents. Eight years old. She'd never seen such pain, relief, anger and terror on their faces.

Brand was not there.

He had been standing at the corner, smiling at her… talking to her… and now he was gone.

Jesse pushed his way through the undergrowth, cringing as it scratched at his face and hand. "Bloody hell… I must be mad." he said.

"Were you here just now?" Nikki gasped, realising how crazy it sounded.

"Huh? Taken me a lifetime to get through there."

"I saw someone."

"Who?"

Who? Nikki shook her head. Not to deny that she had seen him — because she *had* — but simply to dismiss the conversation.

Nikki took a good look at the hedge. There was no way Brand could have pushed through there, no way, not without making a noise and not in the time it had taken her to find her footing and turn the corner. And Jesse would certainly have met him. She scanned the hedge, the tangle of bare branches holding clots of rotting leaves, the thorns and the twisted stems that had been growing for maybe a hundred years, denying anyone access... let alone such a tall, big man.

At any moment she expected to see him staring back.

"Nikki?"

"Huh?"

"You alright? You look like you've seen a ghost. And your head's bleeding a bit. You didn't did you? See anything?" For the first time Jesse looked afraid, a fear that encompassed rejection and loneliness as well the more immediate threat. Perhaps Nikki shouldn't have been ignoring him. She knew how things were with Jesse.

"I'm fine, Jesse. Thanks." She wiped her forehead and her hand came away smeared red. Not much. Just a scratch. It had felt worse at the time. "I'm going to go through this way." She nodded past him, wondering what the fuck she was doing and realising the truth instantly: she was *making sure*. If Brand was not here, then she was seeing things, hallucinating... fantasising? Actually finding him hiding back there would be less scary.

"Rather you than me." He squeezed by her, and did he cop a feel? Did his hand brush along the top of her thigh and across her crotch as he tried to negotiate the tangled roots and mud and bed of rotting leaves?

Nikki shook her head. Now she was paranoid. "Beat you back to the door!" she said with a smile, but as she turned from Jesse the smile dropped away instantly. Just what the hell *was* she doing?

She pushed into the hedge, levering the first big branch away from the wall of The Hall and slipping through. She scratched her arm and cheek straight away, bringing morse-lines of blood to the surface. It isn't far, she kept telling herself, not fair at all. She was glad that there were no windows on this side of The Hall, otherwise she may see Mandy staring out, giving her the finger, rapping on the window to scare her. Or perhaps it wouldn't be Mandy. Maybe Brand had reversed the situation and was inside The Hall right now. Waiting for her to return. Brushing Mandy's cheek with the back of his hand…

She tried to push through faster but the hedge thwarted her efforts. It reminded her of a picture-book she'd had as a kid, the story of Sleeping Beauty and how her castle had been overgrown with rose plants to deny anyone access, a prehistoric forest climbing the walls and joining above the roof. Her dad had sat beside her and read through that book a hundred times, and it was always one of the final pictures that stuck in her mind: the valiant prince hacking through the gnarled trunks and stems in his search for the sleeping princess. His quest was to wake her with a kiss.

Would she feel different about things, she wondered, if Brand were to kiss her?

She was halfway through — it would take the same time to go both ways, now, a couple of minutes at least, too far in for anyone to help her if something went wrong, if someone reached out and grabbed her ankle or brushed her throat with a blade — when she heard his voice.

"Sexy girl."

Nikki jumped, gasped, caught her breath and felt her heart take a few wild leaps. She looked over her shoulder, her hair catching on a branch as she did so, and when she turned back Brand was standing right in front of her. He'd pushed through from the other end, his face was scratched in several places, his hands — one resting on the mould-covered wall of the building, the other holding back a heavy branch so that he could look at her — were criss-crossed with bloody trails. But he was totally unconcerned. He looked as much at peace here as anyone could anywhere.

Sexy girl, he'd said. And now, however much Nikki had been thinking about him, whatever illicit thoughts had entered her mind as she lay awake at nights, she was scared.

"How did you get here so quickly?" she asked.

Brand shrugged. "I know short-cuts."

There was no way past him. She could go back the way she had come by turning her back… but that was something she would not do.

"What are you doing here? What do you want?"

Brand smiled and stepped closer, letting the branch fall back into place and lock them in together. He stood inches away, looking down into Nikki's upturned face, breathing at her, his breath stale and old like a bedroom in the morning. Oh God… she could reach out and touch him… .

"I'll be around for a few days," he whispered, filling her head with his voice. "Your father and I have a bit of business to discuss, all hush-hush, don't tell anyone, it's on the quiet. And especially don't tell mention it to your old man… he'd go mad!"

"My dad?"

Brand nodded. "So you're alone this afternoon? In the house?"

"Mum and Dad are in work." Nikki felt a peculiar tingle in her chest, fear and apprehension and a buzz of excitement. Was he making a pass, planting suggestions? "Jazz is coming back with me, though." It was a lie made true as soon as she said it. She'd had no intention of asking Jazz back… but now she would. For the whole afternoon. Not because she thought he could protect her from Brand, but simply for the company.

"Will you fuck him?"

She felt herself reddening, her cheeks flushing and her belly growing warm at the thought. A man talking about sex in such a frank way was not something she was used to. The realisation brought home just how young she really was, and it scared her a lot more because of that. Mostly, she thought of herself as an adult. Right now she was simply that little girl behind The Hall once more.

"Maybe," she said, pleased with the answer.

"He's a waste of space, you know."

"What?"

"Your boyfriend, Jazz. A waste. Something useful could be occupying the space he takes up. Breathing his air. Having his… energy." Something had changed with Brand… perhaps his eyes were darker or his scar paler.

Nikki shook her head, flitting from excitement back to fear in an instant. She was breathing hard with the effort of trying to keep up, trying to figure out what he wanted, where he was coming from, just why he was here at all.

"I could free that space," Brand said. He leaned forward so that his lips were an inch from her forehead, hovering above where she had cut herself. "A moment of your time, sexy Nikki, and maybe I'll do it for you. Hmmm, that could scar." Something touched the cut. It may have been his breath, or perhaps the tip of his tongue, a cool touch on the dribble of blood still seeping out. She recoiled.

He turned away.

"See you around."

Then he pushed between the hedge and The Hall and was gone.

Nikki tried to follow but branches snagged her clothes, holding her back. It took her a couple of minutes to force her way through to the front of the Hall, panicked moments filled with conflicting emotions and ideas, feelings in a pot brought to the boil by Brand... and then left to cool naturally, spewing their heat into the air, settling with a cold greasy fear on top.

Jazz was standing where she had left him. He glanced up as she emerged, eyes widening slightly at the sight of her bloodied skin. She leapt into his arms. He staggered back in surprise.

"See him?" she asked quietly. "Did you see him?"

"Jesse said there was no one there," Jazz said, breathing cigarette smoke into her face.

"Your parents in?" she asked, trying to keep her voice level, burying her face into his neck so that he could not see her wide eyes.

"No. Dad's in work and Mum — "

"Let's go to your place for the afternoon, then." She felt him tense slightly, then he held the back of her head and nuzzled into her neck. Yes, she thought defiantly, I am going to fuck him. She pulled away and looked around. If she had been expecting a rebuke, it did not come.

Ten minutes later they had packed their gear, left Jesse and Mandy behind and were screaming along the road back to Jazz's place.

Nikki held on tight.

CHAPTER FIVE

Of course, the footprints had not left her mind for one minute.

Megan was good at keeping her thoughts internalised, not opening herself up to analysis and criticism. God knew her every move, every thought, each and every image that flitted across her mind was there for Him to see, so if there were any apologies to make she would make them to Him. True, sometimes she felt the need to share her thoughts, that's what family was for, but the more private ones — and there had been many of those lately, some darker than normal, some more secretive — remained hidden. Her mother had told her that this was the best way to be. She had been sparing in her advice, but the one thing she had insisted upon was that Megan need not bother other people with her own fears and woes. Keep them inside, she had said. Handle them yourself. They're your thoughts and yours alone, that's why God gave you your imagination and your inner workings. Keep them to yourself, and to Him.

So she had listened to her mother and slowly, over the years, built a screen around herself. It was invisible, this screen, constructed of secrecy and silence, and it was mirrored on the inside so that when she looked she saw herself staring back. Nobody else could see it, though Dan knew for sure it was there. He tried to scale it, tunnel through or ease his way around without her knowing, but Megan would smile and whisper softly that nothing was wrong, everything was alright, there was no need to worry because if there was anything wrong she would tell him.

That was where the very idea of the screen fell down. Because it made Megan lie. It made her say that things were well when they were not. It forced her to smile when she was crying inside, laugh when she felt like screaming.

It repressed everything… and then she had truly found God. There was no hiding things from Him. He knew it all. He was, in a very real way, the sink for all her fears and anger, all the secret, silent terrors she felt but was too afraid to share, even with Dan.

Sometimes she slipped a little, and then she saw what damage could be done. "I want to move back to the city," she had said. Tension. Anger. Yes, just one tiny crack in her defence and their love was on the line. But occasionally things just had to be said.

"Going to lunch," Megan said to Charlotte.

"'Kay." Charlotte was painting her nails, her usual lunchtime pastime. Megan wondered when the girl found time to do anything, such was the effort she made getting ready.

She left the office and breathed in the crisp air, enjoying the sense of cold spreading into her lungs, the cool prickle on her tongue. There was a small mound of unmelted snow against the wall outside, and she glanced at it as she passed by. No prints, thank God. No prints in there. But she certainly had not forgotten those devilish hoofprints spread across her garden, lined over the roof in an arrogant display of ownership where none had been granted. She offered up a prayer and closed her eyes as she zipped up her coat.

Megan looked back at the patch of dirty snow, afraid that from a different angle she would see a print punched deep down, the shreds of skin at its bottom begging her to pick them up…

She had a choice of what to do for lunch. There was Magenta's, the little village café, but that was likely full of kids enjoying their last free weekday afternoon before school started again after Easter. She may even bump into Nikki and Jeremy in there. She'd embarrass her daughter just by existing in the same room as her, and she had no wish for a confrontation, however pleasantly adorned it may be. Or she could go to the pub in the square, sit in the corner with a basket meal and read the paper while the old folk drank halves and stared into the past where it stained the dark ceiling timbers.

Or she could go to church. And so thinking, she realised that this was what she had needed all morning.

Tall Stennington was somewhere between a village and a small town. Its residents referred to it as a village, its businesses — the solicitor's she worked at amongst them — preferred the term town. Better for business. There was the old part, with buildings dating from three hundred years ago or earlier, cottages whitewashed every couple of years, winding roads really too small for vehicular traffic, a village square taken straight from a postcard, cobbles fighting in vain against the encroaching influence of Tarmac roads, walls leaning drunkenly, giving the impression of imminent collapse even though they had probably been that way since before she was born. Then the newer part of town, with council houses surrounding a small business park, a whole slew of tastelessly built offices and shops snaking out from the village square to the main road, and the new, post-modern church.

This was where Megan was headed.

Tall Evangelical Church was built of redbrick, had a roof four times as high as its external walls and a blue neon cross that, when lit, was visible from way outside the village. It was a true blot, and there was much gossip of how it had received planning permission, rumours ranging from a huge back-hander to the local authority, to the planning officer in question's unusual relationship with the vicar and his wife. For Megan, its appearance did not matter. The signs outside, exhorting devotion to Jesus, held no import for her. The colour of its walls, the carefully maintained gardens, the six-foot boundary wall that failed miserably in keeping the local youths out... none of this mattered. All that concerned her was that this was home from home, the house of God. A refuge in plain sight.

The one place where she could let down her guard.

"Oh Jesus." Megan never took the Lord's name in vain, but often uttered it as a kind of invocation. If something scared her or shocked her she called on His help. "Oh my Jesus!"

At first she thought the shape was a new cross, leaning against the railings in front of the church while its mount was prepared inside. But as she drew nearer she saw hair flitting in the gentle breeze. Someone was tied to the railings, arms out, feet up off the ground, limbs twisted in and out of the up-rights in a manner that must surely mean broken bones.

Then, as she came to a halt several yards in front of it, the body moved. Its arms slipped from between the iron railings, it slid to the ground and looked up at her.

"You dog, why hast thou fellated me?" Brand said.

Megan could not speak. She opened her mouth but could not breathe, as if the air had frozen around her and Brand, solidifying, allowing only the twisting of his face as he smiled, the satisfied sigh as he stretched his limbs — joints clicking, bones creaking — the only sound. She could not move, either, because he was looking at her. In the frank sunlight she could see his scars... several of them, evenly spaced across his face, certainly not random. Sigils, signs, wards... they were *designed*.

She knew this was sacrilege, yet she was fascinated.

She'd read about small rodents caught in the gaze of a co-bra, pierced by its eyes and scared into a terrible paralysis that only ended as the snake struck.

Going to bite me, Megan thought, he's really going to bite me. Brand's Grin widened and she believed it, for a crazy moment she imagined him leaning forward, clamping his jaws around her exposed, cool neck and chomping down on carti-lage, carotid artery, muscle and flesh, shredding...

Then the image passed and she stepped back quickly. Her heel caught on the path edging and she was falling, Brand grow-ing before her as he rose in her vision and the sky surrounded him. She wheeled her arms and cried out, stupidly embar-rassed.

Brand grabbed her. He filled her field of vision now, just as he had that first moment they'd seen him out in the snow-storm, impossibly huge through the windscreen. She was ter-rified. "There is plenty covered that shall never be revealed," he said, smiling, "and hid that can never be known."

"Let go of me," she hissed, but he had her. His right hand was closed around her left bicep, his left curved back under her right arm and pressed flat to her back. Her breast nudged his wrist. His eyebrows raised slightly, lifting one of the scars — it was shaped like a serpent with three heads — although he was not looking at her face any more. His gaze had been stolen by something across the street.

"Unlucky for some," he said.

Megan struggled away from him, almost stumbling again but righting herself this time. He was looking over her shoulder, his amused expression doing nothing to dispel the threat he exuded. She looked. There was a small dog with something in its jaws. It was flinging it into the air and catching it again, and Megan realised after a few seconds that it was a bird, probably dead already but still being toyed with, nipped, holed so that tiny droplets of blood spattered the grey concrete it was not being allowed to rest upon. The hound seemed neither excited nor bloodthirsty, merely interested, curious as to what would happen were it to catch the bird again, fling it again, catch and fling one more time, and so on and on.

"A charming village you live in," Brand said. "No, really, I'm not fucking with you, a lovely little place."

"What do you want?" Megan asked, suddenly angry. How dare he scare her? And here, by the church... how dare he? "Didn't you get your lift?"

Brand frowned and looked skyward, finger touching a ragged mark on his chin. "Hmm. Now then, did I get my lift? Well... .yes!"

Megan backed away a little more. His arms, they'd been between the bars, she'd seen them there but now they were whole and healthy again. A contortionist perhaps, using his unusual joint structure to shock and frighten?

"Well you can't have gone very far," she said.

"No I didn't. My lift arrived, I asked a small favour of them and they threw me back to the storm, back into the teeth of snow and ice, into the freezer, thinking perhaps that I was warmed enough by their meagre hospitality to survive the night out there on my own."

"You were being weird!" Megan couldn't help justifying herself. She glanced past Brand to the church door, wondering if she could run there before he had a chance to grab her

again. Her arm throbbed where his fingers had pressed in.
Her breast tingled where he had nudged it, like the last dregs
of a local anaesthetic.

"I was being honest!" Brand shouted.

Megan ran toward the church.

He shouted again, louder, spittle tickling the back of her
neck. "I only needed a moment, just a small moment, just a
few seconds — "

His voice followed her, though she could not hear his footsteps. Surely someone could hear him shouting, someone would
see?

" — spent the night wandering through the snow — "

She reached the door. It was open to her, as always.

"That poor cat." It was Brand's voice but it was inside her
head, as if he had taken her space and spoken with her mind
but not her mouth. *That poor cat.*

She turned and started shoving the big door shut, but
stopped when she saw him. He had backed up to the gate in
the railings, staring up at the spire and the unlit neon cross.
"Fucking monstrosity," he said. Then he looked down at Megan
and smiled that dreadful smile once more. "He's forsaken you
to me." And although it was merely a whisper, and Megan's
heart was thumping, and there were agitated voices behind her
in the church, she heard his words as though his breath gushed
them across her skin.

Megan slammed the door shut on his grin. Perhaps that
would break it. She moved to the full-height window next to
the door, but it was as if the scene was printed there from
some cumulative image of the church garden: no Brand; neutral sunlight; the grass cut; the flowers tended.

No Brand. Yet again, he had vanished in the space of a
second.

"That poor cat," someone said behind her. She spun around,
wanting to shout but unable to find her breath. Leave me
alone, the silent shout echoed in her mind, just leave me alone,
go away, get lost… Brand had frightened her. His coldness,
his mirthless humour, his emphasis slipping from one subject
to another, all combined to disturb. Those terrible scars cut
into his flesh with intent, gruesome tattoos using his own dam-

aged tissue as ink. And his eyes. Blue, but dark. Bright, but bland. The eyes of a corpse that doesn't know it's dead. His arms, twisted but straight again... and the way he'd been looking at Nikki in the car...

There were three people gathered in front of the cross, none of them Brand, all of them female. And they were looking at something down by their feet. One of the women had her hands to her mouth, the other to her ears, and if the third had not been smoking a cigarette she could have completed the threesome by covering her eyes.

The woman holding her ears shook her head once more. "Poor, poor thing."

"Who the hell — ?"

"I'll get onto Father Peter about this, you know," the smoking woman said. "I'm not having sickos breaking into our church and doing this, it's just not... fair." She turned and looked at Megan. Megan had seen her a few times in church, but did not know her name. "Not fair at all."

"What happened?" Megan asked.

The other two women looked up and moved back for her to see. Megan walked between the rows of chairs, inhaling and taking comfort in the familiar smells of well-thumbed Bibles and old prayers tumbled into dusty corners. She glanced back once, but the doors were shut, the handles were still, and if Brand did want to come in at least he would be faced with the four of them now. He would not find her on her own.

There was something on the floor at the women's feet. Megan could only identified it as a cat because one of the women said so. The face still had whiskers, she supposed, and the dry leathery nose was there, and the fur was black and white, but splashed a dark, crispy red.

"Poor cat," someone said once more, but Megan thought it must have been an echo.

She gagged. Her mouth filled with bile, her stomach rose up and clenched tight, muscles hardening. "Oh shit."

The creature was on its back. Its legs had been snapped to the side so that they lay flat against the floor, and rusted nails had been driven through its paws.

"I know who did this," Megan said. *That poor cat*, Brand

had said. Or had he? Had his lips really moved or had the words only been imagined?

"Who?" said the smoking woman. The word blew out in an angry puff.

Megan looked up. She smiled at the other two women, only now recognising them: Jane Weeks from the council estate and Marjorie Bellamy, the just-retired nurse who ran the Women's Night at the social club. Then she looked at the smoking woman and shook her head, almost imperceptibly, as if to dislodge a sticky memory.

"I said who? Who would break in here and do... " The woman nodded down at the crucified animal, taking another heavy drag on her cigarette.

"No smoking in here," Megan said.

The woman stared. "It's to calm my nerves," she said very slowly, as if talking to a child in a foreign language.

"Do you really know?" Marjorie asked.

Megan shook her head and pressed close to one of the tall windows. "No, not really," she said, her breath misting on the glass. She turned one way then the other, trying to see as much as she could. On this side of the church the railings gave way to the old boundary wall. A path ran behind, high trees standing like sentinels on the other side, and there were a couple of breaches where frost had shattered stone over the years. The wall had been here long before the church. Some said they had built on the site of a slaughter house, but even the oldest people in the village claimed not to remember that far back.

Nothing. No one. The tall trees shifted slightly in the breeze, still naked and awaiting spring to finally come along and clothe them. Something moved on top of the wall and Megan thought it was a cat, but when she turned to look full-on there was nothing there, not even a shadow.

"We should call the police," Jane said. "This is vandalism. Desecration. It must be a crime, mustn't it?"

"In Tall Stennington this is akin to murder," Marjorie said. "Nothing ever happens here."

Why do you think I want to go? Megan thought, and Brand passed one of the breaks on the wall. She stiffened, pressing her face close to the glass and holding her breath so that her vision did not mist over. At least, she'd thought it was Brand. A black shape, a quick wave of hair, taunting. Nothing now, but then she thought that if she stared at the gap forever nothing else would pass by.

The wall was only four feet high. He must have been intentionally hunkered down to only appear in the gap.

"Anyone got a mobile?" the smoking woman asked.

Megan thought about the phone in her bag but did not volunteer it. If they called the police they would come, see the cat, find Brand wandering around outside, question him, and he would mention her name and the brief lift her family had offered in the snowstorm… No, she did not want that sort of trouble.

Didn't look at his feet, a voice said in her head, the voice she recognised as her Honest side trying to pierce the lies she blanketed herself beneath. *Didn't look to see what shape they were.*

"Not me," Jane said.

"Nope." Marjorie glanced at Megan.

She shook her head. "Someone should move it," she said. She imagined touching the cat and retched again, trying hard to keep her mouth shut and her face neutral. She swallowed and felt the bile burning its way back into her. Turning back to the window seemed to provide some privacy, but it meant she had to look out into the church gardens, between the rose bushes and the small trees that barely seemed to grow.

"It's evidence," someone said behind her, but she ignored them. She needed to pray. That's why she had come here this lunchtime, to pray for help and protection from whatever had passed them by in the snowstorm. Not the Devil — of course not — but something *had* happened to their family, she had felt it then and she could still feel it now, a prying eye trying to see past her shell and probe inside. When Dan attempted to winkle a truth from her she could feel it, sense his concern or curiosity working at her, and it was easy to shield against that. Now, she was not entirely sure what was happening.

She did know what Brand was trying to do.

She needed to pray.

Megan went and knelt before the cross, forcing herself to stare up as she did every time, hating the symbol of His pain.

The voices of the women drifted away, her senses turned inwards, the black space behind her closed eyelids grew, her own breathing came heavy and closer than ever, and in seconds Jesus was breathing along with her.

She muttered her prayers but only to give them weight. She was never loud enough for others to hear because her prayers were private, known only to her and God. She honoured Him forever, occasionally asking for help, more often simply revelling in His being there for her, exhalations of love and devotion and humility.

Today, things felt different. "My Jesus, I don't know exactly what's going on, I want to leave this place and Dan doesn't want to go, and there's the prints... those footprints over our house... and Brand — "

Something touched her leg. It was so unexpected, so personal — and she was immersed in prayer — that she screeched.

"What!" someone shouted, but Megan was trying to catch her breath, looking down at her leg where she'd felt fingertips brush at the fine hairs there, dreadfully, hopelessly sure that there would be nothing but the thin red lines of nail scratches.

A spider. She watched it scurry across the polished timber floor and disappear beneath the first row of chairs. It was a normal house spider, not huge, yet she was sure she heard a *tappity-tappity-tap* as it made its escape.

"Just a spider," she said, and then something darkened the window to her left. She glanced up but there was nothing there. "Did you see that?"

"Yes," Jane said. "Euch, I hate spiders."

"No, the window, there was... " Megan trailed off, realising how paranoid she would sound. A spider touched my leg, I know who did the cat, something at the window... She went to the window and looked out. Opposite the church on this side was a row of old cottages, whitewashed and thatched, small windows often containing the original distorted glass. *Glass is a liquid*, she remembered someone saying, *it runs with time*. Between the church and the cottages was a narrow road, wide enough for one car at a time, no pavements, no border between the road and the church. The bricks along this façade were scratched by wing-mirrors, and on more than one occasion the congregation had been startled during a service by the low growl of a new rut being carved by an unwary driver.

No Brand. No signs at all. Again Megan pressed her face to the window and looked left, thinking that maybe she'd see him walking up the slow hill towards the village square. She sighed, the window misted, and the spider ran across right by her face. She did not screech this time but she did take a step back. It scurried along the mullion and down to the sill, and then headed off across the wall towards the next window. Megan squeezed past the end chairs to get there. Behind her, the three women were again discussing the dead cat as if Megan was no longer with them.

The next window darkened and remained dark. From this angle Megan could not quite see out. She did not know if she really wanted to, but still she jumped onto a chair and climbed over to the next one, looking at the window all the time, not minding her footing.

Brand's face disappeared just as she came near enough to see. He'd been grinning, she was sure. Her heart stammered, and just as it kicked back in with a painful punch she went tumbling, slipping and landing on her side on the connected chairs, then rolling to the floor. The fall was hard enough to knock the wind from her. Unable to breathe, her throat painfully closed and her chest burning, Megan hauled herself into a sitting position to look at the window.

Sun shone in.

Hands closed around Megan's arms and lifted her up. She caught her breath, and even though she knew that it was the women helping her she couldn't hold in the scream. Fingers dug into her left arm and a hand nudged her breast, reawakening the tingle from where Brand had touched her, making her puke, spattering her skirt, the chairs and the floor with what was left of her breakfast.

"Oh Jesus," someone said.

That's right, Megan thought, and then she heaved again. She was bathed in cold sweat. Trickles ran down her side, from her forehead and into her eyes. Her stomach ached. It felt like the worst hangover of her life.

The women helped her sit on a chair, exuding concern but still careful not to touch where she was speckled with her own puke.

"I know it's come as a shock," Marjorie said, "someone doing something terrible like this. But really, dear, it's just some poor stray moggie. Kids, I expect." Every word was tainted with doubt.

"It's not that," Megan said, but she would not — *could* not — elaborate. It's the face at the window, the grin, those scars and their hidden meaning, the very fact that he's even still here.

A shadow passed by the next window along. Megan looked up, even though she really did not wish to. There was nothing there but the spider, hanging from the frame on a thread of silk, its legs kicking at the air as if swimming.

His hand touched me, she thought, remembering the sensation of the spider brushing her leg. Much too hard to be contact from the spider's legs... much too *personal*.

Megan stood, scrambled over three rows of chairs, took off a shoe, waited until the spider had passed the glass and had bare plaster behind it, and then crushed it with one slap. There was a slight sucking noise as she took the shoe away to view the remains. It was little more than a stain.

Someone shouted outside. Or perhaps it was a crow cawing in the trees beside the church. Either way, she hoped it hurt.

"I have to go," she whispered, "I'm due back in work."

They tried to stop her, told her she needed cleaning up. Megan wondered whether it was concern for her or the mess that needed mopping. She did not care about that, not now. Maybe later she'd return. Just before opening the outside door she turned to the cross, closed her eyes and muttered one last prayer. He always listened. He always helped. He would see her home safely that night.

Megan walked back through the village to the office. The scent of vomit accompanied her, diluted by the breeze but still there. She should really go home. She could phone for a taxi, go home, clean up and spend an afternoon reading or cooking a meal, the things that always relaxed her. But behind all these thoughts was the fear of being alone, and her Honest voice reminded her of this. Dan would not arrive home until after six that evening, and Nikki could saunter in at any time between then and midnight.

She did not want to be alone in the house.

If they lived back in the city there would be plenty of people around, but not out here. And now that she knew for sure that Brand was still around, her fear was very, very real.

The road twisted and turned between houses, high stone walls and car hardstandings. Every time she saw someone that was not Brand the relief was intense. She absolutely refused to glance over her shoulder. She tried to tread softly so that she would hear footsteps if they approach from behind. She hugged her coat around her, partly to cover the vomit stains, partly to provide some sense of warm safety that was a hangover from childhood.

A curtain twitched to her left but when Megan looked it was still, not even the shadow of a watcher behind it. She hurried on. The sun was warm on her neck although the air was cold. Maybe someone was looking at her there, heating her skin with his gaze…

She looked back at last, unable to help herself. The street was deserted apart from a couple of birds pecking at tiny dead things on the road. One of them looked up and started hopping her way. Megan hurried on.

The road opened into the village square and there were people there, old and young, wandering from shop to shop, others hurrying back to work. Magenta's stood in one corner, music and smoke squeezed out by the throng of teenagers. Maybe Nikki would be in there? Megan would like to see her now, but the idea of approaching her daughter and her friends covered in vomit and looking a mess… she'd never be forgiven.

So she turned right and left the square quickly, passing by the blocks of council houses and heading for the office. The road here was straighter, but there were alleys and driveways and nooks and crannies, a hundred different places from where Brand could be watching, a dozen corner from which he could emerge. She looked down at her feet, counting the steps, each number taking her closer to work.

"God help me", she muttered, "Jesus, see me safe." He heard. He listened. He took her back to the office and into the arms of Charlotte, young vain Charlotte who sat with her for the next three hours. Then, around five o'clock, Megan decided it was time to call a taxi and go home.

THE BOOK OF LIES

What you see is what you get.

Never has a worse lie been uttered, never have words been formed into such a meaningless, vacuous sentence. Seeing is believing, *there's another, but it's not quite as bad or misleading. You can see and believe, but often the truth will out when more is known, or told, or gleaned from the blackness of lies.*

What you see is what you get...

You can know someone as well as you know yourself (which, sometimes, is not as well as you think... more of which later), but seeing them is not knowing them, smelling or tasting or touching them does not let you into their soul, their core, that place where they are what they are, no matter how much you, or they, or anyone tries to change them. You are all blueprints, changeable but stolid in their foundations. You are what you are. You certainly are not what you see.

There are eye complaints that cause hallucinations; drugs that inspire visions; mental states that change what is seen to something different, something not there when you think it is; the poison of a certain frog's skin can blind; distilled potato spirits can induce sightlessness amongst those who think they are seeing all. States of being which are lies, where sight is being devious and truth is more elusive that a glance here, a nod there. Because truth sometimes wishes to elude. That is its nature. Sometimes, truth itself is a lie.

You may see a bird in the street and know it's a bird, but who can tell what it's thinking, or who is thinking for it? You can see a spider going about its gruesome business — paralysing, injecting, liquefying — but are you sure it's only a spider? Can you say for sure that it does not have its own arachnid thoughts about you?

So what are you getting? Not what you're seeing.

So often you are getting far, far more.

CHAPTER SIX

Brand had been on his mind all day. That sense of victory he'd had when he left the bar — the bar and that bastard stranger, squirming in his own blood — still existed, but it had slipped sideways into unease. Something was not quite right. Dan sensed people smiling behind his back, and whenever he blinked the darkness behind his eyes was filled with brief images of Brand, Brady and Justin playing pool together, laughing, talking about what a fool Dan was.

He knew it had not happened. But he also knew that it *could* have. Who, after all, would ever tell him?

He'd tried to throw himself into his work, but whenever he used a pen or a keyboard his hand hurt, the bruises flexing and driving memory-spikes into his brain along with the pain. Flashbacks haunted his day, a slide projector's screen spliced into his head forcing unsought images his mind's eye. Some he was pleased, even happy with: Brand kneeling on the floor; blood glistening; Brady's eyes as he watched Dan leave. Others — darker, hazier, older — he did not welcome so much: Megan covered with her own blood, her eyes white and wide and shocked; Brand in the back of the car with Nikki, his hand creeping slowly across the seat towards his daughter's thigh.

Nikki smiling back at the stranger.

Some were memory, others twisted versions of memory, and although Dan was certain he knew which were which they still disturbed him greatly. He had taken lunch in the pub in the village square with a few colleagues, but there was a pool table there and a chirpy barman, and all it did was to remind him of Bar None.

It was not until mid-afternoon that Dan began to realise why he could not keep the incident from his mind. Over and above the extraordinariness of what had happened, and the bullish satisfaction at beating someone in a fight, and the sense of achievement he felt about defending his family's honour, was the overwhelming certainty that there was still some distance to go. Things were incomplete. He may have given Brand a lashing but he was still here. Dan was positive of that. *See you around*, the voice had whispered as he left the pub. He knew it had not been Brand uttering those words; it *could* not have been. Perhaps he'd just been warning himself that things like this rarely ended so suddenly.

Bastards like Brand had to be told two or three times until they saw the truth.

The final hour in work dragged by. He knew what he was doing and where he was going next. Doubt had vanished, replaced by a plot with a grim certainty as its ending. Grim, but satisfying. That comforted him. He liked to have a plan.

Dan passed through Tall Stennington on his way home. He loved this little place. It was dark now, but that just added a new sheen to the village, the cosy warmth of lit windows spilling into the dark and holding it back. Streetlamps had been installed only recently, though their light was fragmented by waving branches, hitting the pavement like shards from a shattered mirror. Even the industrial units and offices looked appealing at night, adding a shiny modernity to the village that leant more emphasis to its *olde worlde* charm.

He passed by the ugly church which Megan attended thrice-weekly. It looked huge and foreboding in the dark, its steeply pitched roof casting a massive silhouette against the sky as if striving for God, even when empty. Dan had never been inside.

Fifteen minutes later he pulled up in front of their garage. The house was dark and silent. Dan was pleased. Nobody home, no one to ask what he was doing in the woods, in the dark, on his own. Good. He had something to finish in there, someone to look for, and it would not be easily explained. Even if he told Megan that he was feeling pretty good about himself for the first time in years, the reason would not impress her. I beat up someone in a pub, darling, and now I feel great, now I feel as though I could take on the world. And you know what? I did it all for you.

No, nothing good there. He could disguise it as protecting his family but this was, in reality, all for himself. It was for the little boy who'd been constantly harassed and bullied in school, mentally at first, then physically when the thugs decided that verbal lashings were no longer enough fun. He still had the scar on his knee from when they'd pushed him into a ditch, thrown dog shit at him, kicked him back down when he tried to climb out. A rusty shopping trolley had added insult to injury after they left him to his own devices, slashing at his leg as he scrambled up the slippery slope to the footpath. It was not the only slippery slope he had been on… the bullying had driven him deeper into himself, tying him to his home more and more, afraid to go out but even more afraid to stay hidden. He knew that was the coward's way, but he'd never been a hero. He knew that to hide himself away would be to let them win, but he still had to go to school. He lost either way.

He'd been an ugly and awkward kid, so lacking in confidence that he spent hours in front of the mirror trying to see someone else looking back. He thought that by will alone he could change that face, clear up the acne and give the hair some sort of life and style, encourage poise and confidence simply by willing it at his own image. The mirror turns left to right, he used to think, but why not up to down? Then he'd answer himself out loud: It does turn up to down, and back to front as well, because in the mirror I'm someone different. In the mirror, I'm someone who'd fight back.

That night in Bar None, his mirror-self had manifested at long last. Perhaps it was guilt — more likely desperation, and eternal anger at himself for not being there for Megan — but whatever had finally turned him inside had made him realise that there *were* victories to be had in this world. They just need taking.

The house was dark, the woods were darker, but Dan was going in there to make sure that bastard Brand had gone for good. To ensure that he had done the best he could to protect his family. And to grab that victory for himself, one more time. That was all he really wanted.

Dan took a torch and a baseball bat from the garage, parked the Freelander and set off across the garden. He passed the dead apple tree and climbed the fence just where those damn footprints had seemed to vault it. The field between their garden and the woods was common ground, and so it had never been subjected to any agricultural preening. Clumps of shrubs and trees were dotted here and there, like hairy moles on a giant's rugged face. The grasses were long and rough. Seed pods hitched a ride on his trousers as he approached the woods. The ground smelled damp and his shoes squished in the grass, a dirty water rising up over the leather if he stood still for too long. He carried the bat in one hand — he'd bought it the month they moved here, with a vague idea that he, Nikki and Megan could do some pitching in the fields, but it had never been used — and the torch in the other. The bat swished through the long grass as he swung it, reminding him of child-hood walks in the country when he simply *had* to have a stick to swat at nettles and brambles, the longer the better, and some-times it would become his favourite stick and he'd take it home and use it again and —

The woods were dark as hell. It was almost five-thirty and the sun had truly left him. He felt his home behind him, watch-ing and wondering just what he thought he was doing. The other house stood dark and lifeless. When he'd come home he'd been pleased at that, because he didn't want his neighbours to see him plodding across the muddy field like some mad-man. Now it made him lonely. He was the only one around, no one else within shouting distance, only him, the woods… and Brand? Was he in there? Dan really didn't have any rea-son to believe he was anywhere nearby, in fact he began to wish that maybe he *had* scurried away already.

Dark, the whisper of water dropping onto its carpet of leaves, breathing out the staleness of damp rot, the woods bade him enter.

He turned on the torch. The light did not penetrate as far as he'd hoped, even though the trees were leafless, many of the shrubs likewise. He followed its beam between trunks, keeping to the vague path that ran through the woods to the lake on the other side. There were night sounds in here already, secret whispers he never heard during the day because sunlight brought so much more background noise. Now, the calls and cries and rustles were much more individualised, as if presented purely for his benefit. He smiled in the dark and the confidence rose within him. Brand was not in here. No way. He'd be long gone by now, tail between his legs, a split-egg bruise throbbing on the back of his head as a reminder that he couldn't just intrude into someone's personal space, talk about their family as if he owned them.

No. He was gone.

Dan realised that he'd been stepping quietly. He started stomping louder, brushing against bushes and walking faster. No need not to warn whatever lived in here of his approach. He'd seen foxes, badgers and deer, as well as dozens of species of birds, and he had nothing to fear from any of them. He moved the torch lower to try to see beneath bushes, searching for the animals that would be so scared of him, hiding away, cowering just as Brand should be were he here.

Dan surprised himself by giggling.

A shadow moved the wrong way. All noise ceased as Dan froze, one foot raised to step over a small fallen tree. He looked left where he'd seen the strange movement, shone the torch that way, succeeding only in allowing the same thing to happen to his right. He spun around that way as well. Movement. Surely more than shadows dancing with the torch, but while trying to convince himself, doubt took root. The quicker he turned to and fro, the more the shadows slipped behind trees, sunk to the ground, hiding away after allowing him the briefest glimpse of something wrong from the corner of his eye. And was that whispering he could hear? Sibilant plotting or water dripping through the trees? If it was water it fell in startling symphony. It was telling him to be afraid, though its own voice was fearless.

He backed away from the darkness he would have stepped

into next, had he kept going. Black eyes watched him, so many that they formed night. His torch flickered and dimmed. The reduction in intensity allowed him to see further, realising that brash light made his surroundings darker. He switched it off, but only momentarily. Better an oasis of light than a desert of dark. He reversed faster, feeling the path behind him with his heels and only noticing that he'd left it when he backed into a tree. A cool touch between his shoulders, the kiss of a bare branch against his scalp.

Calm, he thought, calm, there's no one here, just the torch playing with shadows. Again he turned off the torch briefly, only to see variations of dusk and dark dancing between the trees. The stream gurgled over to his right, a jaunty song, time-less, unafraid of the night. As he should be. As he had never been. The darkness was a source of his own inadequacy, a hiding place for defeats known and yet to be known.

Not so soon, he thought. Please, not so soon after some-thing so positive, a victory so total. He could stay and delay the inevitable — a panicked exit from the woods, the tang of fear emanating from him, his eyes wide and his clothes torn — or he could go now, still in possession of some of his bluster, keeping one single thing in mind: the impact of the pool cue on the back of Brand's head. Smashing those foul thoughts. Sending a shockwave through the bastard's ideas about his fam-ily, and shattering them.

Gripping the torch until his fingers hurt, Dan hurried back through the woods. He was sure he was going the right way. He had to be going the right way *so badly* that he convinced himself there was no doubt. Keeping the beam aimed at the ground just before him he refrained from running, breathing loud and deep to try to mask any sounds that may be about to come from behind him, or to the side. He was fleeing, true, but it was an orderly retreat.

By the time he reached the edge of the woods he was cer-tain that he had been following someone the whole time.

At last he found an excuse to run, because as he neared the house he saw that the outside lights were on, and Megan was slumped on the doorstep. He had never seen a dead person outside a hospital. He was sure he recognised one now.

"Oh honey," she said, "I've been sick."

"You're a mess."

Megan almost found it possible to laugh. How could Dan call her a mess when he looked like he'd run a marathon? He was sweating in the cold, face red from exertion, eyes driven wide. His trousers were wet to the thighs from running through the field. There were scratches on his neck and face.

"What have you been up to?" she asked. Any hint of amusement dropped when she saw the baseball bat. "Dan... ?"

"Dog," he said, because it was the first thing he thought of. He'd been running and his mind had been racing with him. Now confusion settled like a mist as blood slowed in his veins. "Dog. A big dog was sniffing around when I got home, and I thought of the Wilkinson's rabbits and chicken, so I... followed it across the fields. Chased it." Chased? Followed? He should make up his mind.

"With the baseball bat?" Megan considered what she could have done today, had she been in possession of a baseball bat. Beaten Brand away? Really?

"It was a big dog," Dan said, as if that explained it all. An unexpected flashback hit him then: feet raining down on him and the warm wet tickle of blood running down behind his ears, the ditch water soaking into his clothes where he lay, the grinning, faceless faces above him mouthing obscenities simply because they could, because he was an easy victim. And then the woods just now, dark and frightening without reason.

Dan stopped breathing, just for an instant. He wondered what precisely he would have done had he *really* found Brand in there, sleeping beneath a rough shelter or sitting inside a ragged tent eating food cold from a can. Would he really have struck him with the bat?

And how many times?

"I feel poorly," Megan said. And she did. Being sick had purged nothing. The fears were still there, the suspicions taking on gnarled certainties as her mind tossed them around, way down deep where even she could barely reach.

"Let's get you inside." Dan dropped the bat and torch and

helped Megan to stand. "Please tell me you didn't walk home in this state?"

"Got a taxi. Charlotte cleaned me up the best she could, but I think these clothes are ruined."

"You smell like the morning after," he said, trying to sound flippant.

"Feel like it."

"Why didn't you go inside?"

"Left my bag in work with my keys. I opened the garage and saw the car, and I guessed you'd gone for a walk or something. So I thought I'd wait."

Dan unlocked the front door, turned on the lights and stood aside to let Megan enter. Christ, she was a mess. Her clothes were spattered with tea-coloured patches, she exuded the sweet aroma of vomit and her face looked pale and tired.

"Want me to run you a bath?" he asked.

Megan nodded. "First, I need a drink."

"I don't think — "

"Tea, I was thinking. Don't worry. I won't hit the bottle until at least seven o'clock." She smiled, but it seemed that flippant was something neither of them could master this evening.

Dan started upstairs and Megan went into the kitchen. There were used dishes in the sink and half a cup of coffee on the worktop. The familiar signs of family pleased her, injected some form of calm into the places inside where her thoughts were still raging, where ideas and fears were swirling around each other like sperm and egg, just waiting to conjoin and form something else. Something new. A certainty she could not bear but must face. "My sweet Jesus," she muttered, "help me here and now, be with me, help me do whatever it is I have to do." She looked around for spiders but there were none. The window, offering a wide view of the garden during the day, was now a reflection of the lit kitchen. She looked very small. There could be anything out there watching her, and even if it stood only a few steps from the window, it would still be in the dark. She drew the blind, enjoying the rattle of its drum because it was something else familiar.

"Dan?" she called. He answered faintly from upstairs. "Why

did you follow the dog into the woods, precisely?"

He didn't respond for a while. She heard the taps go off and footsteps moving out onto the landing. Even then the answer took a few seconds, and she knew he was leaning against the landing balustrade, looking down at the hall floor and thinking what was best to say.

"It looked wild," he said. "A dog like that can be dangerous."

Megan nodded to herself, not replying. She filled the kettle, watching the chaotic swirl of water. Devil's dog, she thought, and she dropped the kettle into the sink. Her breath caught in her throat, stalled by the sudden realisation. The dog... the bird starting to follow her in the street... and that damned spider. Literally damned.

Brand had been watching her all the time.

"Oh my God," she gasped, falling to her knees and clasping her hands under her chin, resting her forehead against the kitchen unit to stop herself slumping to the floor. She started praying but kept her eyes open, glancing around, making sure she wasn't being watched. By anything.

Dan stirred the bath. Bubbles caught on the hairs of his arms, the hot water tingled the stretched skin of his bruised hand and wrist, he closed his eyes and enjoyed the sweet aroma of pine forests in the summer. The dark, that's all he had been afraid of, and though he was angry with himself for fleeing, the fact that he had ventured into the woods in the first place was a small victory. Now he had Megan to look after. And Nikki would be home soon.

He would lock the doors and smile a small, satisfied smile, because his family would be around him.

Nikki and Jazz had spent that afternoon in his parents' house.

When they arrived Nikki had been scared but invigorated, the strange experience behind The Hall having dislodged something in her mind, shoved aside certainty and normality to allow in other, more exciting stuff. Nikki loved the unusual, the bizarre and the plain weird, and she loved even more anything that caused deviation from the norm. She knew what normality did to people because she knew her parents. Love them she did, but sometimes they could barely find the time to speak to each other, let alone interact and share and love. She just didn't want to get like that. She could see it in her father's eyes as he sat watching TV in the evenings, a dull blankness that reflected the dancing colours of the screen without taking them, giving his eyes a sad colourless hue. And her mother, when she started spouting about God and being saved and Jesus and His sacrifice, Nikki wondered whether it was only she who saw the desperation in her mother's expression, the signs of wanting to be known and loved and understood.

She guessed not.

She guessed that was why her Dad watched too much TV with those sad, dying eyes.

Brand had scared her but she was excited, and although she'd wanted to be with Jazz — his company more than his actual presence had given her some comfort — still her thoughts were of Brand. Several miles away from The Hall, his apparent disappearing act in the bushes behind the tatty old building seemed less important, less *impossible*. He was a big man, totally in control, confident of his abilities and his looks, and he made her feel like a little girl again. Maybe that was why she was so interested. Around Jazz she felt like a woman, because she was in control and he was falling over his feet for her. With Brand, she was the youngster. He was the one with power.

Jazz had wanted to make love but Nikki had shrugged him off. They had lain on his bed kissing and cuddling, and although she knew just how worked up he was — she could feel it down there, pressed against her hip — she felt no inclination to do anything about it. Even if she imagined Brand lying there next to her instead of Jazz it did not work, because his actions were all wrong. Jazz pawed at her, scratching her breast as he pulled her bra down, biting her nipple instead of kissing, panting instead of breathing heavily, licking her ears and making disgusting slurping sounds as he tried to force is hand down the front of her jeans. Brand would be... experienced. Not gentle, but strong. So Nikki closed her eyes and let Jazz feel and pant and gurgle, because in a way she was glad he was there. She thought of branches scratching her face as Jazz bit her neck, tried recalling what Brand's breath smelled like as Jazz struggled to take off his jeans.

She had asked him to take her home. It was almost tea time, and for no apparent reason she suddenly wanted to see her mum and dad, have tea with them, chat, look for a spark of life in her father's eyes, a glint of normality in her mother's. She almost laughed at the unfairness of it all, imagining just what Jazz was thinking of her — he stood from the bed with his cock sticking out and his face flushed and hangdog — but she really hadn't done it to spite him. She watched him push it back inside his jeans, cursing as he zipped his fly, trying not to hate her as he shoved by and shrugged on his jacket.

She'd apologised and he had accepted with a shrug and a kiss. "I'm not being a bitch, Jazz," she had said. "I just need to get home. I need to talk to Mum and Dad."

He had driven her home on his bike, taking corners slightly too fast, pushing it to its limits and just beyond, as if purging his sexual frustration and confusion through speed and danger.

Yes, she needed to talk to her mum and dad. But as they pulled up in front of the house, she knew what there was one thing she could not mention: Brand. And although her dad must know about him (*your father and I have a bit of business to discuss*) Nikki certainly didn't want them to know that she'd seen him again. Just in case. Just in case she was destined to see him one more time.

Nikki kissed Jazz goodbye and promised to call him later for a chat. She apologised once more, said she wasn't a teasing bitch , she just didn't feel like it. "School tomorrow," she said. "I'll see you there."

"Love you," Jazz said.

Nikki kissed him again, smiled and went inside. She smelled cooking. The TV was rattling on about politics and flag-waving in the living room. She was home, and she was glad.

"The wanderer returns!" her mum said as she entered the kitchen.

"Hi Mum." Nikki kissed her on the cheek, then stared at her for just too long. She smelled of pine forests.

"What's up, honey?"

"Nothing."

"I was sick in work today, that's why I look a bit peaky. Okay now, though. And starving! I'm doing us a stir-fry."

"Lovely," Nikki said. *Sick in work... peaky...* she looked ill, not just peaky, and ill beyond sick. Her mother's eyes flitted from side to side, never quite alighting on her face, as if constantly looking for something over her daughter's shoulder. She turned back to the cooker and stirred the onions, mushrooms and peppers in the wok, always glancing up at the wall, the windowsill, the junction of wall and ceiling, the corners of the room, the window. And her smile, though quite natural looking, looked as fragile as a crystal spider-web, ready to shatter at the slightest provocation.

"How was band practise today?"

"Disturbed," Nikki said without thinking. She cringed, but her mother was looking elsewhere.

"Most of your songs are, from what I understand."

A joke or misunderstanding? Either way, Nikki was off the hook on that one. She felt the need to give her mum another peck on the cheek, which brought a genuine grin to her mother's face.

"Blimey, I am honoured this evening," she said.

"I'm going to say hi to Dad, then I'll go get changed. Give me a shout when dinner's ready, slave-woman."

"Okay honey." No response to the joke. No real display that she'd even heard it. Nikki frowned, shook her head and went into the living room.

Her dad was sprawled in the armchair watching the TV with the usual, not-quite-watching-this expression on his face. He seemed distracted, when he was usually simply spiritless.

"Hi Dad."

"Nikki! You grace us with your presence."

"Had that from Mum. She okay? She looks weird."

Her dad flicked channels from one mindless soap to another, grimaced, found a quiz show and seemed content. "She's a bit poorly," he said, leaning forward in his chair. "She was sick in work today."

"Did she go to church lunchtime?" Nikki wasn't sure why she asked, but it seemed important.

Her dad shrugged. "Don't know. Didn't think to ask. You know, I... I'm not really concerned whether she did or didn't."

"I wanted to come home so we could all have tea together," Nikki spurted, "I thought it would be nice and we don't do it much, I know it's usually because I'm out but I thought it would be nice."

Her dad smiled and Nikki was pleased. It made his face younger. "It will be," he said. "Good thinking!" He stretched back in the chair then and flicked over the channels a few more times. Nikki felt dismissed.

Askew. That's the best word she could think of as she walked upstairs. Today, there were things going on beneath the surface. She thought of the lake across the other side of the woods, how local legend had it that it was bottomless. Yeah, right, but she'd often stood staring at its calm, mirrored surface, wondering just what was happening way down there on its bed, what creatures stirred, lived, died. Same here, same now. A surface reflecting relative normality, with depths... perhaps bottomless... where a million unknown things crawled. Squirmed. Slithered.

For some reason, those slimy words felt just right.

Dinner was tense. For three people who knew each other so well, the lies and deceptions came thick and fast. Megan, Dan and Nikki all went to the table knowing that there would be talk about their day, all intending to miss out the portions concerning Brand, because none of the others knew. Only Nikki had seen Brand, only Megan had met him again, only Dan had beaten him at Bar None and pursued his memory into the woods earlier that evening. They all lied to the ones they loved, and although lying by omission had been their intentions, the untruths spread and grew like wet rot, until they all *knew* that they were lies but could no longer prevent them.

As they left the table, each blamed themselves.

That night, Nikki dreamed of Brand. She rarely recalled her dreams, but as she woke sweating in the dark — maybe she cried out, maybe not — it was still there in her mind, fresh and wet and violent.

She meets him behind The Hall, but this time he goes for her, hauling down her jeans and touching her roughly, bending her over to enter, growling as he does so, his legs longer than they should be, he's tall, too tall, and his white scar is blazing red.

Even as Jazz and her father push through the bushes and see what is going on she cries out, because she loves every thrust, every scratch, every animal second of it.

He's a waste of space, Brand grunts behind her in his real voice, a voice she hasn't heard yet. And as she smiles up at her father and Jazz, she wonders just who her lover is referring to.

Dan dreamed of Brand as well.

They are in Bar None again, but this time the pool cue slips from his grip and hits Brady on the shoulder. It pierces him there and arterial blood sprays out across the room, giving fake cadavers new blood. Brand grins at him and grasps his throat, lifting him until his head touches the ceiling, shoving him up so that his skull cracks against a timber beam, again and again, and all the while the others in the bar — Brady gushing blood, Justin smiling in the corner, Morris the barman — are willing Brand on. He's violent, he's always so violent, they say of Dan, but as he goes to protest Brand's fingers close into his throat and his fingertips meet inside Dan's flesh.

He woke fighting Brand off, and in their dark bedroom in the middle of the night he was being punched and hit.

Because Megan had been dreaming of spiders and birds and serpents, and when she jerked awake there were a dozen of them using the holes in her body, or making new ones.

THE BOOK OF LIES

Sweet dreams are made of these.... Life and death and sex and love and hate and spunk and blood and puke and shit and food and wine and tears and spit and mud. Dreams are life, real life, not simply reflections. Dreams are honest.

No morals in dreams. No deceptions in there because honesty provides their landscape, candour their atmosphere, and when you breathe in dreams you're exhale all the lies you've ever felt or lived or said as dead things, shells, to be blown away on the breeze. There must be a hill somewhere, a dream hill, against which the carcasses of all lies are drifted by the wind. It's can't be a very nice place. It must smell of decay and rot and evil, because lies generally are. Generally.

I don't want to ever go there. No one should ever have to go there, because it's not a place for souls. Lies are soulless. How to mix the two?

Make love in a dream and you come while you're asleep. No faking. No effort. You come because you're enjoying it, because there are no lies in your dream like yes, I like that, do it like that, even though you don't and you're only agreeing because you don't want to hurt your lover's feelings. In your dream you say no and suddenly it isn't happening anymore, you're doing it as you like it, as you've always liked it... or perhaps how you want it, and as you've always wanted it. So you come in your sleep. And the worst thing you can do when you wake up is to feel ashamed, because it's an honest orgasm, the best little death.

Fight in your dreams and the outcome is the only way it can ever be. You may lie to yourself when you're awake, say that everything is right and this is the way it has been and will be, but the true victory... or defeat... is won or lost in your dreams. Trust them. Heed them. They're there to be read and understood and, one day, lived out. If you do not fear God, then fear your dreams, because they're how He talks to you.

Most of all, if your dreams reveal things to you, heed them. Did Mozart compose in his sleep? Did Shakespeare dream his plots and his characters? Likely. You dream your future whether you like it or not, because your dreams are the concentration of all possible outcomes. Know them. Understand them.

Oh, and there's a spider in your heart, watching you.

CHAPTER SEVEN

Nikki returned to school the following day. It felt like the first day of spring. The sun was warming, not just a smudge in the sky, and a few brave snowdrops and daffodils were scattered on the grass verge at the school entrance. Trust the weather to improve just as school started again.

As she climbed off the bus, stared across at the sixth-form building and saw the unmistakable trio of Jazz, Mandy and Jesse, she suddenly felt much older. A teacher walked by and Nikki said good morning, feeling equal for possibly the first time, sensing that she could easily talk to them about drink and sex and drugs and all the issues that adults were supposed to be so good with, but were usually just as fucked up about as kids.

She walked around the circular road to the sixth-form block, feeling eyes upon her. Never the over-confident one, she looked down at her feet until she was nearer, then glanced up at her friends. They were busy in discussion, Mandy leaning against the wall, Jazz gesticulating wildly. The band, obviously. They could always argue about the band. She still felt that prickling of her skin once more, the weird sense of being observed. Looking over her shoulder, she noticed a gang of kids over by the middle block, third- and fourth-formers. They were watching her, giggling, pushing each other in clumsy displays of machismo, one of them grinding his hips and pushing and pulling his fists down by his sides. She sent them the finger — it only encouraged the display, she should have known that —

and moved on.

It gave her a perverse thrill, even though the boys were only thirteen or fourteen, several years her junior. Not a sexual feeling as such, more a mental perking-up, a confidence boost that lifted her spirits the closer she came to her arguing friends. She'd never felt like a sex object before. She smiled as she realised it had put a spring in her step and a swing to her hips.

"Morning all," she said. "All keen to get back to school, I see?"

"Hi Nikki." Jazz smiled at her even though she could see he was still pissed off. He worshipped her. She had a brief flashback to yesterday: Jazz standing in front of The Hall while she explored behind, meeting danger, meeting Brand; then back at his house, his mouth gnawing at her neck, clumsy hands trying to pique her interest. His adoration went only so far, it seemed.

"Hi." She kissed his cheek and it felt warm already.

"You two tore off pretty quickly yesterday," Mandy said. "Left me and Jesse holding the audience!" She smiled prettily.

"Sorry, I just… scared myself rooting around behind The Hall. Wanted to get away. You get the gear packed up alright?"

Mandy nodded. "Eventually."

"What did you think of *The Origin of Storms?*" Jesse almost whispered, as if apologetic for actually speaking.

Nikki smiled. "I loved it. Powerful. Great lyrics, fantastic. It'll blow their socks off!"

"Whoever 'they' may be."

"Mand, we'll get a gig soon, you know that. We can walk into a pub anywhere and get a gig for free, but we need to choose the right place."

Jesse had already gone pale. "Euch. Playing live… "

Nikki felt eyes on her again, a surreptitious stare, not from one of her friends. She glanced around at the gang of younger boys but they were wrestling on the ground, throwing each other's rucksacks around, generally paying attention to no one but themselves.

"You coming to my party tomorrow?" Mandy asked.

"Huh?"

"My party. Tomorrow." She sounded vaguely desperate.

Nikki nodded. "Oh, yeah, yeah, damn right. You think I'd miss your eighteenth? Hey, at least you can drink legally there." She sensed Jazz smiling next to her and guessed what was going on in his mind.

"Mum and Dad are away for the night, they wanted to leave the house free," Mandy said. "More fool them."

"And it's a big house!" Jesse said.

Still that strange sensation on the back of her neck, like a hot breath touching her from a few inches away. Brand's breath, Brand's touch. Nikki stepped back from her friends and took a good look around. There was nobody suspicious over by the school entrance, only kids pouring off a double-decker and a couple of teachers waiting to drive in. She turned a full circle, glancing at the lower block, the middle block and then the sixth form building between the two... and then she saw the shadow.

It shifted a second after she'd set eyes on it, keen to be seen. What surprised her most was that it was inside the school, the first floor library. The blinds twitched as it sidled out of sight.

Nikki knew she wasn't seeing things.

If it's him, why doesn't he show himself? she thought.

"Giving us the slow spin, Nikki?" Mandy said. "What, you had plastic surgery? New skirt? Haircut? Yeah, looks nice whatever it is."

Nikki shook her head without taking her gaze from the library window. "Sixth sense. Someone's watching me."

"Just like yesterday," Jesse mumbled.

"Watching us, you mean?" Mandy was the only person Nikki knew who had a voice like a raised eyebrow.

"Yeah, right, us."

Jazz moved closer to Nikki gain and put his arm around her shoulders. She did not shrug him off, but her coolness must had bled through to him. His arm was stiff and tight, the hold possessive, not affectionate. She felt like a new guitar slung under his arm rather than a person, his girlfriend. She knew she wasn't a trophy girlfriend — far from it — but she had also known for a long time now that Jazz's ego was a complex, fragile thing, and a reasonably attractive girl on his arm may well mean more than the girl herself.

"Can't believe we're back in this shithole for another term," Jesse said.

Nikki smiled and slapped him playfully around the head. "Not just another term, the *final* term. Stress and exams and saying goodbyes."

"Yeah, exams, tell me about it."

"Mum and dad still getting at you?"

Jesse nodded, blushed and looked down at his feet.

"Well I for one can't wait to get out and away," Mandy said.

Nikki frowned at her. A sense of time hit her all of a sudden, hard, minutes passing, the sun moving, her own flesh and blood and mind ageing. "And what about the band?" she said.

"Hey, it won't stop it," Jazz said. "We'll still practise and get a gig, won't we?"

"'Course we will," Nikki said.

Mandy laughed, a cruel knife slicing through Jazz's naïve optimism. "Yeah, like how?"

The bell rang to announce registration. Saved by the bell, Nikki thought, but as she glanced once again at the library she wanted to go home. To enter into that building would be opening herself up to danger, stepping into something she should be running away from. She'd be acting like a scream-queen in one of those horror films, investigating the blood-smelling cellar instead of running like hell, going toward the monster, not away from it.

But she could do little else. Normality and mundanity still ruled her, even though she liked to think otherwise. She had exams to study for, and when she noticed that the shadow had gone the danger seemed suddenly distant and foolish.

That lunchtime, Nikki went to the library.

For her English A-level she was studying *A Midsummer Night's Dream* and Golding's *Lord of the Flies*, but however much she stared at the pages of the novel today, closed her eyes, tried to put herself on the island with those tribal, lonely and very human boys, she could not picture Piggy or put herself in

Ralph's mind. She read the same page four times before giving up and staring at the words, trying instead to make sense of whatever strange sentences her mind may form from them. The big room was never really quiet, especially at lunchtime, but Nikki was in a world of her own. The noise she heard was the rasp of dry skin across the Freelander's upholstery. The smell was the musty staleness of Brand's breath. And instead of the warm breeze of a tropical island on her face, or the dryness of the school's heated air, she felt the stinging caress of branches as she pushed her way behind The Hall.

Someone opened the door and she glanced up, startled. It was a fifth-former returning some books. Nikki knew the face but not his name, and she probably never would. Here was a boy she had shared the same school with for years, but she would go through life without knowing him. He would live, marry and die, and she would never hear about it. He may be a success or a failure, but nothing he did would ever touch her life, none of his accomplishments — so important to him, meaningless to anyone else — would ever matter to her. That's something her father had once told her: nothing really matters. In the scheme of things we live, we die, everything moves on. She hated that idea, and sometimes she hated her father more for telling it, because it was something she could not get out of her head. In that respect, at least, she often found herself jealous of her mum's faith.

Eventually, as she knew it would be, her attention was drawn to the blinds where the faceless watcher had been standing. That was why she had come here, to look and see and smell, try to sense whether it really had been Brand standing there spying on her. There was no reason it should have been him, no logic in it... but if it had, that was more terrifying than anything. It meant that he was following her still.

And why follow *her* when his business was with her father?

Nikki had never thought of herself as particularly brave. Her life was generally so safe and ordered that her level of bravery was not something that had been put to the test. She's never faced a gunman in the village post office, never pulled someone from a burning car wreck, never had to watch a friend or family member die. If she was truly brave she had yet to discover the fact. The only time her courage had been put to the test she had failed. At least, that was how she still pictured it.

Her mother in the hospital. Nikki as a young girl, holding her daddy's hand as they went to visit. Her mother's face as she saw her daughter... her damaged, bandaged, almost unrecognisable face... and Nikki's instant reaction was to scream, snatch her hand from her father's grip and flee the private room, crying and dribbling snot and *wanting her mummy back*.

What still inspired shame was that one glance back to see her mother crying fresh tears, the salt-water diluting dried blood and dripping pinkly onto her hospital sheets.

No, Nikki had never felt brave.

She stood, scraping her chair and drawing amused glances from the other pupils in the room. Her book flipped closed as she left the table, as if in reaction to her ignorance. She'd see now. She'd go to the window and sense his presence, maybe even put herself in his place, be exactly where he'd been, look out and see where she'd been talking to the guys earlier that morning... maybe even see herself out there now, staring up in fear at the shadow staring down, staring up, staring down...

The blinds were dusty with lack of use. The sill had been painted a dozen times, badly, and its only adornment was a collection of dead flies. Nikki glanced at them and wondered if it hurt when they died and if any other flies missed them. She picked one up, the Lady of the Flies, and crunched its dried shell between her fingers. It was not a pleasant sensation. There was no moisture there, but she was destroying the remains of something that had once been alive.

When she twisted the control wire and opened the blinds, she saw a huddle of flies in the corner of the sill, as if blown there by a breeze. Every one of them was crushed. Wings were scattered across the dull gloss like faded daisy petals, legs gave the paint a crazy effect, bodies were shrivelled raisins in the spring sunlight. Looking down, she could see the place where she'd been standing that morning. The double-glazed window's seal had gone and it was misted on the inside as if someone had just exhaled between the panes.

It had been Brand. She could not smell him or taste or feel him here, but there was something else that convinced her he'd been here. Not a sixth sense, nothing so melodramatic, but a certainty derived of the course of events over the last few days. Maybe she'd been watching too many crummy detective shows, reading too many stalk-and-slash horror books, but it made sense for the watcher to have been him. Anyone else would have been pointless. Anyone else and…

… and she'd have been disappointed. Even though he petrified her, she'd have been disappointed.

She heard the final footstep behind her. A hand touched her shoulder; lips opened with a terribly loud *pop* as whoever it was went to breathe or shout in her ear; she heard the quick intake of breath; the hand tightened almost imperceptibly, an unconscious *now you're mine* gesture.

Nikki screamed: "Get the fuck away from me!"

The library went from a place of calm and relative peace to a room full of potential chaos. Tables scraped and chairs tumbled as people stood, the librarian stumbled from her office as if thrown and Nikki spun, lifting her arm and swinging her elbow around before her. She aimed high — aimed for Brand's throat, pictured his Adam's apple squishing — and struck Jazz on the temple.

Why would I want to hurt Brand? She thought. But it was pure instinct. And instinct told her that it was the right thing to do.

Finally given leave by their surprise, the others in the library began to make a noise. A few pupils scurried around or across tables to get closer to the action, laughing in base excitement. The librarian still stood in gaping, dumbstruck amazement. Nikki's scream had been like an explosion in the silent night, and now her violence against Jazz, her boyfriend, was a shock upon shocks.

Jazz hit the floor quickly, crumpling as if struck by a car. His hand clasped Nikki's shoulder tightly before he fell away. His fingers snagged on her blouse and almost pulled her down on top of him.

"Jazz!" Nikki breathed, hoarse with shock.

"Nikki, what the hell… ?" He curled up on the floor and

held his head. His left eye squinted shut as if trying to cut out the pain leaking into it from his bruised temple.

"Jazz." It *had* been Brand. She'd heard him approaching her from behind... or perhaps she'd only sensed him, sensed who she'd wanted it to be. It had been his hand on her shoulder, big and warm and strong... or maybe Jazz, foolish young Jazz had merely been trying to scare her. Nikki sniffed. There was a faint smell in the air, subtle but foul, like the stench of old food in a dustbin.

"You idiot!" Jazz shouted.

Nikki went defensive. She couldn't help it. She felt calm and relatively composed now that she knew it wasn't Brand, but there was also a heavy, angry atmosphere in the room. It didn't come from the pupils, or the librarian... or from poor, ineffectual Jazz. It permeated the air like invisible smoke, solid on her chest and stinging her eyes. It was a strong, cloying haze of rage... and it scared Nikki. It scared her a lot.

"What're you doing creeping up on me like that, Jazz?" she said. "You're the bloody idiot! What do you expect me to do, turn around and give you a kiss?"

"Wouldn't want a kiss from you, stupid bitch!"

"Good job," she said. "Not getting one."

"Good!"

"You mind telling me what's going on?" the librarian finally managed. She was a meek little lady, a dormouse who rarely spoke above a whisper, even when she was not in a library. Her voice was raised to mutter-level in surprise.

"Mind your own!" Jazz snapped, and she jerked back as if pushed.

"Jazz, leave it out," Nikki said, seeing what was happening, recognising his imminent explosion but unable as ever to prevent it.

For some reason she glanced back at the window sill and saw the flies there. The crawling flies.

No bits, no pieces left.

She'd even crushed the shell of one herself.

"The flies," she said, then trailed off. The whole window misted, faded and misted again, as if the room was breathing in excitement at the fight about to erupt within. Nikki glanced around to see if anyone else felt anything strange. All eyes were upon her. Theirs, and someone else's. She still had the crazy, unsettling feeling of being spied upon.

Ironic, considering she was the centre of attention.

"Fucking bitch!" Jazz whispered.

"Brand would never say that," she said.

"Who?"

She glanced back at the window and away again, remembered where she was and what was happening. "Eh?"

"Who? Who's Brand? Who's he, your bit on the side, is he? You two-timing me, you bitch?"

Nikki grimaced and turned away from Jazz — pathetic, squirming Jazz, shifting on the floor and kicking his legs and whining like a kid. "Don't be stupid."

"Do you mind taking this elsewhere?" the librarian said.

"She's not fucking him anymore!" one of the watchers said.

Nikki walked away. She had to because she didn't want a scene, even though there'd already been one she didn't want it made worse, and there was something very wrong in that room now, something warm and clammy that had nothing to do with central heating and nerves and the red-hot vibes of hate and embarrassment, and hatred for being embarrassed, rising up from Jazz. Everyone stood still and watched her go, but she knew she was being followed.

"Nikki!" Jazz hissed.

She opened the door and heard him scrabbling to his feet to chase her. There were amused giggles from the pupils, a whispered reprimand from the librarian. *Those flies*, she thought, but already she'd rationalised it away. They were there before, just disturbed from behind the blinds by all the commotion. Lazy with the cold draft from the window, sluggish in the air, crawling on the sill was all they could do, avoiding their dead dried cousins... .

Jazz shouted something else — something nasty and sick and imbued with threat, trying to save face in front of those amused observers — but Nikki let the door swing shut and she made no effort to hear anymore. She hurried downstairs and wandered the corridors for a few minutes, passing but not seeing other pupils and teachers. She felt someone following her, keeping out of sight, matching her footsteps in an effort to avoid detection. Whoever it was kept quiet. Jazz would have been shouting.

Lunch was ended by the bell and Nikki made her way to the theatre for her afternoon English lecture. The school was buzzing now as pupils and teachers went to their next lessons, and she risked a few glances behind her along corridors and through glass doors. Amongst so many people, she saw no one.

The teacher talked them through the play and they discussed honest Puck, and Nikki would never see Jazz again.

That evening, Jazz rides home from school.

He's a seething jumble of emotions; an embarrassed love-lorn teenager with a hard-on, shameful plans for revenge clouding his vision as the motorbike rumbles through the lanes. He sees Nikki's face as she turned and elbowed him in the head, and his heart drops and his limbs loosen at his feelings for her, her beauty. He blinks and sees her face again, grits his teeth, wants to punch it, needing to hit his anger into her because she embarrassed him so badly. But of course he never will, even if he does find the chance. Jazz has never been violent or abusive, but perhaps because of his inadequacy he is more aware than most of those who are. People will hear about today. They'll laugh behind his back, smirk because he'd been decked by a girl, call him a pussy... and he will mist away in their estimations like breath on a windowpane. He can feel himself changing now, as if the speed of his angry ride is tearing bits of him away, flipping them to the wind to let the air eat them up.

He is not concentrating enough on the road. It's not a particularly fast bike, but he can wind it up to sixty along these country lanes if he tries, and today he really tries. It's fast enough. He's usually such a careful driver, but some things need more than care to avoid them. Some things need an incredible stroke of luck, or reactions faster than light, or God on your side. And sometimes even that is not enough.

He rounds a bend and sees something standing in the road.

For an instant it's just a shadow thrown down by a tree, but as Jazz approaches the shape solidifies, coalesces out of nothing into something… into a man. A tall man with long dark hair and a smile that should look pleasant on his face, should look welcoming. Perhaps it's the speed of his approach, or Jazz's confused state of mind… or the ugly, bleeding wounds that hide the man's expression along with the truth.

That smile just looks rotten.

Jazz shouts. The noise explodes in his helmet but barely leaks out. He squeezes the brakes and knocks down two gears, the motor screams, Jazz screams again, the man opens his mouth as if parodying Jazz's shock…

The bike swerves and leaves the road with Jazz still astride it. They leap the ditch and the bike forces its way straight through the hedge, motor still whining, startled birds and last year's dead leaves exploding into the air on either side.

Jazz is left in the undergrowth like a butterfly pinned to a board.

Shock steals his breath, his comprehension, and for a few seconds he can only remember the guy's face as he skidded by at almost forty miles per hour. His face, and how much he looked like someone Jazz had never known and could never know. How much he looked like no one.

Then the pain kicks in.

Decelerating from forty to nil in the space of a hedge has virtually merged him with the shrubs and bushes, making a mockery of his protective leathers and driving leafless twigs and shards of split wood through into his flesh, knocking bones aside like so much play-dough and embedding themselves in organs, stomach, skull, bowels.

He's no one, Jazz thinks, because it is all he can think. It's all the pain allows. He tries to breath but it does not work. He opens his eyes but he can see nothing because there are twigs piercing both eyeballs.

He's no one, he thinks again.

Hands touch his shoulders, reach up to his neck, down his back to his legs. A fist closes tenderly over his crotch.

"A waste of space," a voice says from out of nowhere.

Help, Jazz thinks, and it is neither a request, nor a statement. He thinks of Nikki but all he sees is the laughing, bleeding face of the shadow that should have never become a man.

And then he knows that there can be no help because hands start pounding at him, pushing him deeper into the hedge, twisting him further onto the branches. He opens his mouth but a hand covers it, holding in the scream. Making him die in silence.

THE BOOK OF LIES

Chance does not kill, otherwise what chance would anyone have? Chancers would be killers, media games of chance gladiatorial blood-lettings of epic proportions instead of the mindless exercises in mass-control they really are. The horses? While they're running the minds of the gamblers are not... their imaginations, their views of the worlds are dead, but they are not dead themselves. No, chance is a duller, not a killer. Believe in chance... rely on it... and you remove yourself from the world stage. No need to kill you. You're nothing. Ironic, then, that chance's very arbitrariness makes life one long game of chance, and a game that kills is meaningless and... unfair. And saying that life is unfair is no defence, because life is impartial. What can be fairer than that?

Luck does not kill. Where chance is sought, luck is possessed. Good luck and bad luck may well be inherited, genetically or created by circum- stance, but they merely form opportunities for chance to kick in and change lives, for good or bad. Good luck is a blessing, bad luck a curse, but only in the perspective of a human. Again, nature is impartial. Luck is luck is luck. It doesn't end lives. It doesn't need to. Lives do that.

But fate, now... fate kills. Fate knows all about you, it knows your fears and your weaknesses and your confidences and strengths, and it can be ready for all of them when it decides that the time is right. It can move you like a pawn in a terrible game of chess, sacrifice you for the good of others, drop you from a building you should never have been inside, give you a disease that no one has ever heard of. Luck and chance are impar- tial. Fate is active. It picks on people. Almost as if it thinks about things too much...

Fate can be standing in a road where nothing or no one could or should be standing. It can put a cat in a trap, but how do you know it's there without looking? And without looking, how can you tell whether the cat is alive or dead?

And fate always gets an invite to parties.

CHAPTER EIGHT

Megan remained home that day. Dan rang into the office for her and spoke to Charlotte, told her that Megan was still feeling sick, and Charlotte sent get-well wishes for him to pass on. His wife merely nodded and smiled because she knew she should. It felt forced. Her mouth was a lump of metal she was trying to bend into an impossible shape.

Dan fussed and made her breakfast and they both kissed Nikki as she left for school. When they were alone he sat quietly and looked into the half-empty cup he held in his hands. There was no truth in there, Megan knew, just cold coffee. But still he stared, his forehead lined with thought, eyes half closed. His knuckles were white. He didn't know how to say whatever it is he needed to say.

"I'm going to the loo," Megan said, rising from the table and groaning at the pain in her stomach. She must have pulled a muscle yesterday while she was being sick.

"What were you dreaming about last night?" Dan asked. Megan was almost relieved. If that was all he'd been struggling with she needn't be worried, needn't concern herself about Brand and whether Dan suspected. Not that there was anything to suspect. Or feel guilty about, other than lies.

"I don't really recall," she lied again. "Animals, I think."

"You were batting your hands around and hitting me."

"I've already said sorry."

Dan looked up at her and smiled. "I'm not after an apology, honey. I'm just worried about you."

"Dan, I feel rough. Must have been something I ate, or something. Haven't you ever had bad dreams when you're ill?" She leaned against the wall and shifted until the pain in her stomach lessened. She had to get to the bathroom, just to check one more time.

"Yes, I have," he said. "It's just... since you said you wanted to go back to the city, it's all been a bit weird."

Megan looked at Dan, her husband, her love, and she suddenly wanted to tell him everything. Not only the stuff about Brand and yesterday and how it had messed her up, but the idea that he was around all the time, watching her vicariously... that bird, that spider... mad but true, it had to be true. And she wanted to hug Dan and ask him not to be so worried for her because God was on her side. He had kept Brand from the church yesterday when he could so easily have come inside and hurt her —

(*the cat, what about the cat, crucified on the floor of the church, legs snapped back?*)

— and there was nothing to fear when God was on your side. He had been looking over her shoulder as Brand reached out and grabbed her and touched her breast. He had seen him, and He had marked him. Megan was good. She had nothing to fear.

She wanted to hug her husband and tell him not to be so scared and guilty and not to torture himself about that terrible attack that had drawn them out of the city and into the wilds, the wilderness, this place where she knew no one and where no one knew, or wanted to know her. Because Dan thought about it every minute of the day. It was plain in his eyes, obvious in his voice when he spoke to her, evident in his tensed body as they made love. He hated himself for not being there to help her. Ironically, she loved him more for that.

But she could not tell him any of this. He may ask, but she could not say. Because she had to protect herself and her family. And silence, as her mother had always taught her, was the best protection.

"Honey, I feel rough," she said. "I need the loo. Hey, don't worry." She turned and left him staring after her, feeling his gaze on her back and all those unsaid things hanging like a barrier between them, stretching now as she widened the space, more impenetrable for that.

She went to the loo, sat down, then had to stand and lean over the pan as she was sick. When she saw movement in there, something as big as her thumbnail with clawed legs and a curved stinger, she closed her eyes and flushed the mess away.

Dan thumped on the door. "You okay, Megan?"

She mumbled a yes. Then she stripped her bathrobe and nightdress and ran her hands across her body. She was looking for her dream-wounds, knowing that they could not possibly be there but desperate to check again, for the third time that morning. She touched her ears and nose and mouth, looked at her fingers, no blood. She squeezed her nipples and ran her hands down between her legs, from the front and behind, checking her palms and fingers for blood, seeing none. She twisted as far around as she could to look at her back, just to make sure they weren't hiding their entry and exit holes there. Nothing. As she knew there would be… nothing.

Nothing but the thing she had vomited up.

Megan closed her eyes and muttered a frantic prayer, covering as many of her orifices as she could with two hands, keeping things out or holding them in.

God would look after her.

After Dan had left for work — again kissing Megan and mentioning his concerns, again turning away with a frown when she told him that everything was alright — she walked from room to room without really knowing what she was looking for. She checked the front door to make sure it was bolted from the inside, then the windows in the living room, dining room, study, kitchen and utility room. Then the back door in the kitchen — opening and closing the bolts several time just to feel the metallic certainty of them — until she started on the front door again. She looked out of every window at the day outside, the morning chill held at bay by the central heating and double glazing. No sounds, no breezes, no smells wafted in. She may as well have been in another world. And that alien world outside was as still and peaceful-looking as ever, with the neighbouring houses shut up and silent, the woods drawn back further from the house than they had seemed whilst snow-laden, the surrounding scrub-land offering few hiding places for anyone wishing to approach the house unseen. There was the main lane, and that was it. No opportunities for creeping up on her. No ditches, no hedges or secret tunnels…

He was not out there, because if he had been she would have known about it already. She wondered whether he really needed to be out there to see her, to hear her or taste her. She ran her hands through her hair, sure that she would shake woodlice and fleas onto the laminate floor in the hallway, but apart from the night-time knots it was clean and clear.

Megan thought briefly about the thing in her vomit, but it had been a piece of food from last night, given life by a hang-over from her nightmare. Things don't live inside you, not things like that. Her stomach twinged at the thought. She could not decide whether the pain was real or imaginary.

In each room she searched for something as she checked the locks. She was not sure what, only that she would know it when she saw it. For now she did not see it, did not know it. In a way that made her more nervous. Confronting dangers she could see or sense would be preferable to living in fear of something she could not. God was with her but sometimes, she knew, pain and fear were His way.

She spent the first hour after Dan had left patrolling the house, walking from room to room downstairs and up, lock-ing, unlocking, re-locking doors and windows, staring at the still scene outside, wondering all the while just what Brand had wanted yesterday. The more she thought about it the more sour the taste in her mouth. He had scared her very badly and she resented that. It made her angry that he could come be-tween Dan and her, because that's exactly what the stranger had done. She had dreamed badly last night and lied this morn-ing. Now she was acting like some paranoid, disturbed idiot, reading more into things than she possibly could or should.

Megan went back downstairs to the kitchen, made a cup of tea and continued lying to herself. Talking out loud helped perpetuate the idea that she had been talking and thinking her-self into a panic, rather than reacting to simple fact and actions. Brand had threatened her, but with effort she did not see it that way. He had scared her, but with a little bit of thought and some creative screening in her mind, all his frightening aspects were hidden behind his superficial appearance: that blank, strangely unattractive visage he presented; those grue- some scars. By the time she'd finished her second cup of tea she was almost feeling better. She was aware that she was con- structing lie upon lie to protect herself, just as she had to hide herself from Dan, but she was so desperate for comfort that lies seemed better than the truth. However elusive she was making it.

And as she finished pouring her third cup of tea she heard the footsteps upstairs.

A daddy long-legs fluttered down from the ceiling and alighted on the back of her hand. Megan jerked in surprise, knocking the cup to the floor. It shattered and spilled tea like brown blood. The long-legs remained where it was, its touch barely felt but its weight more than she could bear.

He was watching. Seeing her with whatever multi-faceted eyes this thing had. Viewing a dozen images of her, each one of them changing as he did more to haunt and hunt.

The footsteps again, across the landing, nudging one of the wardrobe doors in her bedroom.

"Oh God," she whispered, bringing her right hand down to enclose her left, feeling the flighty tickle of the insect's wings for the split second before she exerted enough pressure to kill it. She ground her palm against her knuckles, wishing she could crush it so much that it would not be there when she looked.

"Leave me alone, leave me alone, leave me alone… " Here, on her own, she found that the make-believe no longer worked. She could only lie to herself so much before the truth began laughing in her face.

The thing was a smudge on her skin. Banging from up- stairs again, random and seemingly without design. She felt the insect's insides as a breeze kissed them cool on her hand. Her heart thudded, breath came in short painful gasps, tears blurred her vision. It's not like him, she thought. Running around, banging, not like him. He'd be more… composed.

She should leave, open the door and flee, but to where?

Out in the open she was just as vulnerable as in here. At least she knew her own house, felt confident here, if not comfortable. And he was invading her territory. The bastard was in her *house*.

Hardly believing what she was doing, Megan grabbed the large carving knife from the knife block and went out into the hallway.

A cloud of rooks darkened the landing window and she wondered which ones were his.

"Help me Jesus," she whispered, "be with me, guide me, touch me, help me, help me… " She mounted the staircase. Whoever or whatever was upstairs must have heard her because the noises ceased. She was pleased in a way, but it also meant that she could no longer locate their source. She thought it had been on the landing initially, but then it had sounded more like wardrobe doors being nudged, or the partition between the bathroom and Nikki's bedroom being scratched and scraped.

"Leave me alone!" Megan shouted, surprised at the venom in her voice. Surprised also at how confident she sounded. "Leave me the hell alone!" Silence was the answer. "I've got a knife, I'll use it." She sensed eyes upon her, though there was no one in sight. She was almost on the landing now, trying to avoid creaking boards she knew so well. The bedroom doors were all open as usual, but there were no shadows crowding them, no eyes peering out. Still, that crawling sensation prickled her neck and arms, the certainty that she was being observed. "Help me," she whispered again, and the shape ran from Nikki's room.

She screamed and threw the knife, realising as she did so that the thing was small and black, not the tall man she'd been expecting. The blade flew wide of the shape. It darted directly at her, halted and reversed direction before Megan had time to finish her scream.

The cat scurried about on the landing for a moment, confused and shocked, and then it stood just inside the bathroom door. And stared.

She'd never liked cats. They always seemed to mock, she thought, licking their paws and grumbling and sauntering around, never once dropping their gaze because they knew things you didn't. She'd never seen this one… and it not only knew things, it knew *her*, she could see that by the way it stared, looking her up and down, a very human gesture. It had seen her before. Mocked her before.

"Try your best, my love in God will protect me," she hissed. The cat stared, the slits of its eyes narrowed, even though the light levels remained the same. It blinked once, turned and walked into the bathroom.

Megan picked up the knife, followed it in and closed the door.

She couldn't decide whether or not the cat was scared. *She* was. She hated cats and she was terrified, so it should be coming at her, slinking around her legs and purring and laughing in its purrs. But it was hunkered down behind the washing basket instead, watching. For an insane moment she was suddenly sure it was the cat from the church, but that one had been a different colour, and it was dead…

"Whether it's you or not, you won't be there for long," she said, fear giving her voice a gravely edge. Those eyes… they terrified her. Totally dominant and confident. They never wavered even as she stepped forward, grabbed the washing basket handle and dragged it across the floor. "You hear me, you fucking weirdo? I'm not scared of you. And look what I have here." She turned the knife in her hand.

The cat laughed at her. It was a hiss, a baring of teeth, but there was no fear or violence there. It was a laugh. Wherever he was hidden and whatever he was doing, he was laughing at her now.

Megan lashed out with the knife and stumbled back in surprise as it opened the cat from neck to rump. Blood spattered onto the white porcelain wc pan and fur clung to the blade like a line of tiny spiders.

The blood splash dripped and dribbled into the shape of one of Brand's scars.

The cat changed. Its eyes went wide with pain, their colour shifted, and its hissing laugh changed to one of shock and rage. It tried to run but its legs would not function. It slithered in its own leaking mess, paws scrabbling for purchase on the slippery floor, teeth bared again as it hissed and snarled.

Megan glanced at the bloodstain again, but it had run past that shape now, smudged into something more chaotic. "Oh sweet God," she said, appealing for help and cursing at the same time. She had never killed anything in her life, not like this. Spiders and flies and ants, yes, but never something this big. And never so cruelly. A grey shape bulged from the rent in the cat's side, and the more it struggled the more the thing slipped out and caught on its slick fur. The dying creature keened like a baby in pain.

Megan took refuge in the only place she could: blame. "You bastard!" she shouted, sweating and swearing, "You fucking, freaky bastard, look what you made me do, look at it, look at the poor thing — "

She stepped forward and lashed out again, closing her eyes this as the knife stuck home. It jarred in her hand and grated against something, and she let go and stepped away, eyes still closed, listening to the final few jerky movements of the animal as it died on her bathroom floor. When all was silent she looked. The cat was dead. The knife was jammed into the back of its neck.

"It was his, it was his," Megan whispered. She had seen eyes like that before. After the attack, back in the city, people had watched her, friends and relatives regarding her differently. Everyone was fascinated and they disguised morbid curiosity as concern. Walking along the street she had sometimes seen someone on the other side acting strangely, or the swish of hair on a turning head from the corner of her eye as she passed a shop. She had become used to eyes flitting from her as she looked at people, and even more used to the blatant stares. She knew the difference between a casual glance and a determined gaze. Even on a cat.

The shakes were settling in now. Five minutes ago she had been drinking tea, convincing herself that all was right with the world, that any fears she may have were unfounded, constructed from Brand and how he'd unsettled her. Now she was standing in her bathroom over the corpse of a butchered cat.

She noticed for the first time that it wore a collar. She did not read its name-tag.

"It was his," she said again, backing from the room. The way it had been looking at her! The snarl that was a laugh! Wherever he was he was blind to her now, but she was certain he'd still be smiling. Hiding in a ditch or a dirty room, knowing what she had done and aware of what she must be feeling. And smiling. "It was his."

Megan went downstairs and turned on the kettle. She would make another cup of tea. She would sit and drink and stare from the window, looking through the steam from her mug, and convince herself that things were fine.

As the kettle boiled she held onto the worktop, fingers pressed down on its surface until her nails went white and her knuckles felt ready to burst. There was an ant hurrying across the floor just in front of the Rayburn. It did not seem to be coming towards her, or moving away. It was aimless. Of course it was. May be his, she thought, but the fear was bounced back at her and subsumed beneath the lies she needed to create to drown the truth. Aimless and its own thing, nobody else's. For God's sake, how could anyone use an ant?

Or a spider or a bird... or a cat.

Megan laughed and shook her head at her own stupidity, and on the way to the fridge she made sure she trod the ant into a quarry tile. She had to hold onto something.

CHAPTER NINE

Of course, there had been nothing in the woods. That was a crazy thought. Nothing but the buried fear of failure stalking him as he stalked something else, something — or someone — long gone. Because he had beaten Brand and scared him away. He would never see him again. And that was that.

By lunchtime in work, Dan had convinced himself that this was the truth. He was not very good at thinking around problems like this — his thoughts were scattered, without order or definition — but that morning, poring over figures he could not see and letters that remained unread, he succeeded in realising the truth. It was a pleasant truth, a comfortable one, because he had scared the guy away. He had protected his family.... if there had ever really been a threat from Brand in the first place. He was a wanderer. A loser. And now he had lost, he'd wandered away out of their lives.

Smiling, actually a little embarrassed at his fleeing the woods last night, Dan reached for the phone to see how Megan was faring at home. It rang just as he touched it and, enjoying the idea of fate grinning down, he snapped it up.

"Honey!" he said.

There was a pause, a whisper of breath — or perhaps a restrained giggle — and then a voice. "Well yes, as I've already said, I'm sure that's what it tastes like... Honey."

Dan felt a chill prickle his skin and his shoulders actually slumped as failure once again attacked his thoughts. He was scared, angry and shocked all at once. What could he do?

What *should* he do?

"Just you stay… " he said, but he got no further. Brand laughed, loud and hard and hearty, and Dan imagined him leaning back in whatever chair he occupied, holding his stomach with both hands, the phone hooked beneath his chin.

Dan went to hang up but could not. If he did that he'd spend all day wondering what Brand had phoned to say, and if it was something bad… something worse than empty threats… Dan may regret it. What if he'd called to say, *I'm with your wife now, and I'm about to fuck her with a rolling pin and slit her throat?* He'd let his wife and himself down once, and he swore that it would never happen again. So he waited and listened as the laughter subsided.

Brand laughed until he was hoarse, his breath catching when laughter turned to tears, voice screeching, the plastic telephone receiver shaking in Dan's hand as the speaker within vibrated, on and on. And then he stopped. Instantly, without a sigh or a groan. And his voice was as dark and dank as ever.

"Broke my fucking skull," he said. "All I wanted was a moment of your time, and instead you broke my skull."

"If you come anywhere near my family, I'll kill you," Dan said. It should have sounded melodramatic, but coming from him it was merely pathetic and weak. Not even worthy of a laugh.

"I don't plan to come near your family," the voice said, all innocent and smooth. "I plan to come *in* them. I'll shoot between your daughter's lovely lips, and maybe I'll honour Megan with a good hard fuck. Or perhaps not, considering your wife's track record with pussies."

"I'll call the police," Dan said, voice raised. He thought of shouting louder in the hope that someone in another office would hear, take the hint and make the call. Maybe they could trace this. Maybe they could find out where this sick fuck was calling from and —

"I'm not calling from anywhere," Brand said. "I'm going to make the next few days very, very long for you. Time flies when you're having fun… but when you're watching everything you've lived for destroyed, my oh my, how it must stand still. When everything is happening and you begin to wish you'd given me a measly lift, just think: while for you it's a collection of the longest moments of your life, for me it's not even the blink of an eye. It's a moment between moments. A blank between thoughts. A moment of *my* time. And it's something you'll wish you never had."

The threat out in the open changed everything: the way Dan thought of himself and his family; his sense of justice; his worry over work; his ideas of what was fair and what was not. Everything.

"What do you want?" he managed to whisper.

"Nothing."

"What can I give you? To go away, what can I give you?"

"Giving time is past. I'm taking."

"Please… please… " Dan knew he sounded even more pathetic and out of control, but he was scared, so ball-shrinkingly, bowel-looseningly scared that he could think of nothing else to say.

"Bye!" Brand said, cheerful and jaunty. "See you around!"

"Don't hang up!" But Dan was already talking to nothing, casting his voice along lines that no longer heard, listening to the dull, empty hum of a broken connection. He wondered where Brand had been calling from and what lay between them. There was a link, a solid physical link which, given time, he could follow: leaving the phone on his desk, unearthing the cable, crawling hand over hand, passing over and under roads and fields and houses, until he emerged from a wall and saw Brand sitting there with the phone resting on a table beside him, mouthpiece still hot and wet from his laughter. Brand, his dark eyes hidden by his fall of black hair, his scarred eye closed as he leaned back and knotted his hands behind his head, smiling at the ceiling and relishing the moment.

And given the chance, Dan would kill him.

He put the phone back onto its cradle and rested his head in his hands, rubbing at his temples as if he could massage out the fear and press in a solution. But a solution to what? A total headcase making stupid threats? No, there was more than that. And for the first time Dan wondered whether he was the only one who'd seen Brand since that snowbound night.

"Oh shit!" He snatched up the phone and tapped in his

home number, suddenly certain that he'd be speaking to Brand again in a matter of seconds. He'd speak to Megan and hear Brand laughing down the phone, hear his wife screaming past Brand's hand as the bastard screwed her on the hall floor, leaving the phone off the hook so that Dan could hear everything, see everything in his mind's eye. And this time, Megan would be more out of his reach than ever.

He almost hung up and went to drive home, but the ringing stopped and there was a gasped breath from the other end.

Again, he almost hung up; he did not want to know. He squeezed his eyes shut and winced at the terrible, selfish thought. He did not want to know if anything was wrong. "Megan," he said quietly.

"Hi Hon," she said.

"Megan!" He gushed it rather than spoke it this time, slumping back into his chair.

"I'm feeling a lot better now, if that's what you've called to ask," she said. "I've had a bath, prayed a little, and God and aspirin have settled my stomach."

Dan heard the smile in her voice but he could not bring himself to answer with a quip. "Good, I'm glad, don't want you being sick again. Everything okay?"

"Fine, yes, I've told you. I'm going to spend the afternoon reading. I'm drinking lots of tea."

Lots of tea. Strange thing for her to say, but then sometimes his wife did come out with peculiarities, especially after she'd been praying. Dan had not prayed since he was a kid at Sunday school. He thought seriously about it now.

He needed guidance and help, not just with how to deal with Brand and whatever threat he posed, but how to handle it with his family as well. If he told Megan the truth now, he'd end up having to explain why he'd beaten the bastard around the head in Bar None. Justin or Brady hadn't said anything to Megan yet, but when they next saw her they'd surely mention it, whether he asked them to keep it quiet or not. He'd not heard from either of them since that night. He knew just how shocked they must be.

"Good," he said. "Fancy a cuppa myself."

"Will you be late home tonight?"

"Maybe." *Why?* he wanted to say, but there was no reason to ask and he hated Brand for planting suspicion. Suspicion at his own wife.

"Oh. I just need to know when to get dinner for. Thought as I was home I may as well do it." It was a lie. His wife was lying to him. He didn't know how he knew — face to face he could never untangle the truths from untruths, even though he knew they were always mixed in — but he knew. Perhaps simply hearing her voice, having nothing physical to distract him, meant he could filter the lies that much easier.

"Nice," he said. "That would be nice. What are we having?"

"I'll think of something."

"Sure you feel alright?"

"Super. Looking forward to a quiet night in... get a video on the way home, perhaps?"

"Right. See you later."

"Love you." And she hung up. She never hung up first. She always waited for Dan to put the phone down, she joked that it gave her the chance to offer a parting shot when he couldn't hear, a secret *I love you,* or perhaps a *tosser* if he'd said something to annoy her.

She was in a rush. Had to get dinner ready. No need to wait.

It was two o'clock. For the next hour Dan sat at his desk, waiting for the phone to ring, dreading it, and wondering just what the fuck he was going to do about Brand's threat.

At three o'clock he rang Brady and asked him over to his house. Then he made his excuses to his boss and went home.

The front door was locked. Dan jiggled the handle and it took him back to life in the city, after Megan was attacked and she took to hiding in the dark, bolts thrown and blinds drawn. Out here they'd become accustomed to leaving the front door unlocked when they were at home. It was a foolish sense of safety, he knew, because bad things were just as likely to happen in a sheltered hamlet as they were in a big city. The fact that the surroundings looked pleasant merely hid the danger more.

He rang the bell three times and listened to it echo away behind the heavy front door.

"Just say you've popped by for a social call," Dan said over his shoulder.

"You should be in work. Why would I do that?"

"Brady... " Dan shook his head, knowing his friend was right. "Coincidence. Just pretend."

They stood silently for another few seconds and then Dan rang the bell again. "She can't have gone out. She was feeling rough."

"Maybe she went for a walk. Er... so why *am* I here, Dan?"

"Want to chat to you about something."

"Oh." Brady shifted from foot to foot behind him, and Dan imagined him staring down at his feet, silent but thoughtful. Brady was the strong quiet type. With a nickname like that, who could blame him? "Hey, if it's about that night at Bar None, just, er, forget it. Everyone does something — "

Dan turned to his friend. "It is about that, but not the way you may think. Megan still doesn't know about it, so don't tell her, but I'm glad I hit that fuck. He's been... threatening me. And my family, though I'm not sure.... I don't know whether he's spoken to Megan or Nikki yet. That's why I came home. Megan sounded weird."

"She's been ill," Brady muttered as Dan turned back to the door, bent down and shouted through the letter-flap.

The door flew open and Dan leaped back in surprise.

I'll honour Megan with a good hard fuck, Brand had said. For a split second Dan closed his eyes because he did not want to see, but what he imagined was surely worse than the truth could be.

"Honey," Megan said, surprised. "You're home early. Hello Brady."

"Thought you sounded a bit lonely so I came home, see how you are." Dan could hear the lie in his voice and wondered if Megan could too.

She stood on the threshold, one hand on the door, the other holding a toilet brush. Both hands were gloved. She wore an apron. There was a spot of something on her forehead, a scab of blood from a dried spot, perhaps.

"Doing some cleaning?"

"I really feel a lot better," she said, turning away so that he could not see her face and going back upstairs. "Make me a cuppa, hon', I'll be down in a minute."

Dan and Brady closed the front door behind them and stood in the hallway. Dan could smell the fumes drifting down from upstairs, bleach and bath cleaner and the subtle and disturbing hint of Megan's sweat underneath. She must have been working hard. He glanced at Brady to see if his friend thought this as strange as he did, but Brady's face wore its usual mask of composure and calm.

"Tea?" Dan asked

"That would be nice. And biscuits, please. Drag me out here and keep me in the dark like all the skeletons in your dusty closet, dangling and loose-limbed and ever so handy with pool cues, no doubt... the very least you can do is to feed me biscuits."

In the kitchen Brady sat at the breakfast bar, picked a paper from the small pile ready for recycling, and started reading it as Dan made the tea. "Weird about those footprints," he commented, scanning the local rag from a few days before.

Dan leaned against the sink and closed his eyes, slowly rubbing his face as if dry-washing. He sighed. "That's when it started, really." He looked at his friend, sitting at the bar and obviously feeling slightly uncomfortable with the scrap of strangeness Dan had aimed his way, and for an insane few seconds Dan envied him: lived on his own; only himself to think about; no real worries. "It's all been very odd."

And then he told Brady about Brand, the lift in the snow, the weird feeling he'd had when they arrived home that night, the sense that Brand was still around even though they'd ejected him from their car (*Megan kicked him out, she did it, I didn't help*)... and everything else. He told him everything.

By the time Megan came back downstairs with a black sack full of rubbish, they'd reached the point where Dan knew he had to decide: call the police or not? Brady had suggested it, Dan had fielded the idea and tossed it around, and now Brady simply sat there staring at his friend, his doleful eyes insisting that it was the only option.

Dan knew he looked like a schoolboy caught stealing apples. "Tea's here," he said to his wife.

She smiled too widely and sounded too cheerful. "I'll just dump this in the dustbin." The back door drifted shut behind her. Dan wondered just what game of lies they were both playing.

"You *have* to call them," Brady hissed, Megan's reappearance perhaps urging him to insist upon it. "This guy sounds like a lunatic."

"You saw him."

Brady shrugged. "Well, I saw some poor sod get whacked by a pool cue. And I didn't hear... well, I didn't hear what you said you heard in the bar."

Dan shrugged and stared at the back door. "She's acting weird."

Brady sniffled, his version of a laugh. "No offence, mate, really. But your Megan's always been a little... off-kilter."

Dan smiled without looking at Brady. He knew how right his friend was.

Megan came back in and drank her tea. Five minutes later Dan saw Brady off. They had still not agreed the solution to Dan's problem. Brady gave him a meaningful look as the door closed on him. *Police. You have to. No question.*

"Not often we see Brady during the day," Megan she said as Dan closed the front door.

"He was passing. Dropped in for a cup of tea."

"Oh."

She didn't ask why, or whether he knew Dan would be home, or how strange it was for Brady of all people — strange, shy, quiet Brady — to make an unexpected social call.

She didn't ask anything.

Dan watched his wife wander into the kitchen, rubbing her hands together as if to rid them of a stain and muttering about the damn spiders and flies.

CHAPTER TEN

Mandy's eighteenth birthday party promised to be a wild affair.

Nikki hadn't seen or heard from Jazz since she'd left him on the library floor the previous afternoon. He usually waited for her after school but not this time, and when she'd casually strolled by the place where he usually parked his bike and saw it empty, the relief was tempered by a vague disappointment. However much of a young fool he was, he was a young fool in love, and Nikki was flattered. She liked him. She didn't want to hurt him. His obvious show of petulance was to grab her attention and to strike back, and in a way it had worked; she had wanted to see him. But at the back of her mind as she waited for the bus home was Brand.

The library window had stared at the back of her head as she boarded the noisy bus. She had been so tempted to look around, yet somehow she had refrained. Not that there would have been anybody there. Of course not. Nobody here but us flies, alive and mostly dead.

He hadn't phoned that night either, and when he failed to show the next day in school Nikki became concerned. They'd had a row, true, but they'd rowed before. It was not like him to ignore her like this... mainly because he could not. He was smitten, and she was certain that any brief show of aloofness would have been ended by her failing to fall for it and contact him. She listened for his bike, watched from the window before lessons started, failed to see him arrive, asked Mandy and

Jesse whether they'd seen him. Neither had. They gave no indication that they knew about the scene in the library. If they were covering up for Jazz they were doing an Oscar-worthy job of it. Besides, Nikki was sure that Jesse wouldn't do anything against her. Bless him, he was smitten as well.

Smitten… she liked how Jazz thought of her, but it was certainly not something she had ever felt over someone else. Jazz was nice, he was cute when he wasn't acting the jerk, he had a good body, he was intelligent and witty (again, when he wasn't a jerk). But she certainly was not smitten with him. He told her he loved her and she said it back, because it felt nice and comfortable and she didn't want to hurt him. But if she was in love with him it certainly wasn't the electric feeling everyone made it out to be, and that in itself proved that she was not.

Then she had met Brand.

Now, everything was different. As she set off for Mandy's party she realised that her concern for Jazz existed simply to keep up appearances, for herself as much as anyone else. That lunchtime in school, the headmaster had sent a message to every class asking if anyone had seen Jazz. His parents had been in touch to say that he was missing, they were worried but not too frantic as yet; he had gone missing for a night before, apparently, although this was news to Nikki. Anyone who knew where he was, they asked, please let them know. If he was upset about something they could talk it through. If he was in trouble, they could discuss it. Anything could be overcome. They just wanted him home.

Nikki had looked down at her hands and seen that they were shaking. She'd closed her eyes and tried to picture Jazz as she had last seen him, but the only face she could see was Brand's, a shadow staring from the library window, hidden in the woods, breathing at her behind The Hall, and the longer she kept her eyes closed the more the image of Brand invaded, the dream of him invading her and grasping onto her hips as they made love.

She'd opened her eyes and gasped, drawing curious glances from those around her.

Jazz… what an idiot. If he thought pulling a stunt like this would make her feel bad, he could think again… and again.

In fact he *could* think again anyway, Nikki thought as they pulled up in front of Mandy's house. If he wasn't here tonight, he could just think on forever without her, because she wasn't hanging around. Not for him, not for… Well, maybe there was someone she would wait for.

Feeling no guilt, Nikki shamelessly hoped that Jazz did not show tonight.

She had an idea that someone else would.

Mandy's parents were both solicitors, and their house was a garish display of the wealth their careers had accumulated. Like Mandy they wanted people to know that they were there, and their three-storey home, surrounded by half an acre of garden lovingly maintained by hired help, was painted a bright yellow, just *too* bright to be called 'sandstone'. The windows were large, offering an open view into the family's private life. The front door was sheltered by a huge open porch, more suited to the finest London hotels than a country house a mile from Tall Stennington. Every time Nikki paid a visit she expected a doorman to step out and help her from the car, then take her dad's keys and offer to park for him. The roof was steeply pitched, which drove its pinnacle above the surrounding trees so that it protruded like a castle in an old fairytale. And like any good castle a wind vane spun on top, the wrought iron fashioned into what Mandy insisted was her family emblem: a bear holding a snake aloft. Cool, Nikki thought, though she'd never said this to Mandy. The whole house stood out like a beacon, especially at night when several banks of floodlights lit its facades. Security, Mandy would say if anyone at school quizzed her about it. Display, most people with more than an ounce of sense would know. It was a beautiful house and it deserved to be seen, but the fact of who the owners were made that flaunting crass in the extreme.

Nikki's parents had even postulated that Mandy was sent to a comprehensive school because it gave her more to boast about. At a private school she'd be just another grape in the bunch.

"Don't get lost in the dungeons," her dad said as Nikki opened the car door. She always heard a note of envy in his voice when he made a quip about the place.

"I expect her mum and dad have locked them up and kept the key," she said.

"Hey, maybe Jeremy is in there!"

"Jazz is just sulking, Dad."

"Well I hope he shows soon for his parents' sake."

Nikki leaned over and gave him a peck on the cheek. "Thanks for the lift. He will show, he's just being a big kid."

Her dad smiled past the sadness that she was becoming used to, the mourning for the loss of his little girl. He glanced her up and down — took in her tight top and short skirt — and she knew what was coming, but she didn't object or leave because she knew it was something he had to say.

"Be careful, Nikki."

"I will Dad."

He looked at her so meaningfully that she almost laughed. "You know what I mean."

"Dad!" She kissed him again, leapt from the Freelander before he could start talking about condoms or disease or how boys her age were walking glands, and slammed the door behind her. She waved as he pulled off, wanting to watch the car back onto the main road, but she was suddenly aware that anyone looking from the house would see her.

It was barely nine o'clock and the party sounded to be in full swing already. The Red Hot Chili Peppers were blasting through closed windows. Lights flashed in the dining room, throwing distorted shadows out across the lawn as revellers danced or stood close to the window. The living room windows had no curtains, and Nikki could see a dozen people milling around, sitting in cliquey corners or strolling in and out. Mandy was one of them. Bottle of wine in one hand, cigarette in the other, she was touring her party and playing the hostess, probably asking everyone if they were alright for drinks and suggesting they visit the wine cellar later because she knew where her mum and dad kept the key and she was sure they wouldn't mind, after all it was her eighteenth birthday...

There were rabbits on the lawn, sitting in the pools of light.

They glanced up and down at the house. Ears twitched. Whiskers moved as they sniffed the air. Nikki wondered why they weren't afraid.

She glanced up at the house looming above her and saw lights on the top two floors as well. She wondered whether Jazz was in there somewhere, waiting to surprise her with his coolness. Just like him to turn up and say '*Hi*' as if nothing had happened, kiss her and hold her and display her to his friends like a badge that said '*Hey, we had a row but she loves me so much she's wanting me back already*'. He'd want to kiss and make up, and no doubt he'd already scouted the house and found the quietest corner where he'd try to drag her before midnight. Seduce her with his rampaging ideas of subtlety. Cynical of her, she knew. Nasty. And yet again she hoped he was not here. Thinking the house empty of him made it easier to ring the doorbell.

She rang three or four times before she heard Mandy shout for whoever it was to just come the fuck in. As she reached for the handle something scuttled through the bushes beside the front door and made her jump. A bird, a mouse, a rabbit? Maybe a cat, hiding in there and watching the humans at play. She glanced back over her shoulder at the dark gardens, made darker by the light splashing out from inside.

Was Brand there? Was he watching her from darkness? She was standing under the porch light, he'd see her from anywhere between here and the road. He could be standing there in the open like a tree, smiling at her, touching himself as her eyes passed over him without seeing, promising her something with eyes she could not see and would never be able to understand if she could.

"Brand," she said, and it felt like the first time she'd ever said his name aloud.

The door burst open and Mandy screamed at her. "Nikki!"

"Shit!" Nikki stumbled back two steps and then laughed at her friend. She looked pissed already. She'd be in bed before midnight and Nikki wondered with whom.

"Nikki, come in, drink, eat, music and gorgeous blokes in the dining room, booze and food and gorgeous blokes in the kitchen, dope and gorgeous blokes and Jesse in the living room."

"No Jazz?" she asked as she walked by Mandy.

"Thought he'd be with you." Her breath smelled like an accident in a brewery.

"Nope." She handed Mandy a present — a copy of David Beckham's biography — and cringed as her friend hugged and kissed her.

"He's a jerk," Mandy said. "Forget him... plenty more sharks in the sea!"

Someone came from the living room and bumped into Nikki, mumbling an apology and heading down the hallway to the kitchen.

"And there's one!" Mandy said. "Charles, my mum's boss's son. Take a look at him, Nikki, and tell me what you see."

Nikki watched the tall boy walk carefully into the kitchen, fingertips brushing one wall to guide himself along the way. Too early to be drunk... he'd been on the dope already. She shrugged. "Pissed bloke?"

"Rich cock on legs," Mandy whispered in her ear. "Twenty grand in the bank and seven inches, so I'm led to believe." Then she took a huge slug of wine and stormed into the dining room, immersing herself in music and light and the adoration of her invited friends. "Have fun!" she commanded Nikki over her shoulder.

Nikki went into the living room and glanced around. Like every room in the house it was huge, the three-piece suite swallowed at one end with another couple of easy chairs and a slew of floor cushions by the shelved near wall. The shelves were loaded with books that Mandy had never read and her parents never had time to read, and knowing that only made the room seem colder. There were about twenty people in here, most of whom she was distressed to note she didn't know. Mandy's social life was governed largely by her parents, perhaps as a way of having an involvement in their daughter's life where work otherwise prevented them. This room was filled with friend's kids, client's kids, the offspring of people they knew from their country club. Nikki wondered just how many of them were really Mandy's friends. They sat and chatted and laughed in a cloud of cigarette and pot smoke.

"Nikki!" Jesse called. He was sitting on a settee at the far end of the room, a can of lager warming between his thighs, girls on either side talking to anyone but him. Nikki's heart sank for her friend, both at his predicament — he must know what he looked like — and the eagerness he showed at her appearance. He struggled to his feet and weaved his way between seated and sprawled bodies. "Hey, Nikki. Okay?"

"Hi Jesse. Having fun?"

His eyes shifted and he glanced down at his feet. "Don't know many of them, but they're an OK bunch."

"Anyone here from school *at all?*"

He nodded vigorously. "Most of the sixth form are dancing in the dining room, a few more are in the kitchen. Rumour has it Natalie is humping Pete upstairs."

"Already? Didn't waste her time."

"Does she ever?" Jesse asked, but Nikki could hear the desperate jealousy in his voice.

"Wanna go mingle?" she asked.

He nodded his relief. "Where's Jazz?"

"You tell me."

"Would if I could. Jerk."

Nikki laughed and gave Jesse a friendly hug. "Mandy's opinion exactly. Hmm… and mine."

They left the unknown smokers and crossed the wide hall to the dining room doorway. The double sliding doors were open, spewing light and loud music and the vague hint of sweat from the dancers boiling within. The Chili Peppers had been replaced by a compilation of club dance music, and the ravers amongst them were getting down to their serious stuff. The huge dining table — Nikki had been for a meal when there were twelve people seated there — had been shoved up against the far wall, and now it provided a grandstand seat for people to sit and rest and view the dancers, take the piss or scope the talent.

"I need a drink!" Nikki shouted into Jesse's ear.

He nodded, then motioned her to him. He held her head as he shouted back, his fingers slipping under her hair and stroking her scalp slowly, gently, and probably unintentionally. "I've seen Amanda! I'll see you in a minute!"

Amanda was a snobbish bitch in Nikki's books, full of self

confidence with very little reason. Nikki scanned the room and saw her in the middle of the dancing throng, strutting her stuff, pumping her hips and sticking out her little tits like some major dance queen. Nowhere near good enough for Jesse. But she could never tell him that. "I'll be in the kitchen," she shouted back, leaving Jesse to waste his time.

As she walked past the staircase to the kitchen she wondered briefly whether *she* was good enough for Jesse. She smiled in surprise, but an instant image of Brand breathing into her face behind The Hall — his stale breath tasting sweet in her mouth — wiped a smile form her face. She looked around startled, as if expecting to see him standing at the front door. There was no one there, only a haze of smoke drifting out from the living room, twisting into impossible shapes in the hallway.

She reached the kitchen door to a wave of shouted greetings and playful insults.

"It's the gorgeous Nikki!"

"Nikki likes licky!"

"Nik, you bitch, what took you so long!"

"Sexy girl." Whispered. A loud whisper as if it came from right beside her. She looked around quickly and shook her head. The voice had sounded older than anyone here... older than *everyone* here.

"Nikki, show us your tits!"

"Hi Mike," she said. She liked Mike, his constant haranguing and playful abuse made her feel strangely at ease in his presence, even though she thought most of it was because he felt inadequate with his attraction to her. That's what she *liked* to think at least.

Mike nudged the guy standing next to him, someone Nikki didn't know. "She does, you know. First whiff of alcohol and she gets her tits out. Second whiff she lets you feel them."

"Don't listen to a word he says," Nikki said.

"Drink?" The guy held out three bottles of Bacardi Breezer. She couldn't help laughing, but she only took one.

"Where's Jazz?" Mike asked.

"Anyone else asks me that and I'll personally execute them in public," she said.

"Oh," Mike said, hopelessly feigning disinterest. "Still AWOL."

"Still being stupid, yeah." She took a swig from her bottle and sighed as the sweet drink tingled her throat.

"Fourth whiff?" the guy asked Mike loud enough for Nikki to hear.

"Home run," she said playfully, pushing past the two collapsing boys and inspecting the food table.

It was an impressive feast; Mandy's parents had obviously invested some of their expense accounts into hiring professional caterers. The kitchen table — not quite as massive as the one in the dining room but still half the size of Nikki's bedroom — was covered with a spread that would put most wedding parties to shame. Sandwiches were beautifully arranged; smoked salmon and shredded duck shared space with lamb kebabs and pork balls; a dozen flavours of vol au vents scattered amongst silver dishes of home-fried crisps and boned chicken breasts coated in a variety of spicy marinades. Bottles of wine were dotted here and there, the red corked to breathe, the white residing in gorgeously melting ice sculptures, their reservoir dishes filling slowly with water. Snacks sat on plates with imaginatively peeled oranges and other useless ornamentations, which would inevitably end up being thrown around the kitchen or hidden in cupboards to rot and stink once everyone was pissed. There was even a huge figure '18' cake, the '1' in the shape of a microphone, the '8' a pair of drums, other music-inspired shapes cast in icing and scattered around the base of the cake.

The candles looked too expensive to set alight.

Nikki was pleased to note that there was more than enough food to cater for her vegetarian sensibilities, although all in all the display looked far too lovely to even consider tearing it apart, throwing it onto plates, eating and probably spewing it into expensively carpeted corners later on.

The drinks table was even more impressively weighed down. Bottles of every imaginable spirit hunkered at the back ready to leap out later in the night, while cans and bottles of lager, bitter, cider, alcoholic fruit juices, wines and fizzy mixer drinks were piled on and under the table, and doubtless cooled in fridge as well. A wreck of empties already hung around the full bin. Several bottle had been smashed, their remains kicked into a corner.

Nikki took a handful of crisps and nibbled at them while she surveyed the feast. It was going to be a good party. Lots of her friends were here, there was food and booze enough for a football stadium, and Jazz wasn't around to bug her or cause trouble. She felt bad thinking that, but it was the truth and she was in no mood to try lying to herself.

Maybe Brand would show as well. She hoped he would. That was the truth.

She wondered what everyone would think if he turned up and they walked around arm in arm. She laughed a little, spraying crisp crumbs onto the floor. Then she stopped laughing because she knew just how badly Brand would mix, and how false that image of comfortable companionship would be. Brand didn't want a girlfriend... Nikki doubted he needed one. If he wanted anything from her it was one thing: sex. She breathed in deeply and tried not to imagine them together, but it felt as though his hands were already there, smoothing her shoulders and working their way down and around her body, over her breasts, across her stomach and between her legs, turning warm to hot and dry to wet.

She opened her eyes, drained the bottle in one gulp and went back to Mike and his nameless friend for another.

"So why isn't Jazz here?" Mike asked. "He sulking? How's the band going?"

"Point one, Jazz and I had a row and he's fucked off to try and get me worried and upset."

"It working?" Mike's friend asked.

Nikki stared at him and took a glug from her new bottle. "Do I look upset?"

"Well... you don't look your usual charming self," Mike said.

Nikki went to clap him on the shoulder but she saw that he was serious. "The Rabids are doing okay," she said. "We want to start gigging soon. May even ask my old man if he can get us a gig at Bar None!"

"Cool place for a rock band to play."

"That's what we thought."

Mike glanced at his mate who sauntered off, muttering something about finding the loo. Nikki saw the prearranged signal as clear as day, but she pretended not to. Mike was all right. She didn't mind chatting to him for a while.

Someone touched her between the legs, a warm, hard hand cupping her there and nudging up with a thick finger.

"Fuck!" She dropped her bottle and spun around, ready to lay out whatever sick bastard thought she wore a short skirt as an invite. The bottle smashed and splashed her bare legs with drink and broken glass. She did not notice.

There was no one there.

"Nikki?" Mike asked.

"Huh?"

He moved the shattered glass aside with his foot and held her shoulders. "What's up? Don't you like Metz?"

She shrugged, held her own hands up in a warding off gesture, shook her head. "Nothing, nothing. I'm okay. Need the loo, I think."

She left the kitchen, feeling Mike's annoyed gaze travelling up and down her back. The downstairs loo was locked so she hurried upstairs, finding the first floor bathroom lit and open. She slammed the door and locked it, sat on the lowered toilet seat and held her head in her hands.

Sexy girl the voice had said. She'd heard it. She'd heard it behind The Hall as well, and she knew she had to get Brand out of her mind. He was not going to be here, he had no invite, he didn't know where she was, he had no interest in her. Business with her father, he'd said, that's why he was hanging around, no other reason...

But why find her? Why follow her?

Why spy on her in school?

She stayed there for a while, wondering what had happened to Jazz and why he'd left it this long. Had she really pissed him off that much? She guessed she had. Elbowing him in the head was just a part of it, he'd known her mind had been elsewhere for the past few days. He may be a raging hormonal monster, but he wasn't stupid. Maybe he was staying away because he really wanted no more to do with her. The thought made her feel cheap and nasty .. .and unwanted. She didn't like it. She liked attention.

Nikki checked her make-up and left the bathroom. Glancing up at the second floor landing she saw Mandy, leaning against the banister and flirting outrageously with Mike's friend. Who knew what would happen there later? One thing for sure: today, Mandy wanted to be centre of attention. If she was going to screw the guy she'd likely do it now, so that she could come back down and flit around the party once more, enjoying the fact that word was spreading that she'd already had her birthday present.

Nikki stood still for a couple of minutes, waiting to see if Mandy noticed her. Noise rose from below, darkness hung above, half-hiding Mandy and the guy from view. Nikki stood in between. The couple were whispering to each other, leaning closer and closer, the guy's bottle of lager eventually touching Mandy's breast, a couple of fingers unwrapping from around the glass to stroke her there. When he leaned forward and gave Mandy a kiss Nikki turned and quietly hurried downstairs. It was crazy but she'd felt a pang of jealousy. She had no one here tonight to kiss. Mike was interested but not interesting, a flirt wrapped around nothing, and besides, notwithstanding everything she'd been feeling and saying about Jazz, she didn't feel in the mood for a guilt trip.

Back downstairs she headed for the dining room, thinking to lose herself in the flashing coloured lights, the music that had been cranked up so loud she could almost climb it when she stood at the door. It was a solid force coming at her, a sensory attack that worked at every level… she could taste the spilled booze and the sweat of the dancers, the pheromones of attraction that ruled the dance floor and drew people into shadowy embraces under the table and in corners where the lights did not reach. She went in, elbowed her way through the dancers — swapping shouted hellos and nods with people she knew as she went — and looked around for Jesse.

He could be anywhere. If not in here, then back in the kitchen for another drink. If not there, then in the living room with the dope-smokers, trying his luck once more with the girls on the settee, telling them he was a drummer in a band.

If not there... well, there were fifteen rooms in the house, any one of them could hide a surprise.

It was too loud to talk, almost too loud to think. Nikki leaned against the table and picked up a half-finished bottle of lager. It was still cool so she took a drink, not caring that it was someone else's. She'd been here for half an hour but already she felt more distant — more *removed* — than when she'd arrived. Being on her own was part of it, but that was no different to at least half of those present. The trouble with Jazz contributed as well, she knew, a complex guilt-driven concern that mixed in anger at his behaviour and confusion at her contradictory thoughts about Brand. Be here, she thought, I'm scared of you, she thought. Just another fucked up teenager, that's what she was. Maybe she needed more drink.

Something touched her ankle, an intimate tickle that could have been a kiss. She cursed out loud, her voice lost in the cacophony, and squatted to look under the table. She stared straight into the face of a girl giving a blow job. The guy's hands grabbed at the floor, fisting and stretching, and the girl — it was Amanda, although the guy certainly wasn't Jesse — looked at Nikki without once losing her rhythm.

Nikki stood, embarrassed and feeling more unwelcome than ever. She shouldered her way from the room, not even bothering to return any greetings or comments this time, and headed to the kitchen for something new to drink.

Mike was still there. "Hey, Nik."

"Fucking orgy," Nikki said, then forced a laugh because she realised how old and *responsible* that sounded.

"Oh, and why aren't I involved?"

"Your mate's upstairs with Mandy, and there's something oral occurring under the dining room table."

"Mandy? Blimey. Fast worker. She doesn't even know him."

Nikki shrugged. "Guess she does by now." She indicated the drinks table with a nod of her head. "Alcohol required in excessive quantities. Want anything?"

She saw a smart quip forming on his lips about what he wanted, so she turned and found a bottle of Schnapps. There were shot glasses but she chose a tumbler, filling it almost to the top before dropping in some ice and a splash of lemonade to assuage her guilt. She drank, relishing the tingle of the drink across her lips and tongue, the warmth as it trickled down into her stomach. A pleasant buzz was already blurring her senses.

She turned around and Mike had gone. Playing hard to get. Well, she guessed he knew by now he wouldn't be got tonight, not by her at least.

"Nikki!" Jesse said, hurrying into the room. He grabbed up two bottles from the table, opened them and took a drink. "Hey, I've met a girl. Suzy. She's in a band, she's a keyboard player, electro-crap but still, she likes the fact that I'm a drummer, she wanted another drink so I said I'd get her one."

"Cool." She felt genuinely happy for him. It was the first truly pleasant feeling she'd had this evening.

"See you later." He looked suddenly sober and concerned. "Hey. You don't mind, do you?"

Nikki laughed out loud and spilled some of her drink. "Don't be soft. Enjoy yourself. Hey, Jesse, full report when I see you next, eh?"

Jesse smiled, nodded and tapped his back pocket. He spun around to leave, then turned back and touched Nikki's arm. "Oh, there was some guy asking after you. Tall. Long hair. Scar… I think." He frowned for a couple of seconds, looking vaguely over Nikki's shoulder. "Seemed like he should be in a band." Then he turned and was gone before she could say a thing.

Tall. Long hair. Scar… I think.

"Oh shit." She started to shake, and had to put her drink down before she dropped it. Nerves twisted her stomach, and excitement, and fear, and pleasure at the confirmation that yes, Brand *was* interested in her. Whatever his business with her dad, she counted as well. Tall. Long hair. Gorgeous.

She stared at the kitchen door, expecting Brand to enter from the hallway at any second. She realised that she was alone. Something heavy was thundering through the house, Rob Zombie or Marilyn Manson, so loud that she could feel the laminate timber flooring vibrate through the soles of her shoes. A haze of smoke hung in the air, tinged with the warm odour of dope. She breathed it in and suddenly craved a joint.

Where was he?

Desperate for another drink, she swigged back the remains of her Archers and half-filled the glass with gin. There was a lemon on a slicing board on the table, she cut a perfect half-inch slice and dropped it in the glass, followed by two chunks of ice and an inch of bitter lemon. She swilled it to mix, then took a sip. Strong. Sweet. Refreshing.

Where the hell... ?

Nikki glanced at the buffet table and felt less hungry than she had for a long time. Another drink washed the feeling away. And another drink because he wasn't there yet, and the last thing she wanted to do was to go looking for him. That would appear too eager, too desperate, even though seeing him was all she really wanted right now...

She noticed that the door to the wine cellar had been unlocked and hung slightly ajar. Darkness threatened to spew out.

Nikki finished her gin, poured two inches of whiskey and went looking for Brand.

He was not in the living room. Jesse sat on one of the floor cushions, propped side to side with the girl he'd met — Suzy, was that her name? — laughing and giggling and taking pleasure in whispering into her ear, greater pleasure when she laughed at what he said. The rest of the room was full of strangers. No Brand. He was a stranger she knew.

The dining room was throbbing with heavy metal, shockwaves pounding through the fabric of the building, ornaments rattling on shelves and windows visibly shaking. Nikki worked her way around the dancers, standing on tiptoe to look over their heads, seeing several tall people. None of them were Brand. Her hips nudged the dining table and she bit her lower lip, wondering, just wondering... she hadn't looked at the guy's face, had she? She'd been too shocked and embarrassed. It could have been anyone under there being sucked off.

Holding her breath Nikki squatted down and looked under the table. Only shadows stared back.

She worked her way around the perimeter of the room, stepping on toes and tripping over splayed legs, before she came back to the door. The music pounded at her. It seemed even louder now, but she knew it was because she was getting quickly and pleasantly pissed.

The kitchen was still empty. She refilled her glass, then glanced at the clock. It was past ten-thirty already. Everything had closed in around her in a comfortable, intimate haze, and she found herself swaying as she walked. The thought of food still made her gag, so she drank some more and guided herself to the stairs by running one hand along the hall wall.

Where the hell was he? She thought of calling his name but it would sound strange, she'd be verbalising her interest in someone other than Jazz. Betrayal would be given voice, and although she was sure no one would hear — or even care if they did — she would still feel bad.

What was she doing? What would she do when she found him? And if he'd been looking for her, where the hell was he now? She thought about the open door to the wine cellar and shook her head. Dark down there. If he was waiting for her down amongst the vintage wines and spiders and damp… just too weird.

There was a bathroom, two bedrooms and a storeroom on the first floor. The bathroom was empty, except for a girl asleep in the bath with the plug in and a dribble of water slowly rising around her. Puke stained her front and hung in a clot from her chin. One bedroom was dark and neat and held a distinct out-of-bounds feel. Nikki knocked on the other door — although she'd hear no reply above the pounding music anyway — opened it a crack and peered in. Mandy and Mike's friend were there, and Mandy was having her birthday present, naked and sweating and making enough noise to cover the sound of Nikki closing the door. She smiled and took another drink, looking up at the second floor landing, realising through the alcohol haze that she was turned on. Not from the sight of Mandy riding Mike's mate, but from the chase. Brand was here, somewhere, and every room she entered and every door she opened brought them closer together. Just the top floor now, and that was it. He must be waiting for her up there. In one of the bedrooms.

There were two bedrooms and a study on the top floor.

All empty.

Nikki stood on the landing where she'd seen Mandy and the guy kissing, looking down the stairwell at the hall below, staring at the heads of people passing in and out of the dining room. She felt out of it again, disappointed and cheated because she hadn't found him, he'd issued his invitation and she had failed him. It must have been Brand, surely? Could Jesse have meant anyone else?

Someone walked into the hall from the kitchen and stood there, unmoving, people parting around him as they went about their drunken business.

Nikki held her breath. Black hair. From this aspect she couldn't tell whether it was long or not, but it was black, jet black, and...

He looked up.

Brand.

He smiled, just a twitch at the corners of his mouth that did nothing to the rest of his face, and then he turned and went back into the kitchen.

Nikki ran downstairs. She dropped her glass on the first floor landing and kicked it in front of her, jumping over it as it smashed onto the hall floor and scattered into a web of shards. Holding the newel post she turned a half circle so that she was facing along the hall and into the kitchen. It seemed empty. All the noise and sense of activity came from her left and right, the dance room and the smoking room. Nothing from the kitchen. It looked cold and sterile and dead, the bright light exuding a lifelessness that she'd never noticed before, sheening the worktops with a dirty haze like a faded photograph. She could not see the food and drink tables from here, nor the door to the cellar, but she bet her life there was no one eating, taking a drink or sneaking down to steal a bottle. Just Brand. In there, waiting for her, *expecting* her, and if she didn't go now maybe she never would.

Face it, she thought, this is what I've been waiting for all evening.

Images of Jazz flashed at her, but it was as if she was remembering a holiday romance from years ago, not her current, missing boyfriend.

"Wherever you are, you deserve this," she said, feeling very adult and very cruel as she walked along the hall and into the kitchen.

It was empty.

"Fuck!" she shouted, darting forward and reaching for a fresh glass, pouring more whiskey, mixing in brandy and Schnapps and anything she could lay her hands on, taking one single mouthful of the horrific concoction before a finger almost touched the back of her neck.

She spun around and Brand was there. They were alone in the kitchen. The noise of the party seemed to drift away as he spoke, as if it no longer mattered.

"I've enjoyed looking at you looking for me," he said. "It's very revealing."

"Does Mandy know you're here?"

Brand raised his eyebrows and smiled. His face was only a few inches from Nikki's, most of them vertical. "Last time I saw Mandy she was letting a stranger come in her mouth."

Nikki didn't know what to say. She felt almost embarrassed for her friend. She looked away and tried to take another swig of her drink, but Brand was standing so close that she couldn't raise the glass.

"Would you do that?" he asked.

"What?" But she knew what he meant, and it gave her a chill as she thought of it. Disgusted, horny.

"Swallow come? Suck cock? Eat a stranger's meat?"

Nikki could not meet his gaze. He was disgusting, but not sleazy; crude, but not distasteful. Jazz tried talking dirty to her, but he only ever sounded like a little boy living out his wank fantasies. Brand... he knew what he was talking about. No fantasies here; he had lived it all.

"I'm a vegetarian," Nikki said, pleased with the ambiguity of her answer. Brand's smile gave her a hint of satisfaction, a feeling of control once more. He may be older than her and taller than her, but she wasn't just a naïve little girl.

"Why did you come to my school?" she asked, looking him in the eye. His eyes were cold, black, as if they'd brought some of the outside in.

"I didn't."

"I saw you, in the library."

"Then it was to see you."

"But you just said you didn't come."

"Did, didn't, whatever pleases you. Will it please you if I come?"

"I told you, I'm vegetarian. And I don't fuck strangers."

Brand touched her left cheek with a fingertip, drew his nail across her skin to the corner of her mouth as if tracing his own scar on her face. It sent a thrill down her spine, igniting every disc, settling into her groin and catching fire there.

"You fuck Jazz, don't you?"

"He isn't a stranger."

"He isn't here right now… sounds strange to me, leaving his beautiful girlfriend alone at a party like this."

"What do you mean, 'like this'?"

"Well, we all know what goes on here, don't we? People under the table .. the hostess giving the mostest… and I'm sure there's a lad or two here you wouldn't mind — "

"I'm not a slut, Brand."

He touched her other cheek and repeated the movement, his hands meeting under her chin and tilting her head up so that she had to look into his eyes. His breath was cool and stale, his hands warm and hard and callused. Old man's hands. "Oh, Nikki, but I'm sure you'd love to eat meat."

Nikki felt hot, her stomach tensed involuntarily, she was horny and excited and terrified half to death. She wondered what would happen if she called for Jesse or Mike — or if she simply shouted for help — but the noise and the smell of the party seemed barricaded beyond the kitchen now. No one came in for drinks. No one seemed interested in the food.

Surely that would not last for long?

"Let me show you," he said.

Nikki's eyes widened. What the hell — ?

He took her hands in his and guided her over to the refrigerator. His skin felt hot now, hotter than when he had touched her face mere seconds ago, and she wondered just how excited he was about this as well. Underneath all the mystery and the strangeness and posturing, was he just another bloke looking for a fuck?

Brand opened the fridge and made a show of sniffing at its contents. Then he moved aside some bottles and cans, winked back at Nikki, put his hand inside and brought a plate. There were two raw steaks there, uncovered, swimming in their own pink juices. He held the plate under his nose and closed his eyes, and Nikki was sure she saw the meat change colour as if exposed to a few seconds of heat.

"Blue," he said, picking up one of the slabs of flesh and biting in.

She should have felt revolted. She hated meat. Disliked the taste and texture, abhorred the thought of killing to eat, despised the pompous, self-righteous bastards who showed her their incisors whenever she got herself into an argument about vegetarianism. But instead of being disgusted, she was fascinated. She watched his teeth — they were grey and ragged, again like an old man's — sinking into the meat, their points pushing it down slowly before penetrating, blood welling and squirting onto his gums and lips, dribbling into his mouth, his teeth disappearing and meeting in the middle as he pulled away and tore out a raw chunk. He chewed. His chin was pink with bloody juice. His eyes rolled Heavenward in ecstasy, a line of blood running from the corner of his mouth and dripping onto his chest.

"That," he said, "is worth living for."

"Dying," she said, correcting him automatically.

Brand smiled, frowned. "No." A question and a statement. He wiped his mouth and held out the plate to her. "Care for some?"

She did not, of course. She would puke if she ate it, felt sick even smelling it, but her senses were driven back once again by the alcohol, forced into another room with the dancers and the smokers, shifted away from whatever was happening here in the kitchen. She held the second steak. It flopped over her hand like a heavy, rolled up rag. It was cold and leaking.

Nikki looked Brand in the eye as she put the meat to her mouth and took a bite. A big bite. She tried to give him the look she gave Jazz when she was giving him a blow job, head tilted down and eyes angled up. And for an instant — a brief, drunken instant that must have been a dream — the meat was hot and clammy, there were hairs, and the juice was not blood.

She snapped her teeth together, pulled away and tore off a chunk of steak, chewing and smiling and still staring at Brand. His expression was bemused and impressed in equal measure. His fine scar stood out vivid-white against his hot face.

"Lovely," he said.

Juice leaked from her mouth and ran down her chin, and Brand reached out to wipe it away with his palm. His hand felt like he had a fever.

"Nikki!" Jesse shouted.

Fuck off, she thought, can't you see I'm busy here, can't you see I'm being seduced... But Brand had turned away and left the kitchen, brushing past Jesse, who barely seemed to acknowledge the tall man's presence.

Shocked, sickened, shaking, Nikki dropped the steak. It hit the floor with a wet smack.

"Nik, I'm leaving, I'm going home with Suzy, her parents are away and — "

"Great!" she said. "Excellent!"

Jesse was far too drunk to notice the bitterness in her voice. He smiled, patted his back pocket again and disappeared.

Brand's sudden exit seemed to be the signal for the kitchen to fill up once more. Nikki swayed where she stood next to the open fridge, reached out to grab her glass from the table and swallowed the remaining contents in one gulp. She swilled the vicious liquid around her mouth to wash away the tang of blood; used it to help her swallow the clot of fleshy meat as well. She gagged, closed her eyes, concentrated on the drunken voices in the kitchen as she let her throat work the clump down to her stomach. They were voices she did not know, saying things she hardly recognised.

" — no time to argue — "

" — you know how she is — "

" — so I'll finish it, and send it in, and who knows — "

" — the heating's fucked, but I can do that myself — "

" — sucking his fucking cock under the fucking table — "

" — love that garlic dip — "

She opened her eyes and the kitchen was full, but empty of

Brand. For a few seconds she too felt empty, desperate, determined to find him because he was all she wanted, there were bedrooms upstairs but the wine cellar would suffice, hell, the garage… but then she realised that people were looking at her. They were still talking, but throwing surreptitious glances her way. All but two of them, who were staring as if she'd suddenly grown antlers and turned yellow.

"What?" she said.

"You're bleeding," said a girl she didn't know. She could have been one of the dope smokers from the sofa next to Jazz, or someone who'd only just arrived. They were all just as faceless to Nikki now, drunken teenagers who didn't know a thing, didn't know anything about what was really out there and in here, now, swimming around, dodging the alcohol fugues to dart in and take crafty bites from her mind, her imagination.

She swayed again, wiped her hand across her chin and saw it come away wet… although for a second it was white and sticky, not pink diluted blood.

Nikki suddenly felt unwelcome, an invited who'd become uninvited and untouchable. She didn't know anyone in the kitchen, and she thought that if she ventured through the house it would be peopled entirely by strangers. Mandy would be gone, and Mike, and Jesse and his new girl had probably already left in a sticky embrace, and before long she'd be here with a bunch of people she could never know.

Except for Brand. Surely he was still here. He wouldn't have left her so soon.

Nikki went looking for him. She realised that she was badly, stupendously drunk. She never went the exact direction she intended, her hands reached out to fend off walls and, once or twice, the floor, and people were looking at her as if they recognised her from a 'Wanted' poster. Faces she didn't know sneered. Mouths she had never kissed or seen speak before formed words she barely understood, in languages she could not understand. Something heavy attacked her from the dining room, and after a couple of seconds she realised it was music, pummelling the floorboards and walls and the inside of her skull. She passed by the doors. There were still people dancing in there, and for all she knew one of them was Brand, but suddenly she only wanted to get outside.

It wasn't fresh air she needed, or coolness washing her numb skin, but darkness. She thought that if she could open her eyes and see nothing maybe she'd feel better, if only for a while.

The glazed panels in the front door glared from the spotlights in the garden.

And then she wanted some wine. Blood-red, soft and subtle, heavy and fruity, tangy or smooth, she wanted nothing more than a bottle of red wine in one hand while the other steadied her against whatever rough floor she was sitting on. She could feel the gritty concrete speckling her bum and legs, the cold ground beneath one palm and the cool glass in the other, and she was sliding along the hallway wall and heading back to the kitchen once more. People passed her by, shadows at the edges of her narrowing perception, and the only ridicule she actually registered was the occasional bout of laughter.

The music must have notched up yet again because it gave her a final push into the kitchen. The room was empty once more. The food table had been attacked and scraps of bread, meat and crisps were trodden into the tiled floor. The drinks table had been mixed. Smashed glass lay amongst scattered ice. One bottle of wine was on its side, glugging its contents onto the floor like a slashed artery, slowing to a dribble. And then the room was dead.

Silent.

And the cellar door was still ajar.

Sweet red wine, Nikki thought, and maybe someone had actually spoken it in her ear. She walked across the kitchen to the cellar, peering down the wooden steps to where her shadow already lay on the bare concrete floor. There was a faint light down there, illuminating the racks and racks of bottles and taking on a reddish hue, as if the bulb had been spattered with blood. She swayed at the top of the stairs and knew she must turn around, leave the house and go home. She'd walk or run, hitch or ring a taxi, but she had to get home. Her father and mother and safety were waiting for her there.

But Brand was waiting for her as well. And he was much, much closer.

"Shut the door behind you," a voice said, dark as the shadows it came from.

"There's not much light."

"Do you believe everything you see? Sight is a liar, on occasion. Instinct... lust... fate... they never lie."

Nikki felt the skin of her arms tingling as if stroked, although he was hidden down there somewhere and she could not yet see him. She closed the door, holding onto the handle for a few seconds as dizziness threatened to spill her down the stairs. She closed her eyes but could not see any less or any more, so she opened them again to the red haze. So much light flowing through so much wine... would blood paint this room the same, she wondered? Would my opened veins catch the light in the same way?

"Come down here," Brand whispered, "I don't want you to fall and bleed."

"I'm scared," Nikki whispered, the fact that she found it necessary to lower her voice scaring her more. If this was a crypt, then it was only right to whisper.

It's wine, she told herself, light through wine, not blood, there's no blood on the walls down here.

"It's only right to be scared. Life is very frightening. Your friends up there haven't figured that out yet, because they're still children. Still merrily going along thinking everything is going to be alright. But you... you know different. You know to be frightened. You're a woman now, Nikki."

Nikki walked down the stairs, the wooden boards creaking beneath her weight. Her final footstep onto concrete was silent. "Where are you?"

Brand appeared in front of one of the racks. She had not noticed him there — she was sure he hadn't *been* there — but then he moved and made himself apparent. He still had pink blood from the steak smeared across his chin and one cheek, and the weak light caught it like sunburn. Nikki glanced up at the bulb and saw that it hung naked in the centre of the cellar, the reddish shade picked up from where it was reflected in and out of bottles and racks, carrying a bloody vintage as it aged.

"Nikki," he said, "such a beautiful name for a woman deserving much, much more."

The dark was contributing to her drunkenness, taking away points of reference so that up and down began merging into one sideways slant. She staggered a little and then went to her knees in the dust. She hung her head, embarrassed, but then his hand touched her chin and lifted her face so that she could look up into his eyes.

"You deserve so much more," he said, "because you're beautiful, and although your parents know that, they will not tell you. Telling you would make you a woman and in their eyes you're still their little girl. Even when you've screwing Jazz you're a little girl, because he's such a little, little boy."

His other hand was at the front of his trousers, unbuttoning his fly.

What? Nikki thought. What's he doing? But when she saw it, all doubts vanished.

For the briefest of moments realisation hit her, hard and fast and full of a very sober panic. He's just like the rest of them.

"Just like eating meat," Brand said softly. His face had not changed, his hand was hot on the back of her neck, and as she took him in her mouth she found that it was hot too.

Nikki did not move for a while, just knelt there drunk and swimming in silent disbelief as she thought about what she was doing. At the same time she was hugely turned-on, this beautiful man had seduced her into doing this, he had whispered sweet nothings and told her hidden truths, so much more confident than clumsy Jazz, more subtle than any of those boys upstairs. She began flicking her tongue, but Brand did not react. She continued, moving her head now, but still no reaction.

Looking up, expecting Brand's eyes to be closed and his head back, she saw him staring down at her. The expression on his face was static, the lines around his mouth deeper than ever in this half-light, and his eyes were a deep black, pupils wide to suck in the light.

The only warning that he was about to come was when he pulled back. His breathing did not change, there were no groans or gasps, just that hard, cold look. As his sperm hit her face and chest Nikki jerked back in surprise — it was so cold! Like being hit by flecks of ice. It was freezing on her chin. It ran from the corner of her mouth like blood from the steak, cold and lifeless and useless.

Brand turned and left the cellar before she had a chance to say anything. Before he closed the door on her, he whispered back down: "Think about it, Nikki." Then he was gone.

THE BOOK OF LIES

*History is more important than the future because it's already hap-
pened. What has been affects our lives every day, what will be will merely
be.*

Bullshit.

*The future is more important than the past because it's where we will
live our lives, it's a blank canvas upon which we can perform any act,
change any fact.*

More bullshit.

*The future and the past are equally meaningless because they are
nebulous entities, times that do not exist, containing events which have no
echo because they are gone, or which hold no import because they are yet to
happen. What is important is the here and now, and now, and now, and
the spaces between the nows. A moment is indefinable, immeasurable, so
finite that there is no unit attributable to it. A thought, perhaps? Can a
thought be a unit of time? But what goes to make up a coherent thought…
surely there's no one image there, no one electrical pulse in the brain, but
many thousands? And where does one thought end and another begin?
There is no middle ground, no bridging gap of nothing, because that's not
the way our minds work. By the time you let out a breath, drawing it in
is history, as inconsequential as every breath you've ever breathed in your
past, all those millions of unconscious bodily functions that go to drive you
on toward death.*

*How many moments are there in the space of an orgasm, I wonder?
A male orgasm first, that building of pressure and the explosion of
relief, those few spurts of outright rapture that are long enough to contain*

epiphanies, but which never reveal anything so grand. Or a female petit mort, the bursting of a dam that sends shudders along limbs and a red flush across chests and cheeks. How many thoughts?

How many moments?

How much can happen in such a short space of time?

It's here and now that counts. Between a gasp and sigh, a life can change forever.

CHAPTER ELEVEN

Once when she was fourteen Nikki had not come home.

Dan had walked to her room, still groggy from the bottle of wine he'd consumed the night before, mindful that she had been out to a party and allowed to stay out past his and Megan's bedtime for the first time... be quiet when you come in, they'd said, don't wake us up... and still vaguely unsettled that both he and Megan had fallen asleep, when really they should have been *unable* to sleep. They should have waited up for her. Any responsible parent would have.

That thought had repeated again and again when he saw that her bed was empty.

A search of the house had revealed no sign of Nikki. the front door was still unlocked, her jacket hadn't been thrown over the chair in the kitchen... she was missing. Megan's first tearful outburst was directed at Dan, telling him to ring the police, casting unfair accusations when she really knew that they were both at fault.

A simple phone call to Nikki's friend's house had solved the mystery. Their mother had left Dan hanging on the phone for a while and then come back to say that Nikki was there, asleep on the floor of her daughter's room, and that perhaps Dan would like to come and collect her? She's been drinking, she had said.

Nikki's experimentation with alcohol was the least of their worries that day.

Ever since then, every time Dan walked the corridor to his

daughter's room knowing that she should be in, the fear was waiting to strike again the minute he opened her door. A fear underpinned with guilt and a sense that he was an unworthy father. He wondered how much his life was shortened by worry and dread whenever Nikki promised to be home by midnight.

Today there was more reason than ever to wish her here. A bad reason. Dan was here for Nikki to talk to if she needed that, but she had to be here too. Had to.

He knocked on her door, holding a cup of tea in his other hand. "Morning Nikki." He never waited for an answer before opening her door.

For a second he knew she wasn't there. She didn't answer, maybe opening the door covered her response, after all she's probably still asleep, but I didn't hear anything, she didn't reply, she's not here...

Then he saw the shape hunched beneath the tangled duvet, hair hanging over the edge of the bed and almost touching the floor.

Dan looked down at his daughter for a few seconds, relieved and sad and still just as worried as ever. He always would be, that was his lot in life as a father. To be just as worried as ever.

He put the cup on the bedside table and nudged her shoulder. "Nikki."

She stirred, mumbled something, turned over and sighed.

"Nikki." He nudged her again, shaking her for a second. She woke up, opened a bleary eye and looked at him.

"It can't be morning," she moaned, pulling the duvet back over her head.

Normally Dan would have snatched up a pillow and beaten his daughter with it, hauled her out of bed, jumped on her, tickled her nose with a feather from the duvet, anything to annoy and wake her at the same time. But this morning was not normal.

"Ten o'clock," he said. "Didn't you hear the phone?"

"Nope."

"Was Jeremy there last night?"

For a moment he thought she'd fallen back to sleep. He could not hear her breathing. She froze, still as death, then flipped back the duvet and answered without looking him in the eye. "No, he didn't show. Big asshole."

"He hasn't shown at home either, this is the second night. His father rang me this morning. They've called the police."

Nikki sat and picked up her tea, still not meeting Dan's eye. "Oh."

"Sure you didn't see him? Meet up again, have another row, send him off in a huff?"

"No Dad, he wasn't there. People asked, I asked around too, but no one has seen him."

"Hi dad's frantic. He's been out since four this morning looking for him. One night they can live with, he said, because it's happened before. But he spent yesterday evening ringing everyone he could think of who may know where he is — "

"Didn't ring me."

"It was just after we left to drop you at Mandy's, your mum took the call. And no one has seen him, like you said."

Nikki took a sip of her tea, winced when she burned her lip and stared from the window. She never drew her curtains. Dan was sometimes worried about people watching her from out there, but really, who would? The Wilkinson's house wasn't in line-of-sight of her window, and the chances of there being anyone in the woods... but he didn't want to think about that, about Brand, not here and now. Brand was an unproven threat, whereas Jeremy was definitely missing, a real problem he could face and try to tackle. However little he could actually do about it.

"Nikki, why would he do this? Is he really this immature?"

She seemed to be looking at something out there. "Huh?"

"You know where he is, don't you?"

"'Course not."

"Why aren't you worried then? Your boyfriend's missing for two nights and you're not worried about him."

"I don't think he's my boyfriend any more, Dad." Nikki took another sip of tea and looked over the rim at Dan. Steam blurred her eyes, but he was sure there was humour in them, a mocking humour perfected by teenaged girls for their father, whose only job it was to protect them and try to shield them from whatever threats he knew to be waiting out there for her.

"Get dressed. The police may call in this morning."

"You invited them over?"

Dan shook his head and turned to leave. "Jeremy's dad said he'd suggested this as the first place to start looking." He expected something more from Nikki, some comment, smart-arsed or flippant. But he closed the door softly behind him, wondering what she was looking at so silently. His back, or the woods beyond her window.

Megan was in the kitchen. She had emptied the contents of one of the low-level cupboards and now she was half inside on her hands and knees, sweeping into the corners and scooping out any bits of rubbish, old spider webs and desiccated insects. She'd bag it all up, tie a knot and throw it into the bin, which was already half full with rubbish she'd taken from other kitchen cupboards. She looked hot and tired and dusty. When she refilled the cupboards with saucepans, cans of food and cooking utensils, she did not do it neatly. She was cleaning out, not tidying up.

She'd been working since five o'clock that morning.

"Nikki's awake," Dan said.

"About time." Megan's voice was muffled by the cramped space. Dan could see the muscles on her arm tensing as she bashed at something in there. "Ants," he thought she said, but it may have been something else.

He'd asked what she as doing, of course, but she had merely responded with a tirade about how dirty the house was, how many insects lived there with them, how could he live somewhere so filthy and *alive?* Initially he'd thought it another reaction against living in the country, a horribly un-subtle dig at the lifestyle. She'd already told him that she wanted to move back to the city, but he knew the way she worked. The occasional hint — a reminder of that conversation — would be forthcoming more and more often until they either had another argument, or he capitulated.

Now, he was not so sure. Megan had not knowingly killed anything in her life.

He walked to the bin she'd been filling and picked out a clear polythene bag. She'd barely dirtied it before tying a knot, twisting a strip of wire around its neck and burying it under the others. Almost as if she was trying to stop something from escaping once she'd put it in there. There was a spider, body burst like a rotten currant, its legs tangled with those of another spider, long dead and dried out by time. Dust peppered their corpses. There was other stuff in the bag: hairs; chewed paper; dark objects which may have been mouse droppings or dead, curled woodlice.

"Megan," Dan said.

"Hmm?" She pulled herself out of the cupboard to glance up at him.

"What's wrong?"

"I told you earlier, I'm tidying up."

"Why didn't you just throw this spider out? You never kill spiders."

She glanced at the bag and seemed to shy away from it, just for a second. "It scared me. Dropped on me. I hit it from my hair and killed it." She moved to the next cupboard and began emptying it. One of the boxes she brought out was adorned with spider webs, and she examined it closely to see whether there were any living creatures clinging to it.

It seemed that there were none. Dan was glad. He didn't want to see her killing anything, because that just wasn't her.

"I'm nipping into the village," he said. "Thought I'd chat to Brady about that weekend away we're planning." If ever there was a sore point that would bring Megan into conversation with him, it was this. He, Brady, Justin and Ahmed Din going away for a weekend to London later in the year, taking in a reformed Black Sabbath concert and generally having a fun time. She wasn't too keen. He hated that, but he hated arguing about it more, so it had always remained at the fringes of conversation.

"Okay," she said. He heard a slap in the cupboard and a muttered comment he could not make out. Another one bites the dust.

"Honey, you sure you're alright?"

"Why shouldn't I be?"

"You're... oh never mind." He turned to leave. "I love you," he called back over his shoulder."

"Me too." *Slap.*

And there goes another one, Dan thought.

He was going into Tall Stennington to see the police. He should have done it yesterday straight after Brand had called him at the office, offered those threats. And then after Brady had suggested it as well; he should have done it then. Letting Nikki out last night was madness, leaving Megan alone more so... but he was the man of the house.

He was the protector.

He had to do what was best for them.

"Lock the door after me," he said, but he did not stay long enough to see the look on Megan's face.

Dan drove past the police station. He didn't know why. Perhaps it was some sort of stupid, puffed-up pride left over from that time in Bar None, a confidence that he had beaten Brand once and could do so again. Or it could have been the 'this can't happen to me' distraction, a belief that the phone call from Brand had been full of empty threats, the tall man shamed and embarrassed into verbal abuse when he knew that a physical assault would only fail again. Every second he drew further away from the police station he berated himself, knowing that he was doing the wrong thing, knowing that he should get help just in case... just in case Brand...

He steered toward the kerb and slammed on the brakes, raising smoke behind him. If there had been anyone close they would have hit him, nudged the Freelander up onto the pavement and into the row of cottages leading into Tall Stennington. He was lucky.

It took a few seconds for his mobile phone to find a signal. He tapped his fingers on the steering wheel, revved the engine as if about to head off and do something about his inaction. He wondered where Jeremy was, and considered for the first time the serious possibility that something bad may have happened to him.

He dialled home. It rang, and rang, and rang, and with every ring the scenario became more and more clear: Megan buried head-first in a cupboard; Brand stepping in the back door because she had forgotten to lock it behind Dan; his wife calling him, thinking he had returned early; Brand standing behind her like one of her out-of-sight memories, watching, waiting for her to look up into his dead, deadly black eyes —

"Hello?" Megan.

"You okay?"

"Dan? Yes, I told you, I'm just cleaning up, it's such — "

"Not that," he said, but then he thought what? What do I tell her? Can I really say that Brand is still around, that he phoned and threatened? Can I really ask her to lock the door again without scaring her? In her present curious condition it may affect her hugely, drive her desire to leave this place into a need, and urgent insistence to quit now, go back to the city and sort out all the house selling details, the jobs, Nikki's schooling once they were there. Megan had been attacked before and Dan had not been there to help her. He would not have her live in fear for her safety again, not while he was around. Being scared was his job now.

"What?" Megan said.

"Don't worry." He glanced up as a car flashed by. A child waved from the back window but he was too distracted to respond. "Don't worry, I'll be home soon."

"Say hello to Brady," she said, but her tone was loaded: suspicion; guilt. Fear?

"Sure." But Megan had already cancelled the call. Again, he should have turned around and gone straight back to her. They could talk through their concerns, sort things out... and if it meant mentioning Brand, so be it.

Dan eased back out into the road and drove to the village. Brady's antique shop sat in one of the little side-streets leading off the village square, so Dan parked in front of the library and climbed slowly from the Freelander, slamming the door, looking around, checking in the mirror, watching out for Brand all the time.

He took out his mobile and dialled home again.

It rang... and rang... and rang. No answer.

He hurried past the front of the library and along the street to Brady's shop, starting to breathe heavily now, wondering just what the fuck he was doing, why wasn't he at home with Megan when she needed him, and Nikki, her boyfriend was missing and she'd likely be interviewed by the police today, *why wasn't he at home?*

Dan stood outside the shop and stared in. Brady was sitting in an old rocking chair reading a crumpled paperback. He wondered why the hell he'd come here instead of the police station, but he couldn't find an answer. *Why not?* didn't seem sufficient.

His phone rang in his hand and startled him, and his sudden

movement caught Brady's attention. Dan waved to him and tried to force a smile as he pressed the answer button. "Hello?"

"Dad?" Nikki sounded sleepy. "Did a call-back… "

"You okay, Nikki?" He tried not to sound too desperate but his voice twitched at the last syllable.

She didn't seem to notice. "Fine. Tired. Too much cider."

"Nobody's phoned?"

Brady had opened the door and was looking out at Dan. It wasn't often Dan visited him in the shop.

"Dad, I honestly don't know where he is."

For a few seconds Dan's insides turned cold and his brain blanked. How does she know I'm talking about Brand? A terrible sense of not belonging overwhelmed him, an enveloping feeling of blackness and emptiness, and the certainty that he was insignificant to all but himself, and even then only as an idea of someone he had once been. All his contacts were gone, all his ties to other people, his histories and ambitions and yearnings… and in that nothingness, fear had drained him completely and left him on his own.

Then he realised that she was talking about Jeremy.

"Police not been round yet?"

"No, Dad. I'm tired."

"Don't tell your mother I rang."

"Okay." She disconnected without saying goodbye.

"Dan," Brady said. "You called the police then?"

Dan could only stare at his friend, marshalling his thoughts and trying to make sense out of what Nikki had said, what Megan was doing, how he felt right now. Perhaps there was no sense, no rhyme or reason. Maybe it was all about being a family.

"Dan?" Brady asked again.

"Yeah. Sorry. No, haven't called the police. Er… Nikki's boyfriend has run away from home. His parents have called the old Bill, and they'll probably be chatting to Nikki later. Perhaps I can mention something to them then."

"Your daughter been doing any unexpected gardening recently?" Brady raised his eyebrows, his normal reaction when his own coffin-cold humour offended even himself.

Dan shrugged, couldn't help smiling. "Well they did have a row, apparently. Little runt's not good enough for her anyway."

"And who would be good enough for her? A tall, dark, mysterious prince won't be good enough in your books."

Dan waited to see if Brady was joking. He wasn't; but then why should he? The only time he'd seen Brand was when seen Dan almost brained him in the pub.

"You're not a Dad," Dan said. "She's my little girl." He shoved past Brady and into the shop, looking around at the confusion of furniture arranged into carefully orchestrated chaos. "I've got to look after her."

"So you haven't called the police about this Brand character, so you've come into town to see them, but you couldn't do it because you felt vaguely stupid going to the station and telling them you'd had a nasty phonecall."

Dan shrugged. "It's not really that. I just don't see what they can do. They can't arrest him for anything, even if they could find him."

Brady sat back down in his chair, groaning as his football-damaged knees clicked in sympathy with the aged timbers. "And if they could maybe you're a bit worried about a GBH charge for your unorthodox pool strokes."

Dan ran his finger along the surface of an old pine table and inspected it for dust. Clean as an operating theatre. Brady was meticulous, that was for sure. "I don't really know, mate. I need to sort it out on my own. I need to… protect my family." It didn't sound as melodramatic as he'd feared.

Dan checked the surface of a magazine rack and found a fine sheen of dust, lying there like the myriad memories of its many owners. That's what Brady always said he sold: memories. Wrapped in the confines of old furniture, time passed through his shop and was sold for money, memories of the countless people who had sat in the chairs, walked with the sticks, kept their own little mementoes on shelves, hung clothes in wardrobes, made love in beds. If ever a place was going to be haunted, this shop was it. Full of lost times.

"So what are you doing here while they're still at home?"

Dan wondered why so many of his memories had to be bad. He took out his phone and pressed recall. "I think I came here so you'd convince me to go to the police."

Brady went to say something, but Dan's call was answered and he turned away.

There was silence along the line. An occupied silence, expectant rather than empty. "Hello?" Dan whispered, and the tone of his voice startled Brady into standing. Dan looked at his friend and shook his head. *Something's wrong.* "Megan? Nikki?"

Brady caught his attention and raised his hands, palms up. *What?*

"Anyone there?" Dan shook his head again.

"They're everywhere," a voice said. It was low, husky, bled androgynous by static.

"Megan?"

"They're everywhere, Dan. His spies are everywhere. I found one on my Bible, trying to sully it, dirtying it with its horrid legs. Looking at me. Seeing what I was reading."

"Megan, what's wrong honey?"

"He there?" Brady asked, frozen into a statue by the fear in Dan's voice.

Dan shook his head, shrugged, covered the mouthpiece. "I don't know." He'd never heard himself sounding so desperate. Brady grabbed his coat and motioned Dan to leave the shop with him. "Megan!"

"Dan, I've cleaned up as best I can but there are ways in. There are always ways in. You can't hide forever, can't cover up all the gaps and spaces. If something wants in, it's in. And I've tried shutting all the curtains but I can hear them out there in the garden — "

"Who's in the garden, Megan? Where's Nikki?"

"The birds. Singing and flitting around, eating the nuts and seed I put out for them. They spy and tell him what they see.

"Tell who?"

"Tell Brand. He's still here. Dan, he's watching me."

"Lock the doors," Dan said, a fear realised actually seeming to inject some sort of calm. It was panic, he thought, but if this is how it manifested then he was glad of it. "Go upstairs with Nikki. Don't open the door to anyone."

"Dan? You've seen him too, haven't you?"

"I'm coming home. Ten minutes." He cancelled the call, feeling terrible as he did so. She sounded terrified. She sounded... *mad.*

I'm going to make the next few days very, very long for you Brand had told him. Dan glanced at the clock and saw that it was still only eleven o'clock. It felt like lunchtime already.

"Oh shit, Brady, he's been at Megan. She's seen him and she thinks... those footsteps. Damn it!"

"She thinks what?"

"You know what she's like. She thinks Brand's the fucking devil and he's spying on her. I'm going home. Call the police for me, mate, tell them there's a stalker... a prowler, whatever, someone at my house. I want them there before me or with me." He left the shop in a hurry, clapping Brady on the arm and giving him a strained smile. "I should never have left them alone."

"Give me a call when you get home," his friend said, then Dan was out of the shop and running back to the Freelander. The phone banged his hip, tempting contact, but he knew that to stop and call home again would be to lose vital seconds.

He hadn't been there for her in the city.

He would not let that happen again.

My God, Dan thought, what the hell is she doing? Those spiders in the bag, the birds in the garden. The way she'd been bashing about in the cupboards, as if she was after not only the crawlies she could see, but those *too small* to be seen.

Not for the first time, he realised that he was slightly afraid of his wife.

Dan started the car and circled the village square, pushing his foot down and banging his head on the ceiling as he drove over the little stone bridge. As he left Tall Stennington and motored towards home, it began to snow.

Brady turns back to his antiques and breaths in deeply. He likes to be alone. He hates stress, and other people give him stress. Dan is one of his very best friends, but for the three minutes he was in the shop Brady was on edge, and driven very close to going over by Dan's strange phone call. He is a good friend, yes, but Brady can do without other people's problems.

He rescues the phone from behind a pile of books he has yet to stock on his bookshelves. It's an old manual dialler, something that came into the shop a year ago and which he just couldn't find it in his heart to sell. A few modifications and it was his to use and enjoy. He likes old things. They are less confusing. His trade in old memories is most pleasing of all, because old memories can do no harm. What's past is past.

Brady dials the local police station, reading the number from a tatty phone-book he keeps in a drawer. He wonders just what he'll say when someone answers. How will he explain a threatening phone-call to a friend, and his friend's odd wife who seems to have developed a profound case of paranoia? And the pool cue incident... well, that could do without mentioning.

The door opens and somebody rushes in behind him. It's Dan; Brady can sense the panic in the air. The edgy tension of the room washes over him like a breath of heat from a sauna, his skin prickles and he turns to see what is troubling his friend now, his friend who has already resigned himself to going back to the city because his wife hates it so much out here...

"What now...?" Brady says, but the shadow moves quickly. He does not see the face of the person who hits him.

He falls, catching a table with his shoulder and bringing a stack of books down on top of him. Dust coats his throat with its dry grit, old memories drowning him. He hears a metallic ring as the phone is picked up from the table, and then there is a terrible, shocking impact as it connects with the back of his skull. His face is drive into the floor and pressed sideways, and he notices an old brass bookmark he lost years ago, little more than a vague hump in the dust beneath a writing desk he's never managed to sell and which now —

Another crash on his head, cheekbone now, something gives and his mouth is full of wet warmth, and *some fucker is battering him*, he hasn't even heard the till being opened yet, it's a manual one, won't cause any trouble, they can even take the whole thing with them if they want —

Thunk, again, old memories abandoning him now to sudden truths, it's the moment that matters, not some unknown past and unknowable future, now, the here —

Crash, onto his skull again.

The here and now, and now, and now.

The phone rings one more time, and then there is silence.

CHAPTER TWELVE

Megan stared at the phone in her hand as it emitted its dead monotone. *Dan has seen him too.* She could not understand that, could not comprehend how or why Brand had been at Dan as well… and even less, why her husband had never told her.

"Everywhere, they're everywhere," she muttered. She thought of Dan staring at her as she cleansed the house of Brand's minions, crushing them sightless, denying him access to her family.

But the birds were singing this morning, and she'd seen a couple of squirrels on the old apple tree before she closed the curtains. Now she knew that the curtains would never be enough. Apples were supposed to contain some sort of power — they had magical connotations — but those were pagan thoughts and Megan lifted her face and closed her eyes and prayed to God for the millionth time that day. She asked for lots of things, all of them special. No simple *smile upon me, Jesus* today. Now was a time for desperate pleas for help, calls for His merciful intervention to protect them from whatever devil had been let loose in their midst.

Until now, she had never seen anyone but her husband in her husband's eyes.

Putting the phone down on its cradle shut off the tone and gave her back the quiet. But only partial quiet; there were still sounds from outside as the world stared in, relaying its message back to *him*, telling *him* what she was doing and listening in for *him*, wherever *he* was... .

He... him... that devil.

Megan snatched at the corner of the curtain covering the front door and glazed side-screen. She lifted it slightly, hoping to surprise whatever foulness existed in the garden into revealing itself. But she saw only the garden, flowers borders and bare rose bushes already perking up as spring hinted at itself, the lawns dark green and unkempt and glistening with dew, the apple tree standing silent sentinel at the fence, branches alive with birds as they fed and fluttered to and fro.

And some of them watched the house. She could see a blue tit sitting on a thin branch near the top of the tree, ignoring the profusion of nut-hangers to stare at the house. Its little head jerked slightly left, slightly right as it took everything in.

Megan felt the bird's eyes upon her, even from that distance. She went cold, her skin stretched and tingled, as if Brand had walked over her grave seconds after burying her there himself. She dropped the curtain and backed into the hall, half-expecting the doorway to darken with his presence.

She couldn't understand why Dan had left her alone, not if he had seen Brand. Surely he knew what Brand was? Surely he knew how *dangerous* he could be? And yet he'd left the house, allowing the monster access any time he wanted. He'd left his family alone.

Megan was good at guilt but it was mostly her own, propagated and nourished by her devotion to God, the certainty that she was far from perfect acting as the driving force behind her worship. Her own sense of imperfection, the acknowledgement of her own sins, the sullied soul she called home, all contributed toward the way she was and how she looked at others. Sometimes she despised the fact that her daughter had not accepted Jesus. The girl shunned this chance at light to live a grey life, renouncing God thorough apathy. Sometimes, the worst of times, she hated Nikki for this.

But she hated herself most of all. She should have raised Nikki with God in her heart, but she had failed. Therein lay her worst guilt, a sense that she had failed her daughter and, more dreadfully, God. Failure was a theme with her family, it seemed. Dan had failed her. Ironically she loved him for it more because it had effectively destroyed the man she had married, leaving a redemptive, silent, melancholic person in his place. A love born of pity, but love nonetheless.

If he failed them again, however, she thought that pitying love could easily turn to a heartfelt hate. And he was her husband. She did not want to hate him.

"Where are you Dan?" she whined, sinking slowly to her knees in the hallway. "Don't leave me like this again." Already she could feel her fears beginning their own ethereal assault.

She stood quickly. God urged her to her feet and into the living room, told her to check the locks on the windows and doors. Protect yourself, don't submit... God helps those who help themselves. She crossed the room and pulled the curtains aside, noticing that it had started snowing in the seconds it had taken her to come from the hallway. It hadn't been forecast, it had been a cool, clear day, but here it was. A few errant flakes at first, but they were fat and fluffy, settling on a fence post, the crazy-paving around the edge of the garden, the lawn, then closer still to the house. Megan actually watched the snow thicken and advance across the garden until it struck the house itself. Several flakes landed on the timber sill outside the window, but did not melt.

Birds went about their business as normal, unperturbed by the sudden flurry. A siskin hopped from branch to branch in the apple tree, glancing at the house between each hop as if making sure she was still watching.

Megan dropped the curtain and stood back. The light coming through seemed brighter than it should, reflected and exaggerated by the thickening snow.

"Nikki," she shouted upstairs, "it's snowing." She wanted it to sound like a warning but realised that there should be nothing inherently worrying about it, not really, it was only weather. "Footprints in the snow," she whispered. "Dan, where are you?"

Megan ran back to the dining room and checked the lock on the French doors. She could see across to the woods from here. They were darkening already, even though it was not even midday, only trees at the very edge standing out from the expanding shade beneath their bare branches. The snow became thick and insistent, hazing the air between the house and the woods. It was settling. A breeze came up from nowhere and sent ghostly shapes hurrying through the downfall.

The birds were watching the house. It wasn't just one or two anymore, like the siskin and the robin — it was all of them. They sat along the fence at the edge of the garden, hopped across flower beds, hovered down from the roof and back up, down and up. Megan felt their dark eyes upon her, *his* dark eyes through theirs, and she closed her own eyes and begged God for help and strength.

Receive with meekness the engrafted word, which is able to save your souls.

And suddenly she was afraid no more. A rush of joy flushed through her, an epiphany in this dark time, lighting the way to the kitchen, into the cupboard next to the sink and then to the back door. She carried a broken broom handle, one end viciously sharp from where it had snapped six months ago. Dan had been meaning to fix it ever since, but it had taken up residence in the rear of the kitchen cupboard along with the rusty wok, the bag of bicycle lights and the box of broken plugs. Useless... until now.

"Nikki!" she shouted again, pleased that the fear had gone from her voice. "Nikki, they're watching the house but I'm going to see them off. He might be watching but that's all he can do. I'll show him I'm not afraid, show him we're not to be messed with . He'll leave us alone then. Your dad may have seen him but he won't again, I won't let him come in and scare us, it isn't right, God is with me and He'll help me see the bastard off!" She opened the back door to a rush of cool air, speckles of snow flurrying in before she stepped over the threshold and slammed the door behind her. Nikki had not responded but that did not concern her. She was hungover. Best she stay out of this, anyway. This was God's work.

Outside now, in Brand's domain perhaps, his place where snow was falling again and his natural minions — or slaves — were watching her, she stepped out from the cover of the roof overhang. Snow landed on her shoulders and in her hair like shed skin, kissed her cheeks with lips of the dead, cooled her skin and drew the life from her...

But the idea of Brand was planting these ideas. The snow was white and pure, cool and indifferent. It melted against her skin and took her warmth, warmth she could afford to give because she revelled in the heat of her devotion.

Megan stood in the middle of the lawn and glanced back. She had left vague footprints already, even though it had only been snowing for a few minutes. If it kept on like this, they'd have a fair covering by the end of the day. She looked across the garden and past it, to the neighbouring house and the woods and the lane leading down to the main road, and the only signs of life were the birds and a small dark shape foraging at the wood's edge.

She had God, the birds were spying for Brand. She felt righteous.

Megan walked towards a fence panel where there were several small birds fluffed up against the cold, observing her approach with tiny jerks of their heads. The broom handle swung by her side. There was no way the birds would stay there for her to strike out at, she was sure of that, but at least she'd be seen to be acting. *Seen* in the very real sense of the word. She would not be afraid anymore, she refused, and even though the tall stranger had frightened her and abused her, God was there as he always had been. Now more than ever she felt that. Now, as she was starting to fight back.

Several steps from the fence the birds took flight, fluttered a few panels along and perched again. They still looked at her, still fluffed up, eyes reflecting the increasingly white landscape. She swung the handle anyway and hit the fence with it, but even though the impact resounded through the wood the birds did not move. They watched.

She ran a few paces and swiped out as a sparrow at it took flight, missing by several feet but still enjoying its panicked little flutter, actually certain that she'd heard a cry of distress.

"Stay away from me!" she shouted. "You hear? You see... but do you hear? You leave me alone, I've got God on my side."

The birds chirped. It sounded as if they were laughing.

"Bastard!" she hissed, running at the dead apple tree, swinging the handle around her head and letting it fly at a magpie in one of the upper branches. It missed the bird and clattered back down through the tree, sticking in the ground between exposed roots. The magpie settled again and screamed down at her. She ran for the stick and tugged it from the earth. As she looked back up at the magpie it took flight and shit at her. It missed, just, and splashed down onto the grass.

Megan hurled the stick again, even though the bird was already way too high to have a hope of hitting it.

The smaller birds along the fence began singing again, laughter running from one end of the garden to the other, no different to the normal birdsong but imbued with some darker significance now. Some of them hopped from fence to ground and back again, taunting her with their trespass.

"Get away from here!" Megan shouted, thinking *God help me get them away from here.* She ran to fetch the handle and threw it at the fence, actually believing for a second that it was going to hit a great-tit sitting there staring at her. It struck the timber inches below the little bird. It did not budge. It was watching Megan.

"Get the Hell away from here!" she screamed, running to and fro, ignoring the useless broom handle now and trying instead to scare the birds into flight. The snow was thicker, deadening the noise of her footfalls, making her all too conscious of her heavy breathing, her sprinting heart, the fear rising in her throat as she realised that she could shoo the birds from one part of the garden, but never all of it. They simply went from one place to another, calmly lifting off as she approached and flitting over her head, past the house and down to the opposite end of the garden.

What a sight she must present. Arms flailing, trousers flapping and spotted with snow, hair wild and whipped around her face. Wherever he was, Brand would be laughing.

Megan stopped at the edge of the lawn. The snow had dropped a fine dusting across the grass now, and her prints were evident, crossing and crissing the garden, showing where she had been and revealing how pointless her little display was. At least for now the birds had stopped singing.

Quietly, calmly, she walked to the back door. By the step into the house she saw a snail, trailing its sticky path through a thin layer of snow as it sought shelter under a sill or beside a window frame. She knelt, letting the snow melt through the knee of her trousers and enjoying the cool kiss of water against her skin. She would be warm again soon. She would be dry and warm and she would pray, and Brand and his minions would be out here in the snow, freezing where they sat.

Megan pressed down on the snail's shell and its eyestalks retracted, the edges of its sticky foot curled up. She pressed more, and more, until she felt and then heard the shell cracking beneath the pressure. Then she left it to die.

Opening the back door she wondered how she appeared to him through a snail's eyes.

"Nikki!" Megan stood by the Rayburn and warmed her hands near its hot metal surface. She felt good. She felt that, along with the cold, she had also locked the threat outside. "Nikki, it's snowing, looks heavy."

No answer. Hating herself for it, Megan could not help rushing into the hallway and shouting upstairs at her daughter. I was in the garden, she thought, I didn't lock the back door, wasn't always in sight of it, anyone could have come in, anything —

"Nikki — " Megan sighed and her shoulders slumped. Her daughter was sitting on the landing, staring down between banisters. Tension left her and the warmth of God's presence massaged her cold, aching muscles. He would look after them, she knew that now. She had made a stand, however ineffectual, and proving that she had fight in her would please God. He would help her to defeat whatever it was Brand had brought with him to infect and corrupt her mind, and the minds of her family.

"Nikki, I'm going to ring your dad and get him to come home, but we might need…. Nikki? Nikki?"

Nikki was not moving. She sat with her head rested against the timber uprights, sharp edges pressing into her temples and cheeks and framing her pale face, emphasising the eyes, those staring, blank eyes… staring straight at Megan.

"Nikki?"

Her daughter smiled slowly and sweetly, but it was not her own mind pulling her lips like that, Megan was sure, she was *certain.* Not Nikki smiling at her like that.

"You leave her alone," Megan hissed. She started up the stairs, then darted back down and into the kitchen.

The poker they used for the Rayburn was still hot.

Dan was driving too fast. Even if the snow had not been turning into a blizzard, even if the light had been good and the roads long and straight, even if he had not been eaten with worry he would have been driving too fast. He took corners trusting that there would be nothing coming from the opposite direction. The wheels spun on the road, and he steered into the skids. He needed to get home. Brady would have phoned the police but he needed to get home, now, instantly. He resented the distance between him and his family, cursed the woods and the fields and the hedgerows. Home, with Megan and Nikki, because Brand *was* still around. And he had met his wife.

Not content with the danger of driving madly through ever-worsening snow, Dan slipped the mobile from his pocket and tapped the memory button for home. There was no tone, no signal, not even a sigh of static. The snow had seen to that.

"Shit!" He bashed the wheel with both hands and the car slewed across the road, heading sideways into a curve, straddling the white lines hidden by snow. Dan panicked and over-compensated, the rear end began to go and he had a sudden, sickening image of himself lying dead in a ditch. Brand would stand over him and smile down at his smashed head, walk by his still-steaming body, glass crunching underfoot as his boots left bloody prints behind him... prints heading into the wood directly to Dan's home.

That was no way to leave his family.

It took three long seconds to save the Freelander from the skid. He cut his speed and took long, deep breaths, trying to take control of his runaway heart.

The snow was terrible now, a heavy fall that seemed to be worsening every second. A breeze was picking up too, driving it across the road in sheets, heading more and more toward blizzard conditions. The second surprise snowfall of the week.

A sudden sense of déjà vu hit Dan and he ran with it. He liked the feeling, he always had. This time, however, it changed into of outright dread within the blink of an eye.

The same turn of the wheel; the same nudge of his knee against the central column; a clump of snow slipping slowly down the edge of the windscreen; a bump as a wheel passed over something on the road; the same corner turned...

... the same shape by the side of the road. And then the sensation lifted and the shape was not standing next to the road, it was *on* the road, the shadow of something not there, a place in the midday blizzard where darkness already hung. Instinct and shock took control of Dan's hands and he spun the wheel to the left.

Everything slowed down as he realised he was leaving the road.

The steering wheel came alive in his hands as the front wheels struck the kerb and lifted the nose of the Freelander into the air. Dan could do nothing but sit tight, watching snow still patter at the windscreen and the wipers still clear it as the hedge grew closer, closer... and then exploded as the vehicle hit.

He managed to turn his head, partly an involuntary gesture to defend his eyes as much as he could from a potentially shattered windscreen, but also to see whether the shape was still in the road. Snow fell, swirled by the breeze, twisting and rising and spinning in impossible patterns, circling the place where the early darkness had been and hiding it from view.

If the front wheels hadn't lifted, maybe the hedge would have been thick enough to prevent the car from gouging through into the ploughed field. Dan's stomach dropped as the front of the vehicle rose. He grabbed hold of the wheel again and felt the mechanical distress of the smashed front axle as it spun into destruction.

The top of the hedge parted to let the car through, clawing at its underside. He could hear paint being scored from the side of the car.

Then the back wheels hit the kerb and flipped the vehicle's rear into the air, the bonnet tipped down and Dan saw the field about the swallow him up.

He tensed against the steering wheel, remembered something about it being best to go limp in a crash, then tensed again the instant the front of the Freelander hit the ploughed earth. The impact whipped his head forward so far that he struck his forehead on the wheel. The seatbelt bit into his neck and shoulder, punched against his ribs. He actually smelled mud as a sheet of dirt was flung into the air in front of the car, cutting darkly through the falling snow and splashing against the windscreen and side windows, pattering down onto the roof as the car crashed down fully into the field, gouged through the mud for several feet and then came to a standstill.

After the noise of the crash every little engine tick, gasped breath, trickle of mud along warped body panels and drip of fuel from the punctured tank was amplified by silence.

Dan twisted in his seat to look for the shape that had distracted him.

Him, he thought, it had to be him. But even though the car had smashed through the hedge and formed a second opening from the field into the road, the snow was falling too heavily for him to see beyond it.

Dan's back hurt, as did his neck and ribs. His hands, already bruised, stung where he had been holding the steering wheel when the car hit the field. He touched his forehead and dabbed there gently, expecting blood but feeling only tightly stretched skin, the bump swelling beneath his fingertips. A sense of unreality gave everything a startling clarity. He supposed it was the usual human defence of *this can't have happened to me*, but he really was in a field in a crashed car, steam was hissing from the bonnet in stark contract to the heavy snow, and he had to get out... had to get out now. He could smell petrol.

Undoing his seatbelt hurt more than he had anticipated. His head kept tipping forward to ease the pain in his neck, and he had to consciously keep it upright, muscles straining in his neck and jaw. Every time he breathed he felt something click in his chest. Maybe he'd broken a rib. Maybe it was edging into his lung right now, threatening to puncture and deflate and drown him in his own blood. He'd heard of instances where people walked away from an accident, only to drop dead hours or days later from injuries they hadn't even been aware of sustaining.

He coughed, gently at first then harder, holding his hand over his mouth and inspecting his spittle. No blood. Not yet.

He had to shove hard against the door to get it open. The whole chassis must have twisted, the side panels deformed, because the bottom edge of the door screeched against the sill and stripped the paint down to the base metal. The cold came in, and the snow, and the total silence. No birds sang. No animals scampered around in the hedge or the field. There were no cars on the road. It had been snowing for a quarter of an hour and there was a layer across the ground. People must already be settling in for another long, cold spell.

Last time, we woke to footprints, Dan thought. And Megan was scared and I was dismissive, and now Brand is here again to do whatever it is he plans to do.

Dan backed away from the car and hugged his arms around his chest, holding the pain, keeping warm, trying to make himself feel safe. He had to get home. The road was safer, he knew, especially in this weather, but across country was far quicker. Two miles by road. A mile across these fields and through the woods, if that. It wasn't as if he'd get lost walking a mile across-country.

And he had to get home.

He should ring Megan. She'd be worried, he was worried, he had to talk to her again and try to calm her and make sure she was doing all the right things. Panicking would not help her, praying to God would not lock the doors and snap home bolts. He knelt in the mud, wincing as his neck protested, and looked beneath the rear of the Freelander. There was a steady trickle of petrol from the ruptured tank, but the wet mud was swallowing it up. The door was open, he only had to reach in for the mobile, no sparks, the engine had gone off on its own accord —

Wet mud, and something else. There was a shape under one of the back wheels where it had skidded and ploughed its way into the mud. Something grey, speckled with unmelted snow because it was so cold.

He needed the phone but curiosity had him. And maybe a

dread sense of the inevitable as well, because even as he knelt in close Dan knew what he was going to find.

He wondered if Nikki had known all along. A hateful thought, but deep inside where civility and morals are slaughtered by honest lizard instinct, thoughts so often were.

Only part of Jazz's head was uncovered, and an arm, and one side of his chest. His jacket was torn and patched with black swathes of dried blood. There was more damage to his arm, too, although Dan guessed that some of it was from where he'd just run over the barely concealed body, the wheels must have been still churning to be able to whip him up out of the ground like that, buried not too long by the look of it, not long enough for the ground-creatures to burrow in and make him their home —

Petrol dripped into the dead boy's eye.

"Holy fuck!" Dan fell backwards and tried to scrabble away from the car, pushing with his hands and feet but unable to tear his gaze from the messed up kid. His whole body screamed at the pain but that only made him crawl and kick more, as if to distance himself from his own agony as well as the dead boy beneath his car. His bruised hands and his coat and his shoes all picked up sticky mud, and soon he could barely lift his limbs such was the weight pulling them down. He slumped back to the ground, unable to tear his gaze from the crumpled form beneath the Freelander, willing the snow to fall heavier and thicker so that it would obscure the view and give him blessed whiteout.

Dan suddenly realised how cold he was. The Freelander's air conditioning had buffered him against the chill until a couple of minutes ago, and now that shock was biting home and pain was flaring, the cold bit hard and relentless. His hands were numb. His face and ears stung where the fat flakes struck. And there was a dead boy beneath his car...

Dan had never disliked Jeremy, but he was a teenaged boy going out with his daughter, so Dan justified his distance and suspicion by saying that he was a father. He knew what he'd been like at Jeremy's age. He knew that Jeremy and Nikki got up to more than just hand-holding when they went to parties or friend's houses. And he hated that.

Well, now Jeremy was dead.

He must tell someone. He had to get the mobile phone from the car, call the police, call Megan. That became the one thing he focussed upon — ignoring the pain, the cold and the corpse — because it provided some sort of temporary refuge from what had happened.

As for the shape in the road... a shadow in the snow. And quietly, so that maybe he would not even hear it himself, Dan whispered about how well he could lie.

He stood and groaned, coughed, making noise to kill the dreadful silence. Nothing else moved; only the snow. No shape emerged from the hedge as he approached the battered Freelander. No whisper came in the snow as he drew closer to the open door and lost sight of the corpse. No cold hand fell on his shoulder.

So who killed him?

Dan shivered, as if the voice in his head belonged to someone else. He recognised his own fear coming through, his own voice giving words to the terrible thought that had been circulating, seeking release, since he'd fallen down and seen at the corpse of his daughter's boyfriend.

Who killed him? Who buried him? Shallow grave, always meant to be found, that's what they say on the news. Shallow grave. As if surprised that a murderer has such disregard for their victim; expecting that a decent killer would dig a six-foot hole for the bloody remains of their latest crime.

Dan grabbed the phone and squeezed tight. Even switched off it was a link away from here, and soon he would be talking to Megan. And however odd she was acting, the sound of her voice would help him. He was phoning to warn her — to *scare* her — but at least that would be a positive action. Better than falling on his arse in the mud.

He turned around as he pressed the memory button. He didn't like having his back to the snow, and whatever hid behind it. The electronic beep that told him the number was being dialled seemed loud and alien in the ever-whitening landscape. Snow landed on his eyelids, turning the sky white and forcing him to blink faster than usual.

The phone let out a long, single tone.

Not connected: try again?

He stared at the little display screen, willing it to change, but a snowflake struck and obscured his view. He wiped it away and pressed the redial button.

A car passed on the road. Dan turned and shouted, waving his arms at the high hedge and stomping along in his mud-heavy shoes. It passed by quickly, although it did not seem to be driving fast, as if the snow was distorting sounds from afar and swallowing them whole. He saw the bloody glow of tail-lights through the hedge, and for a couple of seconds he thought the car was braking. They would pick him up and call the police, drop him home to his family while he spewed his story and demanded protection, begged for help.

But then the car was gone, fog lights fading quickly in the snowstorm.

"Jesus, I'm cold." His voice sounded loud, almost an echo, but it provided company. The phone joined him with another long, unavailable tone. "Damn thing." He stared at the screen again and then pocketed the useless scrap of technology, despairing that a snowfall could knock out his only line of communication so easily.

"It's the blizzard," he said. "It *is*." It seemed that today he was good at believing his own lies.

And then every lie shed its insulating skein of disbelief as the enormity of what had happened finally struck home.

Turning the corner where they had first picked up Brand several days ago; the shape in the road, the shape that *was* Brand, forcing him into a skid that resulted in a crash; Jeremy, Jazz, dead and buried and just begging to be found; and Megan and Nikki only a mile away through the woods.

Dan's heart skipped double-speed for a few seconds. He breathed in long and deep, although panic sought short sharp breaths, and sat down again in the mud. Brady would have called the police, he knew that, but he was not *certain*. He had to be absolutely, no shadow-of-a-doubt *certain*.

Whatever had been in the road (Brand, it was Brand and I fucking know it was Brand)... now had a five minute head start.

Dan stood and ran. If he was going to have a heart attack

so be it, but it would happen while he was doing his best to help and protect his family, not as he sat quivering in the mud, afraid of the snow and mourning his inability to believe what was there before him. He was leaving the scene of an accident, fleeing his Freelander smashed in a field with petrol leaking out and a body jammed half-under one of the rear wheels. But there were more important things happening. Deep at the back of his mind there was hope, but almost smothering that was the dark dread that clouded his thoughts, rolling like thunderheads as he ran and tried to see his way through to the light on the other side.

Gusts of wind picked at his clothing, stronger gusts every time, sending sheets of snow waving across the field and driving the cold in deep.

Five minutes head start, but Dan knew the fields and the woods, he knew his way home across country, whereas Brand would have to take the road, especially in this weather —

So thinking, Dan realised that he stood within a whiteout. Ahead of him was the edge of the woods at the far edge of the field, surely, but he was no longer sure which way *was* ahead. All around the snow came down, and although he caught brief glimpses of vegetation in the distance between waves of white, they could have been hedges or trees in any direction.

"Oh shit, oh shit, oh shit… " He carried on running blind until he tripped over the shape in the field. He cried out, sure his toe had broken, already feeling the warmth flooding his shoe as a smashed nail spewed blood. It turned cold quickly. He rolled and stood up, ready to escape into the blizzard if the shape so much as moved, revealed itself as more darkness at the heart of the whiteout. Wind gusted, snow shifted on the thing and Dan tensed.

It was a motorbike. It's front wheel was buckled, fuel tank dented, its covering of snow giving it an even more abandoned look. Jeremy's bike.

"Left for me to find." A wall of snow blew at him in agreement. A hundred shapes swirled and eddied there, changing into each other, swapping forms until the breeze stopped and the flakes found their way downward again.

Dan ran again. If the bike had been left for him, whoever

left it knew that he'd be taking this route across the field.

Impossible, he thought. No way. That was just too much to bear.

The driver's door of the Freelander slammed shut.

Stopping suddenly tipped his balance and he went sprawling, but he lay there in the mud, supported on cold hands and muddied knees, listening. He was not sure which direction the sound had come from — it may have been from the left, in which case he was going the wrong way; or from behind, so that he was still heading to the woods — but even though he held his breath and listened, there was nothing more to hear.

"Wind," he whispered, but there had been no gusts strong enough to do that.

He stood again, trying to shake some of the wet mud from his shoes, scraping it from his hands and the sleeves of his jacket. He breathed softly, still listening. It could have been a car on the road, perhaps, bumping into the hedge, skidding and denting its bumper against one of the stone walls that lined the road further along.

Dan knew the sound of his own car door. He had left it open. Somebody had closed it.

He ran again. Heading straight ahead, he hoped that in his panic he had not spun around and got his orientation all messed up. Two minutes, he guessed, and then he'd be at the tree line. Once inside the woods the snow may be lighter, although without the leaf canopy overhead, not much. And he'd be able to move faster.

One mile, in the snow, direction uncertain. He should be home within half an hour.

He glimpsed a hump in the snow from the corner of his eye. He ran on, trying to ignore or explain away what he had seen, and then the Freelander loomed before him, blue bodywork smudged white, the ragged shape of Jeremy's body now almost totally covered by snow.

"Oh for fuck's sake!" Dan hissed, and he glanced around because his voice was so loud. Then he looked back at the car to make sure it was his and realised how ridiculous and just so fucking *desperate* all this was fast becoming. The driver's door of the Freelander was closed. He tried calling home again.

The long low tone of unavailability interrupted the silent snowfall, so he turned the phone off and jammed it down into his pocket.

Wind blew snow in his eyes and laughed at him.

"That way," he said, turning his back on the Freelander and Jeremy's body, aiming across the field to where he knew the woods to be. Then he started running again. This time he saw the remains of Jeremy's motorbike pass by on his left. He kept running. Even when he heard the Freelander's doors opening and closing, opening and closing, he continued running, panting with fear now, seeing his breath mist around his face and feeling eyes on his back, even though to see him the watcher would have to be no more than twenty paces away.

Dan ran. He did not turn because that would make him stumble and fall, and he'd lose his way again. He ran because Megan and Nikki were in danger and he had yet to hear a police siren, and he was beginning to wonder whether Brady had called the police at all. He ran because of the shape he'd seen in the road, and the knowledge that it had been Brand startling him into a skid, a swerve, a crash, all planned, all contrived so that he would unearth Jeremy's body and then stumble across his motorbike, so far into the field that it must have been dragged there.

Dan's loud breathing seemed to echo back at him. He could hear only his pounding feet and his manic breaths, feel only the cold, smell only the snow. He hadn't realised that snow had a smell before but here it was, clear and clean and fresh, all-encompassing. It seemed so anomalous in this field, which should smell of spilled petrol and fear and rot. Body rot. Dead body rot.

He ran faster. Even though he had heard the doors opening and closing and seen the shape in the road, he felt alone. That was good. If he'd had even the slightest hint that something or someone was accompanying him through the snow, he was sure he'd have just curled up and suckled mud until whatever or whoever it was arrived.

The trees appeared suddenly, thrusting branches out over the fence to impale him in his headlong flight. He ducked and didn't stop running until he bounced up against the fence. He glanced around, and saw that he'd reached the forest. Thank God, he thought, wondering why such words came when he never thought of himself as a believer. That made him think of Megan, and that made him climb the fence, mindless of the scratching thorns and grasping branches of bushes and shrubs spaced along the forest boundary.

Once beneath the trees he paused to find his bearings, tried the phone again, hoping against hope. It was as dead as ever. The snow seemed lighter in here, even though the leaf canopy was a summertime memory and a springtime promise. There was still a layer on the ground but the going was easier, rotting-down leaves supplying the underlay as opposed to turned, wet mud.

"Good, right way, ten minutes and I'll be home." His voice didn't sound so loud in here with trees to lose itself between. Itself and himself; if he rushed in headlong he could end up anywhere. The woods weren't that big, not this side of the clearing where the houses stood, but if he went the wrong way he could end up travelling parallel to the far boundary, and eventually he'd find himself in deeper woods he didn't know. At least he walked in here occasionally. He'd know the three fallen trees when he found them, and the stone bridge across the stream, and —

Footsteps. Fast, pounding, echoing the beating of his heart, as if trying to use his fear as camouflage. Distance was confusing in the blizzard, but Dan turned his head hurriedly left and right. The field. At last, he was being followed across the field.

The snow could part into a sprinting shape at any second.

Dan set off between the trees. A more certain knowledge of who was out there only made him more scared. In this instance he would have preferred mystery, a more ambiguous fear, to this taste of terror spiced by the rotting reality of Jeremy's death. Murder, Dan thought, it was a murder. Bounding between trees, hands held out to ward off branches aimed for his eyes, Dan knew that he should have called the police days ago. What false pride had stopped him? What foolish certainty that he could protect his family had lead them deeper into danger?

"Murder," he whispered. It sounded like a last gasp.

THE BOOK OF LIES

Lost. Loss. Losing. Odd words for an even odder situation. A human foible, perhaps, the idea that mislaying or yielding something — a possession, a memory, a way — is a bad thing, a lessening of the soul or the soul's belongings. It implies that one possessed something to start with, and so it hints at riches. To lose something worth crying about is to admit that one was fortunate, once. Some are never fortunate. Some never experience loss, only forfeit, because something of no value should never be mourned.

Lost. Loss. Losing. Words of the rich and fortunate, the gifted and blessed, words having no real meaning for the basest in society, the silent majority that goes about its chores, complaining only in badly lit drinking houses as they breathe in the disease-laden smoke of others, muttering dismay into half empty glasses which can never be half full, and following routes laid out by those preparing for their own inevitable loss.

Because everything must, eventually, go. You can't take it with you, so they say. And believe me they're right. What they don't know is that you can't just lose it either...

Whatever fortunes you have, material or ethereal, they must go some-where the moment you die.

Anyone who knows that will be rich in seconds. And in centuries, no one will touch them ever again.

Lost. A definite use of the word, a finite judgement, for if something is lost it can never be found again. Most things judged as lost are merely mislaid. A memory cannot truly be lost because everything seen, heard, tasted and experienced is remember and retained, somewhere. It's always there, reverberating and affecting and steering. All that's lost is the ability to retrieve.

But lost in the woods, now, that's easily done. Especially with fear and desperation guiding the way, because these are the two grossest liars, players of nasty games and spinners of wild, misleading yarns.

Lost in the woods…

How about something worse? How about lost at home? Lost in the place you know and love because there's no way to find yourself, rescue your shivering soul from the inevitable outcome of madness. Lost at home, and losing…

Losing. The state of approaching loss, knowing it is coming but unable to avert, dodge or talk oneself out of its way.

Loss is tenacious. Once its empty self sinks its fangs into something, there's no hauling it back.

Well, maybe on occasion. But even then it's simply delaying the inevitable.

Sometimes loss gets lost, just for a moment.

CHAPTER THIRTEEN

"Nikki, let me in."

More crying from behind the door. Megan frowned and held her breath, trying to hear the giggle hidden by the tears. She was still holding the poker. It would smash the lock on the bathroom door, she supposed, but she liked to think that Nikki was still there somewhere. She liked to think that her daughter could fight the bastard.

"Nikki, let me in and we'll talk, that's all."

"You're still holding that poker!" Nikki sounded terrified. Perhaps Brand had left her now, flitting in and out to taunt Megan with a glance, a stare, a look loaded with barely veiled malice.

"I'm only protecting myself, Nikki. And you know that you bastard, if you're still there."

"There's no one in here with me Mum." Her voice was bent out of shape by tears and fear.

"Then there's no harm letting me in."

There was silence from the bathroom for a moment, then a quiet, emphatic, "No."

Her daughter had retreated along the landing as Megan mounted the staircase, that dopey, hungover smile slipping quickly from her face, replaced by confusion and puzzlement as she saw the poker in her mother's hand. *I saw you in the garden*, Nikki had said. *Why were you chasing the birds, Mum? I thought you liked having them in the garden. Didn't you see them?* Megan had replied, looking into her eyes as she searched for a sign of him in there, watching and laughing at her through her own flesh and blood. *Didn't you see what was wrong with them, they were watching me for him.* Nikki had shrugged her shoulders, frowning, arms held out and hands trailing along the landing walls as she walked back toward the bathroom. *Who, Mum? God?*

Megan had not raised the poker because she *could* not. But she'd seen a brief grin on Nikki's face, disguised as something nervous and vulnerable, perhaps, but loaded with Brand's presence, a mocking glare hiding behind her own daughter's confused smile. And for an instant she had been reflected in Nikki's eyes. She saw herself how Brand was seeing her: hair awry, poker swinging by her side, eyes wide and full of her daughter.

She knocked at the door again. "Nikki, open the door now!"

"Those birds, Mum... "

"I didn't touch them."

"You tried to. You tried to kill them with — "

Megan stood back and shouted, raising the poker to point at the door. "He's spying on me! He has been ever since we met him, spying through his minions, casting his evil through the animals, at me. Maybe he's angry that he can't turn me. Furious that he can't leach me away from God!"

"Who the hell are you on about, Mum?"

Megan held her breath and put her ear to the bathroom door, wondering exactly what she'd heard behind Nikki's voice just then. Her daughter's voice, her daughter's words, but something darker sending them. There was nothing. No movement, no breathing... nothing.

"You know," she said. "You know exactly who I mean. Has he got at you?" The thought was terrible, acid in her veins, blood in her mouth, and for a moment Megan was on the verge of being sick. "Has that bastard been at you? Nikki, answer me! Have you been at her, you bastard? I'll kill you if you have." The images came, much as she tried to force them away. Closing her eyes made them all the more vivid. "God help me," she hissed, but she saw Brand abusing her daughter, bending and twisting and invading her, all the while holding his head back and closing his eyes because somehow he was watching Megan's reaction... watching it *now*.

She spun around and saw the blackbird sitting on the sill

outside the landing window. It pecked gently at the glass and fluttered its wings.

Megan threw the poker. It was a good shot. One end glanced off the window frame and pivoted the other end into the glass. It shattered instantly, sharp silver edges and the black panic of the bird mixing with snow that was instantly blown in. It should have escaped, Megan knew, it should have flown away and called back at her through the blizzard. But a lucky spike of glass plucked at the bird, the poker fell back inside and caught its wing, and the frantic creature fell to the landing floor. Glass tinkled around it. Nikki shouted incoherently behind the bathroom door. Snow touched its feathers and melted. Megan was there in two steps, bringing her foot down on the injured bird, feeling its thin body crunch beneath her shoe, turning its feathers wet and sticking them to the floor in the mess of its own inside.

One wing fluttered briefly and then the creature was still. A snowflake landed on its remains and steamed away.

"There you are," Megan said. She could not keep triumph from her voice. She feared pride, but she feared fear even more.

And then she heard Nikki admitting the vilest truths.

"I love him, Mum," she said, words muffled where she had her face pressed against the door. "I can't help it."

It was only when Megan closed her eyes in despair, attempting to speak to God but finding her way blocked by her own fears, that she heard Nikki's *other* voice, her Brand voice. Deep, mocking, things her daughter would never say passing through her innocent lips. "And he loves me."

She picked up the bloody poker, walked to the bathroom door and swung it hard. Nikki screamed at the impact, and so did Megan. It left one blackbird-bloodied hole in the hollow door. The shock smacked her hands and wrists and she dropped the poker. It rattled to the floor, she picked it up and continued hitting, hitting, her eyes still closed and Nikki's other voice — her voice of Brand — sneaking giggles in between her daughter's screams, a shout and a laugh every time metal impacted upon wood, and Megan was begging God to help her.

He gave her strength. She felt the hot bubble of blisters

already rising on her palms but she kept hitting the door, swinging the poker harder with each strike. It bounced from the door handle, she hit again and the handle bent, wood splintered.

"Mum Mum Mum Mum Mummy..." Nikki shouted, and somehow the other words came too as Megan squeezed her eyes even tighter shut. "Bitch bitch bitch..."

Megan opened her eyes. The lever handle and latch were a mangled mess now, surrounded by splintered wood and ready to give in. She bashed three more times and then hit the door with her shoulder. It swung inward... and then slammed shut again.

"Mum, please, don't do this!" Nikki shouted. She must be leaning against the other side, using her weight to keep it shut.

"He's in you, Nikki," Megan said. "You never had God in you, not really, all those times I wanted to take you to church, to see what it was like to love Him and be loved by Him. You left yourself open, *empty*, and Brand has come to take advantage. He's in you. I can see it in your eyes, hear it — "

"Mum, I can't help it, he's so..." It seemed that Nikki could not think of a word for Brand.

Megan could. "He's evil!" she shouted, looking to the ceiling and closing her eyes, exhorting God to guide her.

"No I'm not," a voice said from the bathroom. "Poor blackbird, going to bake it in a pie?"

Megan screamed in outrage, fear, anger, and charged the door.

It burst open unhindered. She held the poker in front of her as she entered the bathroom, searching around for Nikki. Gone, she's gone, he was in her and now he's taken her and I'll never see her —

Nikki was in the bath. It was empty of water, she was fully clothed, but it looked as if she was washing herself. With both hands. One passing back and forth across her breasts, the other delving down between legs.

"Nikki," Megan whispered, suddenly empty of fight and emotion, a blank.

"Brand," Nikki groaned. Her hips rose, her breathing quickened and she bit her bottom lip until it bled.

Her mother was coming upstairs brandishing a poker, staring at her strangely, forehead creased as it was sometimes when she prayed, knuckles white around the poker handle. She was muttering something, probably to Nikki but her voice was so quiet that it seemed as if she was mumbling to herself.

Nikki backed away and smiled at Brand as they stood behind The Hall. Her mother faded and Brand was there, breathing into her face so that she could taste the inside of him, breath flowing from him to her, and he was whispering sweet nothings into her ear without his lips moving. She knew what he was thinking because she knew him so well… she didn't but she dreamed she did, dreams within dreams, a play within a play revealing hidden treachery and unknown dark depths…. But where had that thought come from?

Her mother's voice forced her back along the landing but still Nikki smiled. Brand was in school, looking down from the library window and waiting for her to sense the remnants of his presence that lunchtime, already knowing that she would be where he stood and leaving signs: the flies, so fat and bloated and dead; the silence, normal in the library but this particular species planted by Brand, an enforced silence in his presence, a deference to him, not to knowledge. Nikki had knowledge. She knew as soon as she saw him that she was the one for him, and vice versa. Jazz's hand flung casually around her shoulder may as well have been a spatter of snowflakes, such was its lasting presence.

The point of the poker wavered. Her mother was using it to point, emphasising each word with a little stab at the air in front of Nikki. She backed against the bathroom door and nudged it open with her shoulder. Brand's hand closed around hers in the Freelander, warm instead of cold, hot in intention, sending secret signals as her parents sat in their own exclusion zones. Their disregard for each other was now so old that they were both almost comfortable with it, pretending it was as things had been and always would be. Pretending it was right.

Nikki slammed the bathroom door behind her and clicked the latch shut. Her mother was talking on the other side, trying to persuade her to come to her senses. Fear gave her voice a high lilt. Prayers broke through now and then, interspersed with please to let her go and let him go, her mother talking to two people. Three if you counted God, and Nikki giggled because she had never counted God before...

She began to cry. She didn't actually feel sad or scared or upset, but it was what was expected. "There's no one in here with me Mum," she said, looking at the shower cubicle and seeing Brand standing in the woods, smiling at her, and even though the expression stayed far from his eyes she smiled back. He shifted slightly and then he was at the party, wandering through the gyrating clouds of nobodies to tell her she was somebody to him. The bathroom was bright and white and cool and stank of bleach, but Nikki could see only the glint of Brand's shiny hair in the dark, feel the warmth of the house heating up under the onslaught of so many teenaged emotions and hormonally-driven quests to exchange juices, taste the tang of pot in the air and the electric surge of sexual excitement as Brand sought her through the crowded house. She had not seen him then but she saw him now, always a step behind her as she searched for him, a shadow twisting in strict accordance with her own, always one step away but always, always behind her, so that he was so much in the corner of her eye that she imagined he was a fantasy or a memory. Following her through the rooms and upstairs and back down. His hand reaching out to touch an errant strand of hair, sending a flush of warmth to her groin.

Her mother questioned and Nikki answered. Or maybe Brand answered; sometimes she wasn't quite sure who was saying what and to whom. Then silence for a while, interrupted only by a *tap-tap-tapping* from beyond the door. Glass shattering. Nikki knew that her mother was going mad out there, but she was also certain that she was utterly sane in here, as definite as she had ever been about her life and the thing it was to become.

Whatever that was.

Nikki rested her forehead on the door and smiled. "I love him Mum. I can't help it." She felt a cool hand caressing the nape of her neck, and when she turned around a breath hung condensed in the bathroom air. Brand stepped from the shower, brushing leaves and twigs from his clothing, mud on his shoes, he was in the woods... and Nikki suddenly knew that this was *now*, this was not what had been or would be. He smiled and spoke in a gruff parody of her voice. "And he loves me."

Nikki held her breath, eyes wide, heart stammering in her chest. Had he really said that? Did he really mean it?

Her mother started smashing at the door. Nikki screamed and Brand giggled, and even though Nikki knew that he was not truly there, she reached out to him for comfort. He laughed some more and her mother screamed through the door. Nikki answered in the only way she knew how. Brand... Brand... Brand... there was nothing else for her, not any more. His memory, his idea, approached her and held her hands. He cooled her skin and prickled goosebumps across her body, leading her to the bath and whispering in her ear, bringing back that final memory. It should have shamed her. She put her hand to her face and chin and felt where he had spilled his seed. Those places still felt cold and numb, colder still when he touched his fingertips to them, drawing out the heat and chilling her to the bone, chilling her bones themselves.

Her mother crashed at the door but Brand threw it shut. He spoke to her, Nikki was screaming simply because she knew she should be, and he watched as she lay down in the bath. The impacts on the door sounded different as the wood gave way. Her mother's voice was suddenly louder now that there were holes for it to come through. Brand reached out and held Nikki's hands. His hair swung over his face as he leaned down and started touching her with her own hands. Nikki closed her eyes and smelled spilled wine and damp in Mandy's basement. And then her mother was in.

Nikki heard her name called but it was from a long, long way away. Much nearer was Brand, touching her all over, setting her skin alive and alight with his gaze, guiding her hands with his own timeless, endless touch.

"Brand," she said. In her mind's eye he smiled because he had her, totally.

CHAPTER FOURTEEN

Dan was lost.

He'd been in these woods dozens of times before; summer and winter; spring when the wood ants were forming their mounds; autumn when decay looked so beautiful. He'd walked through sober in the daytime and drunk in the evening, on those few occasions he chose to walk home from Bar None instead of phoning Megan for a lift. He'd tried to find his countryside heritage, searching through dedicated city-dweller's blood for the farming stock of his great-grandparents. Alcohol sometimes encouraged this vain search, and a stumbled journey through the woods would often leave him scratched and bloodied and dirty, but smiling a sad smile at something he would never be able to be.

Dozens of times.

But he'd never seen this gully, this dam of rocks, this wide pool sucking in the snow.

Maybe kids have been here, he thought. Dammed the stream, intending to come back and bust the dam in a secret World War II bombing raid, forgot, left it. But kids nowadays were more likely to be guiding Lara Croft through endless angular dungeons than playing in the woods.

He couldn't fool himself. He was lost.

Dan stood on the bank of the gully and looked down at the pool, wondering where he'd gone wrong and listening all the time for the sounds of pursuit. Since he'd entered the woods fifteen minutes ago he'd heard nothing but his own footsteps and the occasional *shush* of snow falling through the branches from above. Now, standing still, he listened harder than ever. If Brand was still following him he'd be making a noise. Brushing against trees, blinded by the ever-worsening blizzard. Stumbling in holes already camouflaged by snow.

Unless he was standing as still as Dan, only feet away, watching him.

Dan spun around. Snow swirled at him as a heavy gust passed between the trees, flakes forming a solid mass and nudging him back, back, his heels slipping on slick leaves and wet mud, and then he was falling into space. He tipped and stared up at the sky, catching snowflakes in his eyes and blinking as they melted and blurred his vision. The fall seemed to be taking a very long time. He saw a shadow beneath the trees, a place where no snow fell and no light penetrated, a null zone which was not just black, it was nothing... and when Dan heard a laugh he wanted only to close his eyes, but he had to look. Still falling, still tipping back to the sky, he had to look.

His head and shoulders hit the side of the gully first, then his back and behind. He slid down towards the pool. His senses spun with the impact, eardrums heavy and hard, neck stiff and on fire. He clawed his hands and dragged them through the rot of leaves clinging to the steep gully sides. Leaves collected against his fingers as he slid, dragging decayed bouquets to whoever he was going to meet at the bottom. The sky spun, even though he was sliding in one plane now, and surely it had been daylight minutes ago? Daylight darkened by snow (and the nothing between the trees), but daytime nonetheless? Dark now, darker and colder than he had known, and Dan panicked when he heard pebbles splashing into the pool. In seconds his head would break the surface and water would flood his lungs.

He strained to sit, twisted his body, grabbed harder at the slick bank, and in all the struggling he succeeded in turning just far enough so that only his legs and one arm slid into the freezing pool.

"Shit!" Dan gasped, struggling to breathe for several seconds before air found its way past the shock. The water was so damn cold... and it stank. Stagnant. There was a stream run-

ning through the woods, but this pool must have been formed
from the melting snows of a few days ago. Dan didn't know
how long it took for water to stagnate in such conditions, but
this smelled like an open sewer, the aromas of rot and decay
sweeping over him as if breaking the pool's surface had allowed them egress.

He struggled to crab up the bank and away from the water's
dark edges.

Dan looked up to where he'd been standing. The bank was
barely six feet above him, yet it felt as if he'd been falling for
ever. He was freezing. His teeth clattered and his limbs shook.

And he was lost.

He stood and started edging around the pool, making his
way to the far side where the gully wall tapered back down to
the forest floor. He could try to climb back up where he was
now, but last year's leaves and the snow combined to make that
an almost impossible task. Besides... he looked back over his
shoulder, terrified that he'd see Brand staring down at him, but
he was even more scared not to look.

There was no sign of anyone up there. And that void in
the snow must have been caused by the breeze.

Must have.

His feet slipped into the water several times, each submer-
sion seeming to increase the numbness and make him more
and more concerned. He'd never had to worry about frostbite
or freezing or banging his head and drowning or breaking a
limb and lying helpless as a snowstorm slowly buried him, the
snow melting at first as it touched his warm body, but eventually settling as he lost his heat, his heart, his soul to the blizzard. He glanced up constantly, noticing that the level of the
forest floor came lower and lower the further he shifted around
the pool. Eventually he could see over the bank, and then he
turned and moved sideways on his stomach until he could reach
up and haul himself out of the gully. He crawled a few feet on
his hands and knees before standing, trying to hug heat into
himself and prevent it being leeched away by the snow.

He had to move. To stay still would be to submit, and
that's just what Brand wanted. If he sat down and buried his
head in his hands, slowed his breathing and let the snow erase

him from this world, Brand would come to visit him.

Dan could never do that. There was Megan and Nikki, Megan and Nikki, he kept repeating those names in his head and conjuring their faces, trying to see joy and amusement in them, not the fear and suspicion he'd seen in Megan the last time he was with her.

Something ran by him between the trees. It was a shadow against the whiteout, yet still he could not discern its true form. He hunched down, held his breath and tried to stop his teeth from chattering together.

Footsteps. The sound of something sharp scraping across a tree trunk. A smell, some dank odour not belonging to the fresh snow. A growled giggle… or perhaps it was ice in his ears, melting and popping.

Dan ran. He didn't care about making a noise because Brand knew he was here. Neither did showing his fear concern him; it was beyond hiding. He tried to wave curtains of snow aside as he ran, dodged some trees, hit others, fell to the ground and scrambled to his feet again. All the time that shape may have been behind him, inches from his back, reaching for his neck, but he could not turn around to look. He fended branches from his face and let them flip back, hoping they would hit any pursuer and distract them from the chase.

The path dipped and curved, fallen snow conspiring to hide the lay of the land and sending him sprawling several times. Each time he stood and ran on without looking back. He remembered what his father had told him when he was eighteen, just about to go off on an army training day for charity and faced with the prospect of a two-hundred foot cliff abseil. "Don't look down." Logical advice, obvious, so self-evident that no one else had actually said it to him. It had worked. For two hundred feet he'd stared at a rock face three feet in front of him, no danger of falling, no fear of heights. There was only one time, when he looked sideways, that he was aware of the terrible danger he was in: he could see across the treetops to distant hills, a few multi-coloured specks far, far down, people hustling about on another abseil.

Then back at the cliff face. Looking at something so close made far-off things seem less dangerous.

Dan slipped again, fell hard on his side and lay there, exhausted. Pain came from everywhere. He couldn't even tell whether or not he was still on the path. He turned onto his back and looked up, blinking rapidly as snowflakes tangled themselves in his eyelashes, feeling suddenly claustrophobic and hemmed in by the snow. It was keeping him from his family. It had him trapped. He closed his eyes to the danger and remembered the cliff face, and when he opened them again Brand was staring down at him.

"Cold," Brand said.

"You... "

"It's cold. You'll freeze."

Dan tried to sit up but Brand put a foot on his chest and pushed him back down.

"I could hold you here," the tall man said. "Stay for a few hours, let the snow cover you and drown you. Hold you under." He smiled, put on a high-pitched voice. "And he loves me."

Dan wanted to rage at him, hurt him, struggle out from beneath his foot and fight. But all his strength had gone. He'd looked sideways and seen the fear, and now he had to contend with it at last. No chance of glancing away from this danger. No way to pretend it didn't exist. "Why us?" was all he could say.

Brand bent down, putting more weight on his foot and crushing Dan's chest.

Dan gasped for breath and breathed in a mouthful of snow. He coughed, had to wait until the snow had melted before he could swallow it and suck in a breath.

The tall stranger — name known, scarred face known, but still a stranger — leaned over Dan and shielded him from the snow; blocking out the light, too, causing his own little eclipse. Then he smiled. His bad eye screwed horribly shut. "That's for you to find out," he said. He looked up, frowning, as if trying to see something further in the woods. "Snow's getting heavier. Megan's getting madder. Nikki's getting... " He looked down at Dan and smiled, licking his lips with a dry tongue that looked blue in the fading light. "... sexier."

Dan struggled, twisted and turned, eventually throwing

Brand's foot from his chest. But as he stood and watched Brand disappear between the trees and into the snow, finding a darker place than most to stroll towards, he knew that the stranger had allowed him up.

"Come here!" Dan screamed. "Come back and face me like..." *A man*, he wanted to say. *Come back and face me like a man*. But it all sounded so wrong.

He looked down at the snow layer hiding the forest floor. Brand's footprints led away between the trees, evenly spaced, perfectly formed, no hint of slipping or panic around their edges. Dan set his foot in the first print and found it fit perfectly. He followed three or four more, falling into his own pace, finding that Brand had taken the route of least resistance between the trees.

He followed. There was no need to look up and check his surroundings. He didn't even glance across at the three fallen trees to his left. He felt no surprise when the path led him across the little bridge over the stream.

He knew where Brand was going.

Soon, he would be home.

The footprints ended at the edge of the woods.

They had not been obliterated by the snow, although now it was falling heavier than Dan had ever seen. They were still almost fresh, their edges only slightly blurred by fresh flakes, so Brand could not be far away. Rather, they were lost. There was a confusion of prints, Brand's trail leading into what looked like a crossing-point for the forest animals: deer hoofs; a dog's paw prints; a hundred tiny bird marks; even something that looked like the trail a sidewinder would leave in the desert sand. Brand's prints simply led into this mess and did not emerge again.

Across the field, Dan could just make out a dull splash of light; the outside light above his front door. Just up from this there was an even weaker yellow smudge in the curtains of snow; the bathroom light.

Megan and Nikki.

He wished it didn't feel as if Brand had led him here.

Cold, weak, head aching, neck sore, the snow on his clothes bloodied from where he was cut and scraped by his falls, Dan staggered out into the blizzard and toward his family home.

Megan was leaning against the basin, watching her daughter writhe in the bath whilst muttering the name of the demon that had come to take them all, when she heard the noise downstairs.

Someone was banging on the front door.

After her recent shouting, Nikki's crying, the smashing window and then the brief period of silence interrupted only by Nikki's sighs, the sound was louder than ever. The snow seemed to insulate noises inside the house, blanketing the whole landscape, keeping out any sound not relevant. Everything she could hear was part of the nightmare unfolding around her. There was a secret rustling in the attic above her head. Another spy...

The banging again, louder and faster this time. Megan backed out of the bathroom and looked over the banister at the front door. There was a shape behind it, pressed against the glass with its hands shielding its face to see in.

It was Dan. It should have been Brand — all her fear told her that was so, all logic dictated it — but she could see even from here that it was her husband. Come back to help her, again, at last.

Perhaps he would be in time.

Nikki cried out then. So did Megan, but for vastly different reasons.

Megan ran downstairs, checking each tread for signs of a small animal to trip her, a carpet gnawed by one of Brand's rats, a snail sacrificing itself to send her slipping on its crushed insides... and all the way she muttered under her breath: "One more step, God, one more step, God, one more step... "

Jesus saw her through. She reached the front door, threw back the bolts and swept it wide open.

Dan fell in. He was shaking uncontrollably, his hands were bloody, filth and dead leaves clung to the exposed skin of his face. His eyes were wide, too, and they were all him. She scanned his face quickly to see whether there were any insects on the dirt. He stared at her. She wondered just what he'd seen in the couple of hours he had been gone.

For a terrible second Megan thought that he was dead.

"Dan!" she said. "My Jesus, what happened to him?"

Dan wondered who his wife was talking to. He tried to look around to see if there was anyone else in there with them — Brand, she's talking to Brand — but the warm air in the house hit his cold skin and sent him shivering and shaking, so badly that Megan could not even hold him upright. She released him and let him slip back to the floor. He managed to haul his legs in so that she could slam the door. He watched her turn to look at him, forming her question again, and then he saw the bruise on her hand and a scratch on her face, several buds of blood blooming along its length.

"Where's Nikki?" he asked through chattering teeth.

"Upstairs," Megan said, unable to say more of what had to be said. Upstairs masturbating at the memory of that unholy bastard, abusing herself as he has abused her already... it didn't bear thinking about, let alone verbalising. She knelt by Dan's side and reached out to hold him.

Her hands were hot on his skin, so hot that they hurt. He flinched away. She looked at him strangely, his eyes, staring into his eyes like she never had before, leaning forward to actually look deep into his pupils, moving to one side so that reflected light from the landing window fell on his face.

"What?" Dan said. "Megan, what the fuck... ?"

"You're Dan," she said.

He shivered again, and not simply from the cold. "Megan, where is he? Where's Brand? Is he here, does he have Nikki, is that what you're trying to tell me?"

She stood, strode to the base of the staircase and shouted. "He has Nikki alright, don't you, you bastard! He has Nikki, he's had Nikki, and... she won't let him go!"

Dan pushed himself up on his elbows. "Megan, don't say that. Megan?"

She turned and although she had seen only Dan in Dan's eyes, she raised her hand to strike him. Dan shielded his face. She lowered her hand again, slowly, realising not what she had done but knowing what she must do.

Nikki was corrupted. She was tainted with his evil, touched by his grimy hands and thoughts. "He's been at her, Dan," she said. "We have to do something… to help… her." Her tears came then, hot and plentiful.

Dan had never thought he'd be happy to see Megan cry. It was the most human thing she'd done all day. He crawled to her, his shaking subsiding under the need to comfort his wife. He held her in his arms and that made him feel strong once more. Strong enough to tell her.

"Brand's dangerous. I think he killed Jazz and buried him in a field. I crashed the Freelander. He was there, he distracted me, chased me through the woods… talked to me… and I followed him here." He held her at arms length and tried to stare at her, but tears blurred her eyes. "Megan. Has he been inside?"

"His minions watch us, yes," she said, sniffing. "They're here. They've always been here. And they always will be."

Dan noticed the smashed landing window. "What happened up there?"

"He was staring in," Megan said slowly, as if talking to a child. Dan looked scared and cold and dirty, but that shouldn't make him stupid. If he'd opened himself to Jesus as she had he would not retain this damned innocence, this belief that there was simply good and bad, not purity and utter evil. Megan loved pure, she worshipped it, but she had never, ever had a taste of real evil. Not until now. And Dan still could not see it.

"It's the first floor," Dan said. "Was he up a ladder?" *Can he fly?* He almost added, but the crazy idea disturbed him far more than it should have.

"Watching us through his familiars," she said. "He has been ever since we gave him a lift, since the footprints — "

"He's just a sick fuck," Dan said, suddenly desperate for Megan to recognise this. As long as she thought that Brand was something more than human — something in the vicinity of God and the devil — she was useless, wrapped up in her own wild thoughts. And, he thought, it made him distinctly unsettled.

"Megan, the police, Brady should have called the police and sent them here. Have they called? Have they been?"

"Only God's laws stand any — "

"Megan, he killed Jeremy." He watched his wife as the words slowly sank in. Her face seemed to relax, losing its tense edges, a hint of the craziness bleeding away as she turned pale.

"Then we have to kill him," she said.

Dan stood, shaking his head, the ache in his neck turning into a hot throb as he did so. His extremities were tingling as he warmed up and his circulation improved, and he realised for the first time just how much he'd been cut and bruised during his race through the woods. The mud on his hands would not dry because of the blood soaking it. "Police," he said, and went for the phone.

"Dad?" Nikki had heard her parents arguing and slowly, slowly, she'd raised herself from the bath. Her heart hammered but she was at peace. Her breathing raced but her breath tasted sweet, there were no such things as staleness or stress. She felt drained, her legs shook, everything around her glowed with a pleasant hue, a post-coital fuzz which she'd only ever experienced before on her own. Now she was living it with Brand. She could still feel his fingers down there, a recent memory made hot by her. She could feel his lips around her nipples, though they were dry. She closed her eyes where she stood on the landing and she could see his face. No smile there… no real smile had ever touched those eyes, because he was so content inside that there was no need to display it to the world… but his expression was full of love. He loved her. That's why nothing else mattered.

"Nikki, what's wrong honey?" her dad called up.

"Nothing," she said, opening her eyes and staring down into the hallway. Her father was covered in mud, he was bleeding, her mother looked mad and devastated and drained… but Brand loved her, his memory whispered silent nothings of her own imagining, and little else mattered.

"Nikki." Dan did not know what else to say, whether he should tell her about Jeremy, warn her about Brand. If Megan was right and Brand had been at their daughter he should be watching her now, quizzing her and making sure the bastard wasn't loose in the house. Ensuring his family was safe... there were his footprints after all, disappearing at the edge of the woods, and that was only two hundred steps from the house. If he was not already here he must be outside right now.

Nikki started downstairs. She needed a drink. She wanted to tell her mum that everything was all right. Brand was just a guy, that was all. Older than Jazz, maybe, and a little more mysterious, more... adult. But just a guy.

"He's not just a guy, Mum," she muttered as she reached the hallway, frowning as she tried to remember what she'd just said.

"He's evil!"

"You stay away from him, Nikki!" Dan said.

Nikki had never been a stroppy teenager. Headstrong and self-aware maybe, but her parents were generally understanding and quite liberal about most things — although her mum's God hang-up caused friction sometimes — and arguments about going out and other 'growing up things' had materialised only irregularly. But now... how dare they!

"How dare you!" Nikki said. "I'm seventeen! I can see who I like."

"'See'?" Megan said. "I saw you in the bath, doing what you were doing, you dirty little slut! You've been doing more than just seeing him, haven't you, that bastard? He's been watching me, but he's been... *fucking* you!"

"I've never fucked him!" Nikki screamed, immediately wishing she hadn't. She should have agreed with her mother, made her think that she and Brand had made love, that would teach the religious bitch something, make her think her little girl had been done by the tall dark scarred stranger. But his scar wasn't that bad, was it? Why did that feature so strongly when she thought of him, that thin, white scar?

"Just you stay away from him, Nikki!" Dan said again, scared at the tone he was taking and knowing straight away that he had no authority here, not anymore. Something had changed, some fundamental rule of their father-daughter relationship had shifted since they had last spoken. But still he had to try. "He's dangerous," he said. "He... " Killed Jazz, he wanted to say. He killed Jazz. But remonstrating with Nikki was no way of breaking that news.

Dan left his wife and daughter shouting at each other as he picked up the cordless telephone and dialled 999.

For a second there was a ringing tone. He'd only dialled the emergency services once before, the time he'd discovered Megan after the attack, and he'd been in such a state that he could never recall anything about it... didn't know whether there was a dialling tone beforehand, the sound of ringing, what the person had said on the other end. So now when the ringing tone stopped to be replaced by a soft shush of static, it took him a few seconds to realise that something was wrong.

Megan and Nikki were still shouting. Nikki screamed but did not care, she could still feel the cold impact of Brand on her cheeks and chin so all was well with the world. Megan tried to stare past Nikki's strange expression — part anger, most mockery — to see whether Brand was still in there. Dan shook his head, hung up and dialled again. This time there was no tone whatsoever. Not even static. Nothing.

"Phone's dead," he said quietly, but both his wife and daughter heard him. "My mobile isn't working, must be the blizzard. I heard a tone just now. Briefly. Maybe a line's down somewhere." And if I keep on with this, he thought, I'll convince myself it's true. Then I can move onto ghosts, hollow earth and UFOs.

"It's him," Megan said. "He's stopped the phones working."

"Cut the lines?" Dan said, almost smiling at the TV-show melodrama of it all.

"No. Stopped them working." Megan glared at Dan — at the blood and mud on his face and hands and the leaves stuck to his wet clothing — realising what a fine disguise it could be. She glanced back at her daughter and saw the calm mockery in her eyes once again. Maybe he was watching through Nikki, maybe not. It was more disturbing to think that he was not... then that awful, *adult* expression was Nikki's all alone.

"He can't do that," Dan said, still trying to convince himself of normality, disbelieving even though all the evidence was laid out before him. "Not the mobile, it's the storm, maybe he cut the line — "

Megan felt the rage rising again and quietly begged God to ease it. Either He was not listening or He felt the rage was fine, needed, because her limbs turned hot and the skin of her face stretched as she grimaced and began screaming at her husband and daughter. Neither of them really knew the truth... or in Nikki's case perhaps she did, and again that made it all worse. "He's capable of anything! He can do anything, he *will* do anything, to rip us apart from each other. It's God's love he hates, and like it or not that's what we have between us. The love of God! And for the love of God, I'll do anything to stop him!"

"He's just a guy, Mum."

Megan spun on her daughter — for a second Dan thought she really was going to strike out this time — and shouted. "He's just a guy who's killed your boyfriend!"

Silence. Dan was watching Nikki, and so was Megan. The girl stared over her mother's shoulder at a space on the wall next to the front door.

Killed her boyfriend... she shouldn't believe it because it was unbelievable, but believe it she did. She should be shocked, stunned, distraught, terrified, but she was none of these. As she moved her gaze to the frosted glass and watched the strange shadows of snow falling beyond, she felt only content. Jazz... dead... maybe, maybe not. But if he was then there was always Brand, there was *always* Brand, and as she thought of him she felt the heat in her groin again, and her stomach muscles contracted and her eyes closed as she imagined his fingers running down her sides and across her hips.

"Nikki," Dan said. He wondered just what he was going to say to his daughter when she finally turned to look at him. But she didn't. Instead she turned and walked back upstairs. "Nikki, we have to stay together. We have to talk about this." We have to call the police, he thought, how the hell can we call the police?

"I'm fine, Dad." Seconds later she disappeared around the landing and her bedroom door clicked shut.

Megan and Dan glanced at each other, both lost within their own lies.

"God help us," Megan said.

"I hope He will," Dan replied, not believing but needing Megan to keep believing. However much it confused her, right now it was the only thing keeping her herself. "But for him to help us, we have to help ourselves, yes? I have to call the police. I'm going across to the Wilkinsons' to use their phone."

"Dan — "

"Megan, listen to me. I asked Brady to call the police. He can't have done so, otherwise they'd be here by now. If Brand can kill Jazz he could have killed Brady. I just don't know. But if he's still around, I'd rather have the police here to deal with him than… " *Than me*, he was going to say. But that sounded so cowardly.

Was he? Was he a coward?

"I'll go and talk to Nikki," Megan said. "Tell her how much God loves her."

For a few seconds Dan had the horrible idea that his family was in more danger from within than without. He really shouldn't be leaving Megan, not now, not while she was so changeable. And Nikki…

But coward or not, brave or not — good husband and father, or not — he had to get in touch with the police. Maybe they'd have found the Freelander by now.

Going outside terrified him more than staying put. The fear made him feel brave. However wrong, that was the way things were.

"I'll be ten minutes," he said. Then he went to the cloakroom to wrap up warm and try to find the old baseball bat.

Megan mounted the stairs, wondering if she'd ever see her husband alive again. God willing, she thought.

God willing.

THE BOOK OF LIES

Life is a lie. You strive, you struggle, you agonise and seek and despair and laugh and cry... and in the end you die. Nothing will stop that. Spend fifty years eating what you want, drinking too much, fucking at random and living a criminal life of neglect and over indulgence; or live a hundred on a mountain-top, eating lentils and meditating for eight hours each and every day. Either way, you're dead. Your body turns to mush and your soul... well, what I know of souls is just too difficult. Actions speak louder than words. And actions that hurt can scream.

However much you run and hide and conspire and plan, I could open your neck, hold your carotid artery between my fingertips, and with one click of my fingers you're dead. The end. Fuck you very much, goodnight.

Life is such a lie.

Death, now...

It's easy to mislead. It's easier still to shock with the randomness of death, bring it home to dozens by killing only one, because even though death is something most people consider every day — however indirectly — and watch on the television, read of in books, talk about over their fifth beer whilst ordering another and lighting up just one last cigarette, most people rarely have to look it in the face and truly experience its unbearable depths. For most, death creeps up from behind.

You trust far too much. The sun will rise and the snow will fall, and there will be no obstruction in the road when you corner at fifty. You trust your daughter to love you and your wife to live through the freaky time she's been having... you trust forgiveness because it is borne of love...

... you trust that you will never die. Because things like that just don't happen to you...

And you trust your neighbours to be alive when you go to ask an important favour of them.

Shock is an ally, and life is a lie. Death is the only truth

CHAPTER FIFTEEN

There are three sharp raps at the door. It startles them, because the storm has been raging for almost two hours. Several inches of snow have already fallen. The last thing they expect tonight is visitors.

"I'll go," Frank Wilkinson says, groaning as he pushes himself up from the chair. His knee joints pop audibly and he rubs some warmth into them before standing upright. Myra is intent on the Australian soap they're watching and she does not bother to acknowledge.

Frank walks through into their large hallway, wincing with every step. He'd been through a good many winters — seventy-six of them, in fact — but the last few years seemed to have been getting worse. Not so much weather-wise — this year was a freak in a period when milder winters encouraged the doom-sayers to scream of global warming and melting ice caps — but joint-wise. Too much football during his youth, Myra said. Old age, he countered. Either way, he always knew for days before when there was a storm approaching.

Curious. Today, his bones had only begun to ache as he watched the first snowflakes swirling down.

As he reaches the front door the visitor knocks again, harder this time, more insistent. Frank pauses. It's snowing like hell out there — worse than the blizzard of '62, for sure — and they hadn't been expecting anyone. They'd paid the milkman yesterday, the paper-boy called for his money on a Monday, and the half-lamb they'd ordered from the local butcher wasn't due until next week. In a blizzard like this, a surprise visitor could only mean someone in trouble. Dan from across the meadow, perhaps. Maybe his daughter is in trouble or his wife has fallen and hurt herself. "That you Dan?" Frank calls.

"Yeah." The voice is muffled, but it sounds calm enough. Frank throws back the door bolts and unhasps the chain. Damn thing, Myra had insisted on having it fitted when they'd double-glazed the house six years ago, and he had never used it. Always slung it when he locked up at night, but never when answering the door. It just seemed so... mistrustful.

As Frank unlatches the door and it blows open into his face, his first thought is: It wouldn't have done any good. He gasps in surprise, and then again in pain as his broken nose gushes blood. He slumps to the floor, kneels forward as blood splashes down his shirt and trousers and stains Myra's new damn hall carpet... and as Dan pulls the door almost shut, Frank realises that it must have been caught by the wind. Their surprise visitor from over the way has grabbed the door and hauled it back, seeing what happened and trying to prevent any more injury...

And then it crashes open again, catching Frank on top of his skull this time because he's kneeling forward watching let the blood pool on the *Welcome* mat. He lets out a sound between a cough and a scream and the door hits him again, again, pulled closed and slammed open with incredible force six more times.

The seventh time, a hand curls around the jamb to hold Frank's head steady as the edge of the door crushes his temple.

Frank falls sideways to the floor. He can still see, although his sight if fading, and he notices how bad the snow really is, and how dark the shadow standing at their doorway appears set against it. The visitor — it's not Dan, certainly not Dan, he can see that now — steps over his prone body and closes the door, and now all Frank can see is the blue flower-patterned wallpaper of their hallway fading as his sight retreats into the darkness.

Frank reads a lot. He prefers reading to watching television, he finds it more stimulating and it's good to keep his mind active as he gets on in years. He doesn't want to be one of those old people who…

He read somewhere that hearing is the final sense to go before death.

As he struggles to move, to shout a warning to Myra, to slide himself across the floor to protect her from this monster that has come in from the snow, the last thing he hears is his wife screaming, and something hard impacting on something soft.

Dan recalled a film he'd seen a few years back, John carpenter's *The Thing*. The guys in the Antarctic station had guide ropes between buildings so that they could find their way in blizzards, and he'd thought it was a bit over-the-top. The buildings were only thirty feet apart, after all.

Now he understood.

He was lost. Not badly lost, not never-going-home lost. Not even as lost as he'd been in the woods only an hour before. But when he looked back he could see no sign of his home, his garden, the dead apple tree; and when he looked forward, there was no indication at all that the Wilkinson's house stood anywhere out there in the whiteout.

Dan hunched his shoulders and struggled on, wishing he'd found time to pull on another sweatshirt under the ski-jacket he'd grabbed from the cloakroom. He'd been cold before, but since he'd sampled warmth in the house he was no more freezing than ever. One of his mother's expressions came to mind: colder than a witch's tit. The snow was a solid wall, an all-encompassing blanket surrounding and hemming him in, and every step he took seemed to move him to the place he'd just 7been. Nothing changed. An occasional uneven bit of ground beneath his foot marked where the meadow dipped or rose, but that was all. He could see no houses, no trees, no signs that he was anywhere he knew.

It had been like this earlier. And then he'd heard those pounding footsteps.

He turned around, spinning a full circle in case someone was running at him but succeeding only in disorientating himself more. At least up to now he'd been going in roughly the right direction. Now he was completely confused. But he had to go on, he had to call the police. He had to...

Megan had lost it. Nikki was acting weird, and if what Megan had said was true then Brand had got to their daughter, just as he'd promised. Got to her and done God knows what. Dan had come home to protect them, returning from his trip to the police... and having failed in something so simple, he'd let their unusual behaviour drive him back out into the blizzard. Brand may well be out here, he knew that, stalking the snowscape. And he'd left his family alone, and if Brand found their house and made his way inside...

Jeremy was dead. Brand had killed him. *Dead!*

"Jesus fucking Christ, what am I doing!" Dan turned and started running back the way he'd come, or as close to that direction as he could make out. He tucked the baseball bat under his arm, ready to swing it out and use the momentum to smash it into Brand's face if he appeared from the snow, he'd have no hesitation now, no second thoughts, and if it broke his skull and they found him frozen to the ground after the thaw, his blood hardened into a crispy sheen on the grass, then Dan would admit to it and explain, point them in the direction of his crashed Freelander and what lay beneath it —

And then the house appeared before him, the Wilkinsons' house, and the front door swung open just as Dan came to a standstill in front of it.

Brand was there. Come in, have a cup of tea, it'll only take a moment of your time. The thought shocked Dan, almost made him smile, but then he made out the detail.

Snow flurried in around Brand and turned yellow in the light filtering from within. Frank Wilkinson's body lay crumpled on the floor behind him, blood splashed across the light tan carpet. Brand held a fist-sized petrified wood sculpture by his side. Its yellowed surface was stained red, and it seemed to be growing grey hair.

"Oh," said Brand, raising his eyebrows in mock-surprise. "I was just leaving." He dropped the sculpture.

Dan reacted quickly, letting the bat's weight swing it down and twisting his arm to bring it up at Brand's jaw from below. It hit him just as Dan had intended, the loud *thunk* muffled by the snow.

Brand barely flinched. He snatched the bat from Dan's hands and held it straight out by his side. "Like hitting people with wooden sporting implements, don't you Dan?" Then he twitched his wrist and the bat struck Dan hard, high up on his left arm.

It was surprise more than pain that made Dan cry out. The impact was heavy enough to send him staggering, and the two seconds it took for him to regain his balance gave Brand the chance to swing the bat again, aimed higher this time, aiming to connect with Dan's skull. He ducked instinctively, and instead of connecting squarely with his head the bat glanced off. He slumped to on all fours and rolled sideways in the snow. There was no pain in his head, no signs that the baseball bat had done anything more than part his hair, but then as he stood he felt the warm flow of blood past his ear and down his neck. Realisation made him woozy... he swayed, having the presence of mind to move backward, not forward, and the bat swept by inches from his nose.

Dan fell again. He landed heavily on his behind. He saw the tall shadow advance from the doorway, Brand moving in to deliver the coup de grace now that he was helpless on the ground.

Beat him last time, Dan thought. One blow to the head and he was quiet. Taught him a lesson. Can't let it change like this... can't let the bastard beat me like this...

"You're a stupid man, leaving your family unprotected," Brand said, raising the bat in both hands above his head. "Anything could happen to them."

"What have you done to my daughter?" Dan spat, the act of talking driving a sharp pain through his temple and down into his jaw. That side of his head now felt all wrong, too big, not *his* anymore, and he wondered just how much damage had been done.

Brand paused for a moment, bat held high, snowflakes falling around him but appearing to avoid his hair, coat and face entirely. "Compared to what I'm *going* to do... . Nothing at all." Then he swung straight down at Dan's head.

Dan did the only thing he could do. Instinct took over and

brought his left hand up in a warding off gesture, his right hand pivoting him on the ground ready to roll away if he had the chance.

He did not. His hand was held palm-up, his fingers splayed, when the bat struck it. He heard bones crunch — he had a brief image of snapping a handful of twigs over his knee — and felt three of his fingers snap back, fingertips touching his wrist. Pain drove down from his hand, through his wrist, forearm, elbow and finally into his shoulder, jarring all the way as his arm was driven way down by his side. Brand lifted the bat away and Dan fell onto his back, hand held as far away as possible to lessen the chance of contact.

"So frail," Brand said. He stepped forward and stood over Dan, swinging the bat back and forth above his face, a deadly pendulum sinking lower with every arc. "Look at you. I can never figure the ease with which you give in. All of you. It only takes a moment... "

"You leave my family alone," Dan hissed, pain giving his voice a hard, desperate edge he had never heard before. It did not perturb Brand in the slightest.

"Or what? Really Dan, just look at yourself. Lying in the snow, crying like a child — you *are* crying, you know, I can see the tears, they'll freeze on your face when your blood turns cold — and in the space of five seconds you could be dead. Imagine that. You've lived your whole life as best you can, you've looked out for your family... well, most of the time. You've made your friends, choices and mistakes. You strive constantly to better yourself — and I have to tell you, Dan, that sometimes there is no better in you — and you have a nice house. Really. A nice family, too." Brand was looking up now, staring off into the snow as if contemplating something in the distance. "And with a couple of blows I could empty your head across the snow and you'd be nothing. A lump of warm meat rapidly growing cold. Your history and memory freezing on the ground, if the birds don't peck them up first. And you know the worst thing?" He rested the curved head of the bat in the hollow of Dan's throat and squatted down above him, his face within six inches of Dan's. "The worst thing is that your wife and daughter won't know you're dead until somebody tells them."

Dan tried to shift, to nudge Brand away, but every movement pulled the bat tighter into his throat.. The pain in his hand made it difficult to keep still. He thought, I'm going to die.

Brand stood again and slung the bat over his shoulder. "You work so hard to impress yourself on other people, but you only ever really, really matter to yourself." Then he stood back two steps and brought the bat down in a high arc onto Dan's left knee.

Dan screamed. It was high-pitched and out of control, and the snow seemed to echo it back at him. He sucked in a breath to scream again, but the pain, the shock had winded him. He could only squirm in the snow, trying not to touch down his hand or shift his knee but doing both in the blindness of agony.

"That'll do for now," Brand said, and he walked off into the storm.

Dan screwed his eyes shut and tried to keep still. The pain made him squirm and every movement increased it, so the only recourse was to scream. Snow fell into his open mouth and ran down his tongue like spiders. It pattered into his eyes when he opened them, filled his ears where he twisted on the ground, found its way into his clothing and laid cool caresses across his skin. He was hot from the pain, sweating, and that made him colder. Even with his eyes closed tight, everything was white.

His knee was smashed. He'd felt it disintegrate when the bat struck, a sick, slipping feeling as bone parted and flesh gave way. His whole leg was on fire. He managed to raise himself enough to look down at the leg of his jeans, to see how bad it was. Snowflakes melted as they hit blood and helped it flow easier. The ground beneath him was turning pink. His hand was smashed too, and although somehow the skin had not been broken his fingers had, bent back at an angle too awful to view. It had already swelled to twice its normal size, the flesh puffing out to support the breaks, bruising turning his skin black. He sat up carefully, holding all his weight on his right arm until he was sitting fully, groaning and whining through clenched teeth as his leg shifted slightly. Touching the left side of his head with his right had was harder than he'd thought, but when it came away glistening with fresh blood he wished he hadn't bothered. What he'd felt there was entirely the wrong shape.

His left side was broken and bleeding. He felt sick. Vision blurred and danced before him as a sudden faint chilled his pain-hot body.

Brand had left him alive. *That'll do for now*, he'd said, and here he was, alive.

Then the agony let the cold through once more, and Dan realised that he would very definitely die out here if he didn't help himself now. Fainting would give him to the cold. Lying back and waiting for the pain to fade would do the same.

As logic marshalled itself once more he thought of Megan and Nikki. Remembered why he'd come out here in the first place. Realised just where Brand must be heading.

The Wilkinson's open front door was several steps away. They had a phone.

He would have to crawl.

"God loves you, Nikki. Not him. Not that devil."

Nikki had locked her bedroom door. The lock was so old that Megan had forgotten it existed, they must have painted over it twice since they'd lived here. They were normally a very open family, or so she thought. Open and trusting. Well, maybe. She knew that was not the case with her — she was aware of her own truths shielded from the world, and especially from Dan and Nikki — but generally they were quite free with each other. No need to hide anything. No need for locks on doors.

"Nikki, please, open the door honey. Your dad's gone to call the police, they'll be here soon, there's nothing to worry about." She felt tears coming on again but fought them back. They would distort her voice and Nikki would hear, and Megan did not want to frighten her. That bastard had already touched her. She must be scared enough.

Didn't look scared in the bath, someone whispered in her own voice. Megan looked around and saw a mouse at the top of the stairs, staring at her as it sat on its hindquarters and cleaned its whiskers. Snow had layered the carpet from the smashed window, but the cold seemed not to disturb the calm rodent. "Piss off!" she hissed at it, hearing a sudden movement from behind Nikki's bedroom door. She took off a shoe and threw it, but it bounced past the mouse and tumbled downstairs.

"Nikki — "

"I'm not listening to you, Mum," her daughter said. "I'm sitting on my bed and I'm thinking of him, because he loves me and he's going to take me away. I'm not listening to you... swear all you want, beg God for help, He's not listening. If He was why would he have made Dad run out on you again."

"He has not run out!" She stared at the door and considered smashing this one in as well. But breaking down doors was not an answer, Megan knew that. There would always be another door to hide behind.

"What if Brand were to come back now and kill you, Mum?"

"I know that's not Nikki talking!" Megan screamed, alternating her gaze between the closed door and the mouse on the landing... now joined by a spider, rushing across the snow-dappled carpet in rapid stops and starts. From the other direction, in her and Dan's bedroom, something was scratching at the window asking to be let in.

Megan crawled along the landing and crushed the spider beneath her palm. She reached for the mouse but it hurried past her and disappeared into one of the two spare bedrooms.

"Mum," Nikki said. "You 're not doing any killing out there, are you?"

"That is not Nikki," Megan said. "That is not my daughter."

Somebody banged on the front door. Megan gasped in relief. She looked through the banisters and saw Dan standing outside silhouetted against the snow, darkening the frosted glass with his shadow. She ran downstairs, seeing darting things from the corner of her eye. She turned this way and that, trying to catch sight of them — feathery shapes fluttering above her head, slinky bodies slipping along skirting boards, black blurs scurrying across the timber floor — but whichever way she turned they seemed to elude her, moving just outside her field of vision.

The knocking came again, giving her an instant sense of déjà vu, moving her out of the normal and into the abnormal. Usually she enjoyed déjà vu, tried to perpetuate it by submitting to what it made her say, look at, do. Perhaps it took her nearer to God, because it gave her the idea that He was looking out for her, her life watched over beyond her ken. But not now. Now it scared her badly, because even though this all seemed so familiar — from little over an hour ago — there had been no fleeting shapes dancing at the extremes of her vision then. No surreptitious sounds from behind skirting boards and closed doors.

Had there?

Dan was slumped against the door now, the shadow of the baseball bat a dark exclamation mark against the white background.

Megan drew the bolts and flipped the catch, and too late she saw the shadow grow taller and wider as the door began to swing open. She tried to push it closed, but the baseball bat drove through and levered the door against her. She braced her feet against the floor, but there was no competition. When Brand decided the silly little game was over he threw the door open and Megan went tumbling.

"Get out!" she screamed. She glared at him, down at the bat — it was still dripping darkly — up again. "Where's Dan?"

His eyes were full of a dark liquid mirth. His scars seemed to dance, but it may have been the light. "Who?"

"The police are on their way. He's called the police and they'll be here soon!"

"Well then," Brand said closing and locking the door behind him. "I'll have to be an inconsiderate lover and come first. No time to waste with niceties."

Megan tried to stand but he was already there, twisting one hand into her hair and tugging until she slid to her side on the floor. He hauled her across the hallway, whistling all the way. There was no tune to his whistle, no discernible background or formation, but it made her skin crawl and drove her into a dark, Godless panic... a panic where there was no God, because how *could* He allow this?... a dark place where Brand's tune inspired false memories of bad, bad times, where all the truths she tried so hard to believe in were mocked, shit upon, spat upon by this bastard because all truths were lies, life itself was a lie...

"Meet my friends," Brand said. He pulled hard and Megan slid past him into the study.

She heard her scalp rip before the pain hit, a white-hot glaze over her whole skull that set her ears and neck aflame. It felt as if she'd been doused in acid. She went to scream but held back, closing her eyes, blocking out his face and opening herself up to God, using His love and her love for Him to temper the pain. She did not want to give Brand the satisfaction.

"Megan," he said, clocking her on the head with the baseball bat. She winced, opened her eyes. He had blooded his cheeks with the clot of her scalp, and the blood moved. He glanced over her shoulder and nodded. "As I said... my friends." The door shut on his smile and Megan turned to look behind her.

She gave in to the scream. Nothing could hold that back: faith in God; certainty in her love for Him; strength, strength from anywhere. Nobody was that strong.

The room was alive.

Nikki sat on her bed and stared out at the snow, seeing only white but imagining a lot more. She imagined the tree-line, standing stark and dark from the snowfields and providing some sort of shelter for Brand. Because he would stand and watch her window, day in, day out, maybe forever, watch as she dressed and undressed for him, brushed her hair for him, stood naked at the window and turned slowly around for his attention. He would want her, she would feel the waves of lust heating the surface of the snow and sending it into a melt, a billion glittering diamonds of water simmering and then refreezing when Brand started to walk towards the house.

It was all so romantic. How much must he love her to be out in this storm? How much must he really want her, to make him stay around after they'd given him a lift, watch her, follow

her and make sure he could see her all the time? Romantic...
even that time at the party, when his eyes had been hard and
blank as he came... bad lighting in the cellar, perhaps, the light
refracting through old bottles of wine to steal away his look of
rapture. She had never let Jazz do that, but with Brand it seemed
so natural, so pure, so clean. And now that Jazz was gone...
    ... gone...
    A breath of cool air swept under her bedroom door and
gave her goosebumps. Someone had just walked over her grave,
her grandmother would have said. She'd been full of sayings.
There were footsteps on the stairs, slow and heavy, certainly
not her mother. She'd gone to answer the door and Nikki had
sat back, resting on her hands, staring from the window, imagining Brand... and now it sounded as if he'd come for her.
    She smiled and felt her skin prickling all over at the thought
of him touching her. There was a sudden pain in her side, like
a twinge of stitch, but she shifted and it faded. Her smile
faltered slightly. She sat up straight and alert. The cool breeze
under the door was still there. So were the footsteps. She tried
to imagine Brand naked, his cock hard and ready to impale
her, but try as she might she could not see lust in his expression, nor love, nor anything other than that bland mockery
she'd seen before, the smile she'd tried to attribute to love but
which in reality was little more than a passing interest.
    No. He *loved* her. He did, and she'd make him love her
more.
    Perhaps now, this evening, he'd show her the brand he'd
spoken of. And she would see what had been done to him.

CHAPTER SIXTEEN

Dan lay on his right side in the snow. His arm was stretched along the ground above his head. The pain was so bad that he could not keep still between crawls, and he was afraid that he'd roll over onto his back, hit the ground with his ruined left leg and hand.

The snow was already four inches deep.

He'd made about six feet, if that. Halfway to the Wilkinson's front door. He tried focussing on that rectangle of light, but it was tainted by the sight of Frank's body at its base and the bloody carpet beneath his head. Luckily he was facing into the house and away from the door, perhaps turning to look for his wife in those final moments. Dan was glad. He didn't think he could stand Frank's dead eyes watching his struggle.

He clawed his hand again, gritted his teeth and tried pushing with his right leg, shouting in pain but completing the movement because there was no other way. Pain was transitory, he'd read that somewhere, horrible at the time but functional, a biological warning that his body was damaged. In days or weeks he would not remember this pain, it would not *matter*, so he tried to deal with it like that. In a way, it was interesting. It wasn't the pain actually damaging him. He'd already been damaged. Perhaps the cold helped, too. He could not longer feel the toes of either foot.

And he closed his eyes when he pushed to think of Megan and Nikki. He imagined Nikki being attacked by that bastard, pictured himself coming to her rescue and caving the fucker's head in with the baseball bat, carrying Nikki away and soothing her and telling her everything was going to be alright. He did not allow thoughts of her enjoying Brand; any enjoyment was based on his lies, his deceits. Dan would lay his head open and let his smashed brain steam away all its corrupted ideas. And Megan, his lovely, disturbed wife… the only picture he could conjure was as he'd found her after the attack in the city. He would *not* see her like that again. He would reach her before that happened, he would defend her, stand in the way if needs must. Each day since then he'd hated himself a little more for not being there, even though Megan said she loved him just as much, she hadn't blame him, *could not* blame him. It wasn't her blame he was concerned about.

So thinking, Dan felt the Wilkinson's front door step against his fingertips. He grabbed on and pulled, kicking more with his right leg, accepting the pain by shouting and swallowing a mouthful of snow. His shoulder touched the sill and he rolled onto his front; it was the only way he could get in. His ruined left hand flopped uselessly in the snow and Dan tried to burrow it down, hoping the cold would numb shattered nerves and dull the pain.

Frank's body lay just past the swing radius of the door. Dan saw that he could squeeze past it quite easily, but the old man's blood had soaked into the carpet and spread in a large pool around him. He'd have to crawl through the blood to go in search of the phone. It just was not fair.

"Fuck this," Dan whispered, his voice shockingly loud in the silence. He paused for a moment, listened, heard only the secretive hush of the heavy snowfall and a strange, electrical fizzing from somewhere in the house. "Myra?" he called. He did not expect an answer. "Myra?" One more try for luck, one more try, and perhaps he liked the sound of his own voice in this deathly, muffled silence. He glanced at Frank and tried not to see the damage to his head. Dan had never been close to the Wilkinsons — they never had each other around to dinner, nothing like that — but he'd helped the old man dig a soakaway in his garden the previous year, and he remembered the gent's gentle disgust at the way the world was going, his mourning of older, simpler times. They'd shared some laughs and a few cool beers together, and now…

"Got to stand. Got to get the phone." Dan gasped and grunted and swore, biting his lip until it bled to disperse the faintness as he managed to haul himself up, holding onto the door handle then reaching up and curling his fingers over the door head, supporting his weight on his one good leg and pausing to let everything settle down once more.

Brand could be there by now, he knew. It must be ten minutes since he'd left. If he had managed to walk straight to their house through this storm he could be there, inside his house, doing whatever it was he'd come to do. Dan felt like crying, raging at his impotence, but he also knew that this would gain nothing. He kept his anger in and used it instead to attack the pain.

He slid along the hall wall on his right side, trying to move his left leg but finding the pain easier if he simply allowed it to drag along behind him. He held his swollen hand slightly away from his body, fingers splayed in unnatural directions, the skin a dark purple. He reached a corner and turned, resting for a few seconds before carrying on. If he allowed the pain to die down it would be worse when it flared again, so he kept up a continuous movement, cursing and swearing and shouting, unreasonably embarrassed at the words he was using. Frank had hated profanity. He kept glancing down at the dead man, and now that he could see Frank's face the glances were quicker. Dan didn't like the way his head looked.

He knocked pictures from the wall with his shoulder and they smashed on the floor, worsening the scene of violence. Frank and Myra's children would have to tidy them up, he knew, pick up the shattered glass and decide whether to keep the old photographs inside. Frank and Myra on a beach somewhere; a fifty-year-old wedding photograph; a family shot, a dozen unknown faces staring at him from better times…

Finally he reached the living room door. The electrical sound was coming from here, accompanied now with the sharp tang of burning. Easing himself around the door he saw the television, a fist-sized hole smashed into the screen, smoke wisping from the grille at the back. Small flashes lit its insides. And then he saw Myra's legs stretched behind a chair, her feet turned in so that her toes touched, her white dress spattered with red.

"No more," he whined, glad when tears blurred the scene. "No more, please no more." He tried not to see Megan lying there in place of Myra, but once the idea existed it would not go away. "No, no, no." The telephone was on a table several feet away. Dan pushed away from the door frame and hobbled to it, hopped, screaming as his left foot hit the ground and jarred his knee, crying out all the time, "No, no, no!"

He snatched the receiver from the cradle and listened to terrible nothingness. No tone. No static. Silence.

"Shit!" He screamed, smashed the receiver into the phone and listed again, made sure it was connected at the wall, made sure there was not an on/off button on the phone itself, stared at Myra's legs, wondered if Brand had raped her, looked back and saw Frank's corpse watching him with hooded eyes, one side of his face dented and split, smashed the phone again, listened, nothing.

Nothing.

No help.

He had to get back home. He had no idea what he could do once he arrived — *if* he got there through this blizzard and didn't end up frozen to his own driveway — but that did not matter. Megan and Nikki mattered. His family mattered, and seeing Frank and Myra dead in their own house reinforced that more than ever. They had family. He'd knocked pictures of them off the walls as he slid by. They had family, and that was more important than anything. More important than life.

He'd never make it without help. Frank sometimes used a walking stick, Dan had seen him when he and Myra went for strolls along the road leading through the woods, but where the hell.... And then providence smiled, fate — more used to fucking him over big-time — turned a blind eye, and Dan saw the handle of the stick curved over the back of an armchair.

When he left the Wilkinson's house he was crying again from the pain, and the tears were cooling on his cheeks and making his face cold. He tried to pack snow around his damaged knee, but the blood simply melted it and sluiced it away down his trouser leg. He plunged his swollen hand into the snow, but the dark bruising was hot, and it did the same.

Pain, then. He'd have to see the pain through and do whatever his damaged body allowed, ignoring the messages that
told him to *stop, this is hurting you, it's making your leg worse, injuring
your hand more.* The snowstorm seemed worse than ever, load-
ing his eyelashes and driving into his eyes, stinging the exposed
skin of his face like cigarette burns. He could take time to find
a scarf, towel, anything to protect himself more from the storm,
but time was something he did not have.

Brand could be there by now... .

Dan closed the front door on the horrors behind him and
turned to confront those that lay ahead.

The room was alive. Megan was at the centre of their world,
and they had invaded hers.

The study had one wall lined with books, and the shelves
now crawled with life of every kind. Ants created new titles
on book spines, woodlice and beetles hurried along the shelf
lips, spiders slung themselves from above on gossamer threads,
worms slid across the tops of the books, seeking dark. Small
things hurried in and out between the packed books, too small
to see individually but creating a hazy sheen as a whole, a blurring of vision. A troop of snails hung on the undersides of
shelves, extending hesitant antennae into the light. Birds
perched on the upper shelves, pecking at a daring insects now
and then, picking motionless flies off the wall and ceiling. Blue
tits, siskins, a tiny wren, several sparrows, a pair of bull finches,
and in the corner of the room a lesser spotted woodpecker,
beak pointing directly at Megan's face like a threat.

They were all watching her.

A badger sat on the desk, its snout twitching as it took a
good smell of the room's new visitor. Two squirrels frolicked
on the windowsill and the end of the desk, jumping back and
forth, swapping positions but always turning around... to look
at Megan. Under the desk a hedgehog rooted in the bin, turning its head every few seconds to glance at Megan... or to
make sure she was still there.

A fox lay under the easy chair. A stoat weaved along at
skirting level, darting from one item of furniture to another.

Other things moved around the room, some of which she did not recognise, ignorance of nature or shock confusing her... or perhaps they had no name.

They were all watching her, their eyes a uniform blank, and whichever way she turned she was being stared at. Their eyes were not as they should be, they were deformed and full of *him*. She heard him mounting the stairs overhead, but she knew that he could still see her. She wanted to be brave, defiant, wanted to promise him that he'd never break her... but she screamed.

The sound sent a brief ripple through the life around her. A couple of birds hopped from one place to another, the fox lay its ears back against its head and the squirrels stopped leaping, but other than that there was little reaction. She stood hurriedly, screamed again and kicked out at a small mouse sniffing at her toes. It ducked to one side to dodge the kick and started sniffing again.

The carpet was suddenly crawling with things, ant-sized upwards, and Megan went on tiptoes to avoid them. Her balance wavered and she had to reach out to steady herself against the black wall... but it was usually sunshine yellow, the blackness now given by hundreds of spiders, furry and spindly legged, small and large. Her hand hit the wall and they parted around it. She was so scared, she could not scream. There was nothing crushed beneath her hand... they'd moved away like grease under attack from detergent, forming a circle which now closed, closed.

Megan moved back into the centre of the room and tried to stamp down on the things on the floor, screaming again, swiping at her hair because there was something tangled in there.

Still they watched her. Wherever she trod, the creatures moved quickly aside. She hit nothing. Their reaction was too fast, unnatural, but she kept stamping and kicking and scraping her foot along the floor to try and crush and break the things staring at her. She danced, running on the spot, moving across the room and kicking out at the fox. Her foot was not fast enough. The fox ducked its head and dodged to the side, darted past her and stood by the door, watching again.

They were God's creatures turned against her. In the lion's den, Daniel had extracted the thorn and made friends, turned wildness into tenderness. Now she was trying to put the thorn back in, but the reaction was not the opposite. These animals weren't wild, tender, aggressive, or subdued. They were simply Brand's.

"God, God, God," Megan hissed as she danced, kicked and punched at nothing, but He was letting her find her own way because nothing changed.

They sat and stared. *He* stared.

There was nothing left to do but go mad.

"Nikki," the voice said through the door. It made the hairs on her neck stand on end and sent a shiver down her spine, a shiver that remained in her groin instead of dissipating. Fear and anticipation kept it there. Perhaps the greatest part of love *was* fear. And the most powerful part of sex was anticipation.

Nikki was already standing by the door ready to let him in. She touched the bolt and it felt warm, as if he was touching it from the other side. She would feel that warmth soon across her skin.

She drew back the bolt and opened the door. A breath of cool air came in, exuded from Brand where he stood in the doorway. His skin was pale, a bluish tinge testament to the cold, the white scar was raised and his eyes... they were upon her, they were looking *into* her, but they were cold and jet-black.

"Oh God," Nikki sighed, the skin of her scalp tingling. The stitch in her side returned and she went down on her knees before him, but he lifted her under the armpits, taking her off her feet with ease and walking her across the room to the bed.

"Not that," he said. "Hasn't anyone ever told you that variety is the spice of life?"

Even his voice was sex, caressing her with its cadences and sending her heart thumping, her breath racing. He lay her on the bed and stood up, slipping his coat from his shoulders. Snow fell from it and hit the floor, melting into the carpet. He took something shiny from its deep pocket before dropping it, smiling down at Nikki as he turned the knife and threw its reflection across her body. She could feel it, a cool caress as the weak light from outside travelled up her legs, across her groin and over her stomach, as if he was kissing her already. Her armpits were still warm from where he'd touched her. The heating in the house must have gone off because she was shivering and her breath condensed in the air. His touch was warm, the snow did not melt in his hair or on his shoulders, she was cold, when he came it had burned her skin it was so cold… and just what *was* he?

"What?" Nikki whispered, watching the knife, suddenly afraid. It was perfectly polished, its point so sharp that she could not make out where knife ended and fresh air began.

"Watch," he said, and he touched her chest with the blade. He held it between thumb and forefinger and guided it down between her breasts, over her sternum and across her belly-button, exerting no pressure.

Her T-shirt parted perfectly, every thread cut, and she felt the sharp point tracing an invisible line down across her bare skin. She gasped and arched her back, afraid that the movement would encourage penetration but unable to help herself. Brand stroked again with the knife and the front of her bra parted. Her chest rose and fell with her frantic breathing, and every movement pulled the material further apart.

Brand looked down at her face, unsmiling, but she saw the love in his eyes, the glint of lust. He repeated the performance on his own shirt, sliding the knife in above the top button and letting gravity take it down, buttons popping off and tinkling to the floor as the shirt opened up. He was wearing a T-shirt underneath. He split this too, but he must have been pushing too hard because rosettes of blood bloomed on the white material.

"Careful," Nikki gasped, but then she saw his face, saw his eyes turned up slightly, and realised that he was doing it on purpose.

And then, as his shirt parted and she saw his stomach and chest, she realised that he must have done this many, many times before.

"My mark," he said, taking off his shirt and T-shirt and letting her see his torso. Every inch of his skin was scarred. These were not just passing cuts, but deep incisions, gouges, holes. All were healed and closed — all except for the cuts he had just made, old scars bleeding fresh blood. His skin rose in knobs and twisted heals. Every gash must have needed stitching; none had been. "My brand."

"What's your name?" Nikki asked, unsure of where the question came from.

"Brand."

"Who...?"

He straddled her and rested his weight on her hips. He caressed her stomach with his warm fingertips. The movement caused a ripple in his chest muscles, sent old scars dancing. "Who did this? People. Time. So now I live apart from both."

"You're so warm."

"Shhhh," Brand said, lifting one side of her slashed T-shirt and bra with the point of the knife and laying it over her arm, exposing her breast.

He reached behind him with his other hand and touched her between the legs, pushing gently at her jeans with his knuckle. She wished he'd cut those off as well. Then she thought, He will soon.

Nikki watched his face as he stared at her, saw it unchanging as he touched her nipple with the cold knife, and she realised that the duelling scar had vanished. She gasped and bit her lip, tensing beneath the blade, arching her back again. Brand lay the metal flat on her nipple and moved it slightly from side to side, then he jerked the knife away quickly. Nikki cried out, closed her eyes and lay still. His weight still had her pinned down.

She heard her mother screaming from somewhere down below.

When she looked she saw a line of blood running down her breast and pooling on her chest. There was a small cut next to her nipple. Brand bent forward and kissed it, his other hand exerting more pressure, Nikki's chest rising to meet his mouth as her breathing turned to panting, and when his cold tongue touched her warm blood and cooled the nip of pain she gasped, crying out and covering her mother's anguished screams with her own.

He suckled for a while, then sat back up. She could barely see him through the ecstatic haze. His face had blurred. She must be crying. Then her other nipple hardened under the ice-cold knife, and Brand's shadow bent down once more.

He was going to get lost out here in the snow and die. He'd headed off from the Wilkinsons' in the direction he knew home to be, he'd been walking as straight as he could, he'd even bumped into the fence he knew bounded the road between their two properties... but the pain was close to defeating him, the snow was worse, and he was going to collapse and freeze to death. They'd find him in a couple of days, just another corpse between two houses of death.

And that's what made him go on. Falling over and giving in would be too easy. Brand may win in the end, but he would not *conquer*. Dan would fight until he could not even think any more, he'd decided that already, and such determination gave him an unreasonable optimism. *Even if I die you haven't really won*, he was thinking. *You can murder us, but you can't kill our family.*

Dan leaned over the walking stick and dragged his bad leg behind him; it hurt, but less than trying to lift it clear of the ground altogether. He'd never felt pain from cold but he did now. He'd come out with a thick coat but no gloves or scarf, and now the cold was picking at his fingertips, constantly trying to slow the blood circulation, battling back and forth with his warmth until it felt like a million pins were being driven into his fingers and hands and cheeks, pricking right down to the bone. Still, it provided a counterpoint for the agony in his leg and hand. The more he hurt all over, the less extreme the individual pains seemed to be.

Perhaps he was dying already.

He walked; he shrugged snow from his shoulders and shook it from his head; and he remembered good times. Perhaps good times would keep him warm, he mused, or maybe they would steer him back home. If nothing else they would offer a distraction while cruel reality took him toward his death much faster than was fair. He thought about a holiday they'd taken a few years ago. Nikki had been eleven, old enough to seem like a woman sometimes, young enough to still be their little girl, happy to give him a kiss and cuddle in public, not yet concerned about being embarrassed in front of her mates. They'd hired a barge for a week and cruised the Norfolk canals, pleased when they came to an automated lock and equally happy when they had to work the lock themselves. Nikki had been ecstatic when her parents had to take to the bank to open the gates, because then they'd left her to steer the barge into the lock, easing the throttle so gently, nudging the buffers suspended from the walls, so proud when they came back aboard and praised her. The weather had been fine all week, and one day he and Nikki had spent a couple of hours sunbathing on the roof of the barge while Megan steered and supped wine.

Dan and his daughter had chatted about things. The past first of all, and then the future, what she wanted to do, where she wanted to go, who she wanted to be. Dan had lain back and listened, watching puffy white clouds pass slowly overhead and hearing the soft *shush* of water against the hull, a soporific background to his daughter's excited chatter. It was, he'd thought at the time, the first time he had really become aware of her impending adulthood. She was her own person with her own dreams and ambitions and ideas about things. Whatever he said to her from now on, she would make up her own mind. He could advise, but not guide. It had been an extraordinarily happy moment but also extremely sad, knowing that his little girl was not really that little any more, and that from then on the important choices would be her own.

"You're a good girl," Dan whispered into the snow, his voice hoarse from the cold. "A good girl, Nikki, Daddy's good girl. You do what you like, as long as it's good." Pain tried to hobble him, drop him into the snow where ice-cold arms would hold him down, freeze him, leech the warmth from his bones and his mind. But he remembered that little girl on top of the barge and walked on, each step an agony, expecting at any moment to slip away from the walking stick and break another bone.

He closed his eyes and walked, and for a few seconds he was in a warm operating theatre, surgeons rushing around, grim expressions hidden by green surgical masks. They'd let him in, but only on his insistence. The monitoring machines had told them that the baby was in distress, it had to be born *now*, and Megan was crying as she was jerked and wrenched around. Dan stayed close to her behind the raised sheet screen, not wanting to see what they were doing to his wife even though he could close his eyes and imagine it. She cried and groaned and whimpered, and he tried to hear what the nurses and doctors were saying to each other, was it light-hearted banter or serious talked lightened up for his benefit? Every second that went by without a sound terrified him, he was sweating and shaking nearly as much as Megan, and then they heard her cry... her first cry... and he burst into tears, vision blurred so that he didn't really see his daughter as they showed her to him before whisking her away to clean her up. Megan was shaking, shock setting in, but she was smiling too. She was smiling.

Dan opened his eyes. "Like you smiling," he said past blue lips. "Like the idea of you smiling. And you… " He smiled himself, because in his mind's eye was Nikki — a baby, a girl on the verge of her teens, and the beautiful young woman she was now — looking at him with her cheeky lopsided grin. "You may be seventeen, but you're still my little girl."

He struggled on through the pain. His family gave him strength, his love for them and theirs for him. And a few minutes later the stark, ghostly form of the dead apple tree jumped from the blizzard before him, old angular branches holding onto clumps of snow. He leaned against the fence and fell over, crying out as he rolled but picking himself up again straight away.

Three steps from the front door he brandished the walking stick before him, hopping the last few feet to crash against the door. He tried the handle. It was locked.

Dan slid down to the step and felt tears freezing on his cheeks.

It was beautiful. Jazz had never been like this.

Nikki's room had faded around her until there was only her and Brand, the soft bed beneath their bodies, sheets dampened by sweat and becoming more tangled as they squirmed and moved together. He turned her over and pressed himself to her back, biting her neck, her shoulder blades, her buttocks, biting again, kissing her with the knife and it was beautiful, feeling the air touch where the knife had kissed was beautiful, and then he suckled the blood and pressed his tongue into the wound. Every touch of the knife sent a small shudder through her, every wet kiss of knife or tongue or both, by now she couldn't tell which was which…

He said nothing. He just *did*. Did things she had never dreamed of, parted her legs with his knee and lay the knife against the curves of her buttocks, let blood run and then followed it with his tongue. She lifted to allow him access and the knife kissed again, every parting of skin a rapture.

He moved back up her body and entered her, and she gasped

because he was so cold. Her heat made him feel colder still, and as he moved she could feel every inch, every gnarled and twisted scar that covered even that part of him. The only sounds were her own heavy breathing and the rasping of his rough skin against her smooth, lubricated by the sheen of blood... blood... there was so much...

Nikki lifted her head and opened her eyes, twisting so that she could see the bloodstained sheets. Surely that wasn't right? Blood like that was bad, red, danger, and there was so much, was she feeling weak already? Was this really what she thought? Was Brand *really* loving her?

She opened her mouth, not knowing what was going to emerge.

Brand kissed the back of her neck and slid the knife along her side, parting skin as he drove back into her. He stilled and Nikki felt coldness flooding her. Still he said nothing but Nikki gasped, wondering how she could possibly have thought that anything was wrong.

He turned her onto her back again, sliding his hands across her bloody nakedness. His face was blurred, a red smear, she must have blood in her eyes. Nerve endings flared across her body, the knife and his mouth kissing her, blade and flesh, tongue and metal sucking or opening, or both, it was all so beautiful.

Nikki reached for him and found him still hard, cold yet wanting. She drew him down to her but he held back, touching her belly with the cool knife, pushing.

Nikki screamed and smiled. She knew that he was giving the very best he could.

In madness Megan found a strange peace. She had called to God but found Him cold and wanting, holding back judgement on something that was so plainly bad, evil, corrupt. So she turned to something else. She looked to her memory.

And she found Nikki, a bloody wet bundle only just pulled from her body, waved in front of her for a few precious seconds and then taken away again. They would clean her and make sure she was well, Megan knew, but she wanted her baby with her now. Dan hugged her head and cried. Megan knew she should cry too, but she could not. Instead she began to shake.

Her baby, her baby was covered in blood and crying.

"Baby," she said, "I want my baby." They had used knives to open her up, she knew, a scalpel to slice under the mound of her belly so that they could reach in and take out her baby, relieve her distress, rescue her beautiful daughter from the deadly trap Megan's womb had become. But their scalpels may have cut a lot more, gone in too deep, and she had to see her daughter to make sure she was unharmed by the cool blade. "Nikki," she said, because that was the name she and Dan had chosen for a girl. Megan was instantly aware that the first time she had uttered it was in fear. "Nikki, I want Nikki, where's my baby Nikki?"

And then she had her, a warm bundle, a miracle with black shiny eyes looking around in wonder, staring up at her mother's face and perhaps feeling safe at last.

Megan stood in the middle of the study and wept into her hands. And then she froze, a gasp half out, a memory unfinished, because she thought she had heard her baby crying again.

She looked around. The room was empty. There were no animals. He was no longer watching her.

Perhaps he was too involved elsewhere.

"No," Megan said. She darted for the door. The hallway outside was silent, but if she held her breath and listened carefully she could hear something from upstairs. It was a human sound, though she could not tell who was making it, or what was meant by it. No words for sure. A cry maybe, or a scream, or both. A gasp of pain or pleasure.

Her baby... the memory came again of Nikki finally being handed to her, but this time her baby had not escaped the scalpel. This time, the nurses places a slashed and bleeding infant in her arms, and her baby was crying and screaming at the unfairness of it all.

With her first foot on the stairs something made Megan turn and look at the front door. For the third time that day, someone was trying to get in. For the first time she knew for sure who it was. Brand was upstairs with their daughter, so the shape slumped against the glass could only be Dan. For a second she did not know which way to go. God helps those... she thought, and realised that she and Dan together would at least stand a chance. She went to the front door and opened it.

Dan was dead. He must be to look that bad, that *blue*. And the snow around him was speckled red, a pink pattern already spreading from his misshapen leg like ink on blotting paper. There was snow frozen in his hair, if he'd been alive his body-heat would be melting it, and he must have been here for ages because there were icicles hanging from his eyes —

He moved. Her husband turned to look at her, and Megan cried out because it must be Brand doing this, playing the sick puppeteer with poor dead Dan's freezing corpse —

"Megan," Dan said.

Megan knew her husband's voice. That bastard could not contrive that. "Oh Dan, he's upstairs with Nikki," she said, hauling him in across the snow and ignoring his high-pitched keening, knowing that all there was for them to do was to rescue Nikki from Brand's clutches.

She helped him stand. He was crying and whining with the pain but he did not push her away. He also knew what needed doing, and they did not need to say anything else. As soon as he could stand, move, they had to go upstairs. Their baby was up there, and Brand was doing something to her.

Even now, they both thought at the same time, it may be too late.

There was a smash and the door burst open. Nikki turned her head to look at her parents standing in the doorway, and she opened her mouth, sighed and smiled happily as Brand made his own beautiful brand of love to her.

"You'll scar," he whispered in her mind, "and maybe you'll grow to like it."

Megan smashed at the door with the heavy toolbox from the spare room, and it surprised them both by bursting open at the first impact. Dan leaned against the frame and held the walking stick ready. Megan dropped the toolbox, a screwdriver gripped in her fist.

Brand was raping their daughter. That hit home first, but then some odd things about the scene struggled to imprint on Dan and

Megan's minds. The blood, there was so much blood, *too* much…
and Brand's position was all wrong, he held himself away from
Nikki and they could see the knife, keen blade dulled with blood
as it disappeared inside their daughter's stomach.

Nikki turned to look at them. And she screamed. So much
agony and pain and hurt there, so much betrayal. She *screamed* at
the unfairness of it all.

Dan and Megan launched themselves into the room.

Dan staggered with his first step. He knew he was going over,
so with a shout that hurt his throat and blurred his vision he used
his momentum to swing the walking stick at Brand. Its heavy
rubber-coated end struck the naked man's back, skittering from a
knot of grey scars and clattering to the floor. Dan did the same,
holding out his right hand to deflect the fall, his left hand coming
around automatically and hitting the carpet with him. His scream
continued, rising in pitch.

Someone else screamed as well, the sound perpetuating the
echoes of Nikki's cries. At first Dan thought it was Brand but
then realised it was Megan, leaping across his prone form and
bringing her hand around in an arc. The screwdriver was rusted,
as if already coated with in red blood. Its tip was blunt. But
wielded with enough force it would kill.

It would kill Nikki.

Brand would shift aside and it would go into Nikki, finishing
the job he had begun.

Dan could not close his eyes.

Too fast for him to make out — maybe he'd blinked, maybe
he really had closed his eyes to avoid the dreaded outcome —
things changed. Brand had moved from Nikki's body to a standing position, one hand holding Megan's wrist, the other punching
her stomach, two, three times. She coughed and stumbled back
across Dan's legs. Dan opened his mouth at the shock as she
crushed his left leg into his right, but no sound emerged, the pain
was too great to be given vent just yet.

Daddy, someone said, but Dan could only look at Brand where
he stood, a sculpture of scars. The man's face was still blank, no
expression, no scar… the only flawless piece of him. Except for
the black empty pits that were his eyes. If hate had a colour, they
would be it.

Megan picked herself up quickly, ignoring Dan's explosive scream as she heaved herself from his body. Brand was smiling at her. His face was unblemished now, but the rest of his body seemed to be in motion, every inch of him a slowly twisting sigil, all scarred on, each of them taunting her in languages she could not know. She still had the screwdriver clasped in her hand. She could not breathe, she was winded, her stomach muscles knotted tight as steel, but if she only had a few seconds left to live she would spend them killing this bastard who had done this to her daughter…

…she looked at Nikki but tried not to see, it was just too bad…

And she threw herself at Brand.

He batted her away with a simple movement of his arm. And then he paused, looking up, an expression of surprise animating his dead-flesh face. "Oh!" he said, as if an answer to an old riddle had just leapt into his mind.

Dan and Megan stared up at him, and for a moment the room was almost silent. Almost, but for Nikki's sobbing.

Megan wanted to go to her daughter but she was too afraid to move. Dan *could not* move.

"Oh!" Brand said again. He was staring at the ceiling.

And then they all heard the sound of something walking on the roof. Heavy footsteps passing back and forth above them, and then circling them like a hunter circles prey.

"Well," Brand said, scratching absently at the cuts across his chest and stomach, "it seems it's time for me to go." His cock drooped and dripped Nikki's blood to the carpet.

"No," Megan said.

Brand frowned down at her. For an instant he looked almost confused. "Sorry?"

"I said no."

"You don't want me to go?"

"Why come in the first place?" Dan asked, grinding his teeth together from pain.

"I could tell you, but you'd hate it," the scarred man said. Megan lurched for him again but he kicked her once, hard, in the side. She fell winded, and the screwdriver rolled under Nikki's bed.

"And perhaps that's why I will tell you. I came in the first place because I could. I wanted a moment of your time, and you wouldn't grant it, so I gave you a moment of mine. Really, a moment of yours would have made it so much easier."

"For what?"

"For you all to accept me."

"But why us?" Megan said, hopelessness bringing it out in one gasp.

Brand stood, pulled his coat on and stared down at Megan. "If God won't tell you the truth, I will: because. Just because. Just because bad things happen to good people."

"Daddy," Nikki whispered from the bed.

Dan crawled past Brand's legs, waiting for the kick, the stamp, but none came. The noises from above grew louder, the footsteps more frequent and insistent. Whatever was up there had started running. He reached the bed and hauled himself up. And when he saw what awaited him, then he cried. Nikki's bloodied hand reached for his and he held on tight. It was all he could do.

"Best go," Brand said, glancing up again at the ceiling. "Time."

"Bastard," Dan whispered. "You bastard." It was quieter than a sigh, but they all heard it in that room. Even Brand paused for a second, turned to look at Dan… and Dan was positive he saw an instant of disquiet in the mad man's eyes.

The banging again, louder and louder, like the drums of some unknown invocation beating faster and faster toward conclusion. Brand looked up.

Something nudged Dan's leg. Megan, reaching past Brand's feet, past Dan, hand searching.

Brand glanced back down at Dan, up again. They all felt his attention leaving them. All of them, Nikki included, had a sense of joyous relief. On the carpet next to Nikki's bed, the family's blood combined.

"It's been fun," Brand said. And then Megan lurched up and stuck the screwdriver into his neck.

Brand whirled and smacked her around the head, sending her bouncing against the wall, sliding down, fresh blood leaking from her wounded scalp. Her eyes were open but for a few seconds she could not see.

Dan stood quickly and quietly, imagining his pain in the past and forgetting it even while it happened, because he was not letting this murderer go. "No," he said, lifting the walking stick, "you're not going." Brand turned and Dan hit him around the face, feeling the solid impact of the wood against bone, hearing a crunch as something broke. Brand's head jerked back, and then he looked at Dan again. His eyes were the same dark pools of nothing.

The tall man staggered towards Dan and Megan. The screw-driver dripped as blood leaked from the wound in his neck. Megan fell across his path, using all the strength she could muster to heave herself from the wall. Brand tripped over her body and onto the bed, grunting, twitching and bashing his feet in a rapid tattoo on the carpet.

The sound matched the frantic beating on the roof. Slates were cracking up there, the impacts were louder and louder, and then Brand's feet stopped hitting the floor.

Nikki's hand reached out and touched Brand's head. She stroked his hair, ran her fingers down across his face where she'd seen the dashing scar. There was nothing there now but cooling skin.

"You promised me so much," she whispered. Then her hand dropped to the screwdriver and, with one hard twist that made her scream, she drove it all the way in.

Dan hopped and Megan crawled to the bedside. Brand's eyes had rolled up in his head. They were still black.

"Dead," Megan said.

"Maybe," Dan agreed. He grabbed Brand's hair and tipped him to the floor, raised the walking stick and smashed it into the corpse's face, again and again and again until Megan turned away, Nikki began crying louder, the crunching noises turned wet and the beating on the roof slowly ebbed away into nothing.

Dan closed his eyes and kept on hitting until the walking stick broke in half.

He turned to his family, slipping down next to the bed. Megan held onto him, both of them holding Nikki, touching her abused body, trying to comfort her while they wondered just what the hell they were supposed to do now.

That was when Megan noticed that it had stopped snowing.

CHAPTER SEVENTEEN

The phone was working again. Megan called the police and an ambulance, and then she went outside to see for herself.

She called to God for help and tried to feel Him with her. And even though her beautiful baby was lying on a bed of her own blood upstairs, Megan thought she felt Him there, just a little.

The footprints marked the roof in a random, frantic pattern. She circled the house and saw that they were everywhere. Some slates were smashed, leaving gaping black holes in the roof where the snow had showered down into the attic. The holes were like Brand's eyes: empty; lifeless. Pulped now, but no more lifeless because of that.

There were other blots on the roof and it took Megan a while to figure out what they were: dead birds. A magpie, distorted in death where its white blended with the background. A sparrow, several starlings, a few small specks that may have been wrens. Feet clasped at the sky. She could hear birdsong in the woods, even from trees and bushes nearby, but nothing from the house and garden. All the animals here were dead.

Maybe soon, Megan thought, they can come back in peace.

And then, across the lawn and leading over the fence by the dead apple tree, she saw another trail.

Please God it leads to *the house, not* from *it…* But it *did* lead away.

It started on the roof and led away.

Megan looked around at the white landscape feeling the dread of a few days ago once more, the sense that something great was building steadily against her and even God's presence in her heart would offer no protection. Guide her, perhaps. Save her if the threat of death turned into a promise. But not protect her in the here and now. That was not the way He worked.

She went in and checked on Dan and Nikki. Her daughter was still crying, but the wounds in her stomach and side had stopped bleeding. Megan didn't know whether that was a good or a bad sign. "I'm going to the end of the drive to make sure they don't miss the turning," she told Dan, and he merely nodded weakly and tried to smile at her. His face was swollen, his left leg had seized up entirely and his broken fingers had turned an awful shade of purple. *I want to go home to the city*, she thought of saying, but she realised just how unfair that would be right now.

She stepped over Brand's body when she left the room, trying not to see the mess that had been his head. She preferred his expression now to any time she had seen him alive.

Outside, Megan made sure the hammer was secure in her belt and the broken walking stick tightly gripped in her hand. Then she set out to follow the footprints.

They were the same as before. She climbed the fence and tracked them across the field towards the Wilkinson's house. Before reaching it they veered sharply to the left, crossed the meadow and entered the woods. She only hesitated for a few moments. It would be growing dark soon, and although the snow had suddenly stopped the sky promised more to come.

But somehow things felt quiet. Calm. Finished. So she pursued the prints beneath the trees, trying not to imagine what would happen if she met whatever had made them.

Fifteen minutes later she heard the sirens, and she realised that she had left her family in their moment of greatest need. They could be dead back there. Nikki... her daughter, that bloodied, crying thing that had been ripped from her body seventeen years before, bloodied again now... could be dead.

She looked down and the footprints had vanished. They did not fade away or disappear to the left or right... they simply stopped.

Megan dropped the hammer and the broken stick, took one more look around at the woods and then and ran all the way home.

Dan was sitting in the hallway when she opened the front door. People bustled about him, policemen panicking at the mess they'd found in their leafy, lovely village, paramedics rushing up and down the stairs with bags of equipment, studiously ignoring Megan and Dan.

In his lap he had a book. "I found this," he said. "In the study. On my desk. I've never seen it before. It... ."

Megan saw the look on his face and did not want to know. She went to him and hugged him because there was one thing she *did* want to know, the only thing in the world she needed to know right then. It was life or death, this thing, sanity or madness. Hope or dread. She asked.

Dan held her tight and whispered in her ear. "She's alive."

They brought Nikki down ten minutes later. They carried her in their padded tubular chair, her worst wounds patched, blood still speckling her skin and dripping wild patterns onto the blanket gathered around her. One of the paramedics held a drip that fed into her arm. Another one clasped her hand.

She was looking up at the ceiling, her head in constant motion as if following an invisible shadow or silent footsteps. Her eyes were wide and one of them was filled with blood.

"I'm alive," she said. A smile prompted fresh bleeding from a gash on her cheek, one which the paramedics must have missed. "I'm alive."

THE BOOK OF LIES

You never win, because everything is a lie.

Winning is a human conceit. Defeating the bad guy, coming through, emerging victorious in the end... who's to say? Who can truly believe that any of this means anything? Everything is a lie.

She may be alive. They may be alive. And you may be alive. But alive is merely a state of mind, as is dead, and sometimes the two can be so confused..

Because death is a lie, and life is its greatest untruth.

Believe me. Would I lie to you?